SHEILA ROBERTS

·LIFE IN ICICLE FALLS·

MERRY EX-MAS

HARLEQUIN®
entertain, enrich, inspire™

Recycling programs
for this product may
not exist in your area.

ISBN-13: 978-0-7783-1392-2

MERRY EX-MAS

Copyright © 2012 by Sheila Rabe

Printed in U.S.A.

First printing: November 2012
10 9 8 7 6 5 4 3 2 1

For my pal Kathy

Acknowledgments

I had so much fun writing this book! Of course, it's easy to have fun when you work with great people. Huge thanks to my agent, Paige Wheeler, and my editor, Paula Eykelhof. I'm grateful to both of you for your guidance and input. A big thanks to Janet, owner of Blinx on Bainbridge Island, WA, for giving me a glimpse into the busy life of a shop owner, to my friend Susan Sandeno, wedding cake expert, for sharing some of your cake decorating secrets with me, and to Robert Rabe, super chef, for answering my many questions about running a restaurant. A big yeehaw and thank-you to Ed Kerr and all his pals for helping me produce Jake's song, "Merry Christmas, Mama." And to all my friends who are mothers-in-law... None of you were the inspiration for the mother-in-law in this book! Finally, thanks as always to the brain trust: Susan Wiggs, Kate Breslin, Anjali Banerjee and Elsa Watson. You all rock and I hope Santa brings each of you a sleigh load of chocolate.

Dear Reader,

I've got to say, I love Christmas. Love everything about it—the decorations, the goodies, the presents, the Christmas Eve service, even the crazy busyness. I especially love getting a chance to gather with my family to celebrate. Believe me, my family knows how to celebrate. We are fun, fun, fun!

But I realize that for many of us the holidays can sometimes be more stressful than fun, especially when dealing with difficult family members. And when you start adding former spouses to the mix it can make you want to say more than, "Ho, ho, ho."

I'm hoping Cass Wilkes, her friends and their exes will give you a laugh and maybe even some hope. I sure enjoyed writing about them, especially Ella and her ex-husband, Jake.

I must confess, Jake stole my heart. He even wound up with his own country music video, "Merry Christmas, Mama," which I hope you'll all check out on YouTube. He was kind enough to give me a role in it. Of course, he conveniently neglected to tell me about the rude indignities I'd suffer. Oh, well, that's show biz. Not content with a music video, he's got his own webpage, www.songsbyjake.com, where you can read more of his thoughts, see pictures and hear some of his music.

Meanwhile, I hope you'll enjoy the ride as Cass, Ella, Charley and their friends get ready for a crazy Christmas filled with everything from jingle bells to wedding bells.

You can find me on Facebook and Twitter, and please stop by my website, www.sheilasplace.com.

Sheila

1

Once in a while, if a woman is really lucky, the perfect day she envisioned turns out to be just that. This was going to be one of those days, Cass Wilkes thought as she set the platter of carved turkey on her dining table.

She surveyed her handiwork with a smile. Everything was Martha Stewart–lovely from the china and crystal to the Thanksgiving centerpiece she'd bought at Lupine Floral, and her old Victorian home was filled with the aroma of herbs and spices. The dining room window framed a greeting-card-worthy winter scene—her front lawn with its trees and shrubs draped in frosty white and the snowcapped mountains looming beyond.

The snow had done what all good snow should do; it had stopped in plenty of time for road crews to clear the way for travelers. Unlike Thanksgiving last year, the town of Icicle Falls was humming with visitors looking for a holiday get-away. Great for business, especially when you owned a bakery. This weekend, gingerbread boys and girls would march out the door of Gingerbread Haus in droves and money would march right into Cass's bank account—a good thing since she suspected she was going to have a wedding to pay for in a year or so.

A whoop of male excitement came from the living room, followed by cheers. The football game on TV was nearing its end and obviously the favored team had scored a touchdown.

"Okay, that's everything from the kitchen," said Dot Morrison, Cass's mentor and former boss, as she placed a serving bowl heaped with stuffing, along with another full of mashed potatoes, on the table. Normally Dot would have been celebrating with her daughter, but Tilda was on patrol, keeping Icicle Falls safe from…who knew? Their town wasn't exactly a hotbed of crime.

Dot had dressed for the occasion, wearing jeans and a white sweatshirt decorated with a turkey holding a sign that said "Think Outside the Box. Serve Ham." Dot, who owned the town's most popular pancake place, Breakfast Haus, had encouraged Cass to think outside the box years ago, even lent her money to start her bakery. Cass owed her Thanksgiving dinners for life.

"Get those clowns in here," Dot said. "There's nothing worse than cold food."

Cass could suggest a few things—taxes, yeast infections, exes.

Oh, no, she wasn't going to ruin a perfectly good holiday with even a hint of a thought about her ex-husband. That man, that self-centered, undeserving rat who'd tried to lure the kids away this weekend with a trip to Vail, who...

No, no. No thoughts about Mason. It was Thanksgiving, after all, a time to count her blessings.

Three of those blessings were sitting out there in the living room—her kids Danielle, Willie and Amber. Dani's boyfriend, Mike, was there, too, tucked beside her in an overstuffed easy chair.

Twenty-year-old Dani was Cass's oldest and her right-hand woman at the bakery. She'd inherited Cass's passion for creating in the kitchen, and after a year of community college had opted to work full-time at the bakery. Cass had hoped she'd put in at least another year, but she'd had no interest. "I can learn more from you than I can from any college professor," she'd told Cass. When it came to baking, well, what could Cass say? Dani was right.

Amber, her youngest, sat curled up on one end of the couch, texting. A few months earlier she'd been adding to Cass's gray-hair collection, hanging out with the kind of kids no mother wants her child to be with or, worse, become. Thank God (and, possibly, Cass's pal Samantha Sterling) Amber had changed direction and found some new and improved friends.

Willie, Cass's high school jock, was sprawled on the floor, holding the favored stuffed toy of high school boys everywhere—a football. The only trouble she had with Willie was keeping him full. The boy was a two-legged locust.

Then there was her younger brother, Drew, who'd come over from Seattle. Recently divorced (was this tendency toward divorce something in their genes?), he'd been more than happy to spend the weekend hanging out with her family. He'd never had kids of his own, so she'd shared. He made a great uncle and a better father figure than her ex.

No, no, no. Not giving him so much as a thought today.

Cass stood in the archway like a lady butler and announced, "Dinner, guys."

Of course, no one was listening. Another touchdown happened in TV Land. "Yeah!" whooped Mike.

"My team sucks," Willie muttered, giving his football an irritable bounce.

"My dinner's going to suck if you don't get out here and eat it *now,*" Cass warned.

"The game's pretty much over, anyway," Mike said, demonstrating good boyfriend etiquette. He stood, pulling Dani up with him. He was a big boy, a former football star and her son's new hero. Mike was currently employed at the local hardware store, which, as far as Cass was concerned, was ideal. Once he popped the question, he and Dani would get married and live in Icicle Falls, near family and friends, a win–win for everyone.

"You're right," Drew agreed. He shut off the TV and led the parade to the dining room table.

Cass only had to look at a cookie to gain five pounds. Her brother, lucky dog, was tall and reedy, and could eat anything. He was a better dresser, too, always had been. And better-looking. But he couldn't cook, and when he came to town he was her best customer. He was also her best friend, and she was glad he'd come here for the holiday.

The only ones missing as everyone settled around the table were Cass's mother and stepfather, who'd become snowbirds and were with his family in Florida. But Mom and Fred planned to come out for Christmas, and if Cass had to choose she'd rather have her mother with them for that holiday.

Drew reached for the turkey and Cass rapped his hand with a serving spoon. "Grace first, you heathen."

Willie snickered, which earned him the privilege of offering thanks. He barely had "Amen" out of his mouth before he was into the dressing, piling it high on his plate.

Normally she'd remind him that other people might actually want some, too, but not today. Thanksgiving was for feasting and she'd made plenty. Besides, she was going to have an extra serving herself.

For a while conversation consisted of comments like "Pass the rolls" and "Where'd the olives end up?" As plates and then stomachs filled, new topics arose: whose fantasy football team was going to win, how well Cass and Dani's new gingerbread necklaces were selling, Dot's upcoming bunion surgery.

Then it was time for pie. In spite of how crazy-busy Cass had been with work, she'd managed to bake pumpkin, pecan and her brother's favorite, wild huckleberry. "This will be enough for me," he joked, grabbing the whole pie.

With dessert came another tradition, one Cass had started when the kids were small.

"Okay," she said once everyone had been served, "it's gratitude time. Who wants to go first?"

Gratitude. Sometimes the challenge to be grateful had been as big as the word. Often she'd been a world-class hypocrite, encouraging her children to look on the bright side while she indulged in resentment.

It seemed like she'd spent most of her married life in that particular mental state. She'd resented Mason's decision to join the navy when they were engaged. They'd barely set up housekeeping when he shipped out the first time. He'd missed his daughter's birth; Cass's childbirth partner had been her mother. Better her mother than his, she'd told herself. That was something to be grateful for. And she'd been grateful when he got out of the navy. Not so much when he went back to school and neglected his family for his studies. Not so much when he carved out a career that seemed to keep him gone more than it allowed him to be home. Mason had been determined to find the path to success but that path had little room for his family. She was the one who'd always been there to soothe every heartbreak, puzzle over every math problem, cheer at every ball game. And what had *he* done?

Gratitude, remember? Okay, she was grateful she wasn't with him anymore.

"I'm grateful for something," Dani said. She reached into her jeans pocket and pulled out a diamond ring and slid it on her finger.

"Oh, my gosh, you're engaged!" cried Amber.

Cass set down her fork and gaped. Of course she'd known this was coming, but she was a little upset that her daughter hadn't told her before everyone else. "When did this happen?" she asked.

Dani's brown eyes sparkled with excitement. She looked at Mike and they shared the smile reserved for a couple in possession of newly minted love. "Last night. We wanted to wait and surprise everyone."

Well, they had.

"Don't know how surprised anyone is," Dot said, "but I think you made your mother's day."

Of course she had. Why was Cass sitting there like a turkey in a pan? She jumped up and went to hug her daughter and future son-in-law. "This is wonderful. You two are going to be so happy."

How could they not be? Unlike her mother at that age, Danielle had been wise and thoughtful when selecting a mate. She hadn't rushed into a relationship with her hormones on fire and her brain dead from smoke inhalation. She'd held out for the right man. They even *looked* perfect together, Mike with his dark hair and eyes and that big frame, Dani with her lighter coloring and sandy hair and willowy figure. In their wedding garb they'd look fit for the top of a wedding cake.

"This calls for more pie," Drew said with a grin, and helped himself to another piece.

"I'm going to be a bridesmaid, right?" Amber asked her sister.

"Of course," Dani said.

"You'd better dig out your Armani," Cass said to Drew. "Dani's going to need you to walk her down the aisle."

Dani's face lost some of its bride-to-be glow and she bit her lip.

"Hey, I'm cool sitting in the front row with your mom," Drew said quickly. "I don't have to be the one."

Oh, yes, he did. Who else was going to? Oh, no. Surely not...

"Actually, I was hoping Daddy would walk me down the aisle," Dani said.

The undeserving absent father? The man who'd been M.I.A. for most of Dani's life? Cass fell back against her chair and stared across the table at her daughter.

Dani's cheeks bloomed with a guilty flush and she studiously avoided her mother's gaze.

"Daddy?" Cass echoed. It came out frosted with scorn. *Way to be mature and poison your daughter's happy moment,* she scolded herself.

With her sunny disposition and eagerness to please, Danielle was generally easy to get along with, but now her chin jutted out at a pugnacious angle. "I know he'll want to."

Oh, he always *wanted* to be there, but he never had been. Until lately. Now that their children were practically grown. He and his thirty-two-year-old trophy wife, Babette, seemed to think they could have the kids come over to Seattle anytime he swooped in from his business trips and buy their affection with shopping expeditions and Seahawks tickets.

Obviously it was working, and that made Cass want to break the wishbone she'd been saving into a thousand pieces. This wasn't right. How to get Dani to see that, though?

She cleared her throat. "You know he travels a lot."

"I know," Dani said, "but we want a Christmas wedding and he'll be here for Christmas."

"Christmas Day?" Willie made a face.

Dani frowned at him. "What, are you afraid Santa won't come?" To the others she said, "We thought the weekend before."

"That's not much time to plan a wedding," Dot pointed out. "What's the rush?"

Now Mike was beaming like a man with a big announcement.

"Because Mike got a job as assistant manager at a hardware

store in Spokane," Dani announced for him, "and when he moves for his new job I want to go with him."

Everyone at the table got busy offering Mike congratulations.

Except Cass, who was in shock. They'd be moving away. Her daughter would be leaving practically the minute after she got married. The vision of Dani raising her family here in Icicle Falls, of someday taking over the bakery, went up in smoke. It was all Cass could do not to cry. She pushed away the plate with her half-finished pumpkin pie and hoped nobody asked her what she was thankful for.

"Anyway, we just want a small wedding," Mike said. "Nothing fancy."

Nothing fancy? Dani had always wanted a big church wedding. What happened to that?

"And I know Daddy can come that weekend," Dani added.

"You already talked to your father?" *Before you even shared the news with me?* Hurt welled up in Cass, giving her the worst case of heartburn she'd ever had.

"Just to see if he's going to be around," Dani said. "I thought maybe everyone could come up and stay for the week."

"Here?" Cass squeaked.

"Whoo boy," Drew said under his breath.

"There's no room," Cass said firmly. No room at the inn.

Dot shrugged. "You could probably put them up at Olivia's."

Thank you, Dot. Remind me never to invite you over for Thanksgiving dinner again.

"Dani, you know how crazy it gets this time of year," Cass said. "I'm sure the B and Bs are booked solid."

"Olivia still has a couple of rooms," Dani said.

"You talked to her?" She'd told Olivia, too?

"This morning. I just called to ask if she had any left."

"Well, then, I guess that settles it," Cass said stiffly.

"You'll help me plan it, won't you?" Dani asked her in a small voice.

Cass was hurt and she was mad, but she wasn't insane. "Of course I will. And I'll make the cake."

"Well, duh." Amber rolled her eyes.

Dani ignored her sister and smiled happily. "Thanks, Mom."

Cass sighed. She'd even suck it up and be nice at the wedding. It would be wrong to spoil her daughter's big day with petty jealousy.

It's not petty, whispered her evil twin. Cass told her to shut up.

"I know it's a busy time of year," Dani said.

"'Tis the season," Dot cracked.

The season to be jolly. That was going to be hard with her ex-husband strutting around town, pretending to be the world's best dad. It was going to be hard to greet his bimbo trophy wife with good cheer. And she didn't even want to *think* about dealing with her ex-mother- and sister-in-law. If Santa thought this was what Cass wanted for Christmas, he needed to retire.

"This is going to be a pain in the butt for you," Dot said to her later, after the dishes were done and the kids were playing on the Wii.

Cass leaned against the kitchen counter and stared at the contents of her coffee mug—black, just like her mood.

"But you'll get through it."

Of course she would. Exes were a part of life. She'd put on her big-girl panties and cope. After all, it was only a couple of days. Anyway, they'd all be staying at Olivia's place. She'd hardly have to see them.

Cass managed a reluctant smile and raised her mug. "Well, then, here's to getting through."

Dot clinked mugs with her. "Merry Ex-mas, kiddo."

2

It was Black Friday, a big day for retail in Icicle Falls. For Ella O'Brien that made two black days in a row. How different this Thanksgiving had been from the year before.

Not that her mother hadn't tried to make it special. Mims had hauled Ella over the mountains to Seattle for an overnight in the city, and on turkey day they'd eaten their holiday dinner at a high-priced restaurant. Surrounded by strangers. Well, except for Gregory, Mother's longtime friend and fellow fashionista, who had a condo on the waterfront.

Ella hadn't invited the thought that came to her as they were eating, but it had come, anyway, making an unwelcome fourth at the table. *This is pathetically different from last Thanksgiving with your in-laws.* Correction: former in-laws.

That had been a typical O'Brien celebration, rowdy and

exciting, especially for a woman who'd always wanted brothers and sisters. Mims, who had been included, kept a superior distance while grown-ups and children alike had worked up an appetite by running around in the woods playing capture the flag. After dinner her mother-in-law (ex-mother-in-law, darn it) had helped her figure out a tricky knitting pattern.

And later, when it was time for dessert, Mims the fishaterian learned that the slice of mincemeat pie she was enjoying was a hunter's version with moose meat added to the sweet filling and had to make a dash for the bathroom.

There'd been no bathroom dash this year. And no Jake. That was fine with Ella. Really. Mims was right; she was better off without that skirt-chasing, irresponsible, over-grown child. And her life would be perfect once she didn't have to see him every day.

But she missed his mother and his sister and brothers. It had been fun to have someone to call Mom.

She'd never called her own mother Mom. Instead, she'd wound up mimicking Mims's fashion-model friends and calling her Mims. Ella had never gotten the full story on that nickname, beyond that fact that it had something to do with her mother's fondness for mimosas. Oh, and a tycoon and a yacht. Her mother had never wanted to be Mom, anyway. That was simply too unglam. And Lily Swan brought glamour to everything, including motherhood. So that was how it was growing up and that was normal, and that was what Ella told her friends whenever they asked why she didn't call her mother Mom.

And when they asked why she didn't have a daddy, she recited the Swan party line—a girl didn't really need a daddy.

She'd sure wanted one, though, and had watched with long-ing when she saw other little girls riding on their daddies' shoulders or getting taken out for ice cream.

When she'd married Jake and gotten a father-in-law it was the world's best bonus.

Jake's dad always greeted her with a hug and a "How's my girl?" He checked the air in her tires and whittled little wood raccoons for her to put on her mantelpiece in the living room. Mims had pronounced them tacky but Ella loved them because every time she looked at them she could see her father-in-law's big, smiling face.

"We're so sorry to lose you," Mom O'Brien had written in a sweet card after Ella and Jake broke the news. She'd been sorry to be lost. Too bad a girl couldn't shed the hus-band but keep the family, she thought as she turned the sign hanging on the door of Gilded Lily's to Closed.

She was tired—working with people all day could be exhausting—but it was a good kind of tired, she decided as she started to add up the day's receipts. From now until New Year's Eve the shop would be busy. Gilded Lily's was the closest thing Icicle Falls had to a Neiman Marcus or a Nordstrom. It was owned by her mother but Ella managed it. She loved pretty clothes and she loved helping her cus-tomers find a special dress for that special occasion, whether it was a party or a prom, as well as all the accessories to en-hance it. There'd been a lot of enhancing taking place this Black Friday.

Now the business day was over and it was time to go home. Home is where the heart is. There's no place like home.

Bah, humbug.

She stepped out into the brisk mountain air and locked the door behind her. Winter darkness had settled in for the night and downtown Icicle Falls was a-twinkle. Christmas lights decked out the trees in the park and the potted fir trees nestled against the shops, and red ribbons adorned the old-fashioned lampposts that ran along Center Street.

Every weekend there would be a tree-lighting ceremony, and the skyscraper-size fir in town square would come to life with hundreds of colored lights, making the winter village scene complete. With its mountain setting and Bavarian architecture, Icicle Falls was like an animated postcard, quaint and charming—a perfect setting for a perfect life. Except Ella's life wasn't so perfect these days; it was like a dress that no longer fit.

It didn't take her long to walk the half mile from the shop to her two-bedroom Craftsman-style cottage on Mountain View Road. Her dream home. In the summer she'd put two wicker rockers with plump cushions on the porch, and she and Jake had sat out there on warm weekday nights. She'd work on her knitting with their Saint Bernard, Tiny, lazing at her feet, while Jake serenaded her on his guitar. Last Christmas she'd taken great satisfaction in stringing colored lights and cedar boughs along the porch, while Jake had strung lights along the roofline—a team effort.

Ella sighed at the memory. She'd thought she'd have that house for life, had envisioned raising a family there or, once Jake became a famous country star, keeping it as a vacation home.

Her mother hadn't shared the vision. "You shouldn't buy a house so quickly," Mims had cautioned when they first looked at it. "You're both young and you don't even know if this marriage will last."

"Of course it'll last," Ella had insisted. "Why wouldn't it?"

Her mother said nothing, just pursed her lips like a woman with an ugly secret. How had Mims known things wouldn't work out with Jake? What early warning signs had she seen that Ella hadn't?

Whatever she'd seen, she'd kept it to herself, and to show her support (once the decision was made and the papers were signed), she'd given them a gift certificate to Hearth and Home to buy a new couch, saying, "Really, Ella, you can't decorate in Early American Garage Sale. What will people think?"

"Maybe they'll think we're happy," Ella had suggested.

Mims had ignored that remark. "Go look at the couches at Hearth and Home, baby. You'll find one you love, I promise."

Ella did find a couch she loved, and Mims heartily approved of the brown leather sofa with the carved mahogany accents that Ella picked out. "You have wonderful taste," she'd said, and then added, "In most things." Translation: your taste in men is questionable.

"Really, darling, you can do so much better," Mims advised when Ella and Jake started getting serious. "Sleep with him if you must, but for God's sake don't saddle yourself with him for life."

What kind of mother told her daughter stuff like that? Lily Swan, that was who. Mims hadn't felt the need for a husband, so Ella supposed she thought her daughter would see the wisdom of her choice and follow suit. "Men are fun, but not necessary," she'd once overheard her mother say.

How much fun had Mims had with Ella's father? And what had happened to keep them from becoming a family? That, like her mother's age, was classified information and Ella had finally given up asking.

She opened her front door in time to see her own Mr. Not Necessary, her ex-husband, coming down the hallway wearing nothing but his boxers and carrying a basket of laundry, Tiny trotting at his heels. She hated it when Jake did that—not the laundry, parading around in his boxers.

Jake O'Brien had a poster-worthy body and looking at it was, well, distracting. He'd had all day to do the laundry. Why was he waiting until now?

She frowned at him.

He frowned back. "What?"

Tiny rushed up to her, his huge tail wagging with joy, and she bent to give him a good rub behind his ears. "You couldn't have done the laundry earlier?" That sounded snippy, and she wasn't a snippy sort of person. At least she hadn't been before their divorce.

"I was busy," he said.

Probably with some woman. Not that she cared. It was no longer any of her concern what he did or who he did it with.

"Anyway, what does it matter to you when I do my laundry? We're not married anymore."

"That's my point," she said, straightening up. "We're not married and I don't think you should be running around the house in your underwear." Now she sounded both snippy and bossy. She was never bossy. Never!

He stopped next to her. That close proximity still did things to her.

Used to do things to her. Used to! She told the goose bumps on her arms to settle down.

He grinned at her, a wicked, taunting grin. "Does it… bother you?"

She could feel a guilty as charged heat on her cheeks. "It's not proper." Snippy, bossy and prissy—who was this new and unimproved Ella? "You don't see *me* running around the house in my underwear."

"I wouldn't mind."

She upgraded her frown to a scowl. "We may be sharing this house but it's strictly business."

"I am strictly business, and if my boxers bother you, move."

Like she could afford to move? She didn't have any more money in the bank than he did.

"Go stay with your mama."

He might as well have added, "Mama's girl."

She wasn't a mama's girl and she had as much right to be here until the house sold as he did. She was an adult. She didn't have to run home to her mother.

Anyway, Mims had downsized to a condo in the spiffy new Mountain Ridge condominiums outside town and they didn't allow dogs Tiny's size. If Jake thought she was leaving Tiny to him, he could think again. Tiny needed a mommy and a daddy. Even when they went their separate ways, they'd have joint custody of him. And besides, Ella needed to stay to make sure the house was kept in good condition to show. If she wasn't there, potential buyers would see nothing but dirty toilets, dishes in the sink and beer cans on the coffee table, and they'd never be able to sell the place.

Sell the place—the thought of doing that still hurt. But it

was only one in a string of many hurts she'd endured in the past year. For one wild, crazy moment, she wanted to put a hand to Jake's face and ask, "What happened to us? Why are we doing this?" But she knew what had happened, and there was no going back now. The jet hadn't just taxied down the runway or left the airport. It had left the city. The state. The country. They needed to move on, both of them.

She sighed. "Look, we're stuck here until the place sells. Can't we try and get along?"

He regarded her with those beautiful, dark Irish eyes. Roving eyes! "I'm not the one who started all this, El," he said softly.

"Oh?" Who had "started" it by coming home with another woman's phone number in his pants pocket?

There was no point in bringing that up. He'd just stick with his stupid story about the keyboard player dying to be in his band. Yeah? That wasn't all the woman was dying for. The voice message Ella had gotten when she called the woman's number said it all. *I'm not home right now so leave a message. If this is Jake, I can meet you anytime, anyplace.*

For what? A private audition? It had all been downhill from there.

He'd already let his perfect-husband mask slip before that, though, flirting with every little groupie who sashayed up to the bandstand when his band Ricochet was playing. She'd even caught him taking some girl's black thong one night when the band was on break and he was supposed to be getting a Coke. He'd seen Ella coming and handed it back like it was a hot potato. A lacy hot potato.

"That came out of left field. I was so surprised I didn't know what to do," he'd said.

Just like he hadn't known what to do with a certain key-board player's phone number? How dumb had he thought she was? And once she had proof…oh, he'd climbed on his high horse and acted all insulted that her mother'd had the nerve to hire a private detective to follow him. Who could blame her after hearing about the way he was sneaking around be-hind her daughter's back, collecting other women's panties?

But there was no denying what was plain in those pictures—her husband on another woman's doorstep, hug-ging that woman. After being in her house for an hour. An hour! He'd *claimed* that he'd simply stopped by to drop off some music lead sheets. The kind of sheets they'd been using had nothing to do with music. How many quickies could an unfaithful husband squeeze into an hour? She didn't want to do the math. Boy, whoever said one picture was worth a thousand words must have had a cheating husband.

Well, he'd gotten his keyboard player and Ella had got-ten her divorce. They both got what they wanted. "You're better off without him," Mims had said. "He's never going to amount to anything and you'd have been poor all your life. Starving musicians are a losing proposition."

"I didn't marry Jake to get rich," Ella had protested.

"Congratulations, you succeeded," Mims had retorted. Men might not have been necessary, but as far as her mother was concerned, once a girl had one, he darn well needed to earn his keep.

Her mother was right. Jake was immature and irrespon-sible and, worst of all, a cheater. She was well rid of him. Even if he did look hot in his boxers.

He frowned at her again. "Never mind. There's no point talking anymore. I could talk till I'm blue in the face and you wouldn't hear a thing I said." With that parting remark, he marched up the stairs.

Ella turned her back on him. She was not—not!—going to look at his butt.

In fact, she wasn't even going to stay in this house. By eight he'd be gone, on his way to the Red Barn, a honkytonk a few miles outside of town. There he'd spend the night crooning country songs for people who were more interested in brawling and hooking up than listening to his band.

Ella had always loved listening to the band.

Oh, enough already, she scolded herself.

A moment later Jake was downstairs again and on his way down the hall to the kitchen. He'd covered the boxers with jeans but he was still bare-chested and that brought the goose bumps back for another visit. "The kitchen's mine for twenty more minutes," he called over his shoulder.

"Stay there as long as you want." *Messing everything up.* "I'm leaving," she called.

"Got a hot date?"

None of his business. She declined to answer. Instead, she grabbed her purse and started for the door. Tiny followed her hopefully.

She knelt in front of him and rubbed his side. "I promise I'll be back as soon as he's gone," she whispered. "Then I'll give you a good brushing."

Tiny let out a groan and drool dripped from his chin. (Tiny did his share of mess-making, but unlike the other male in this house, he couldn't help it.)

She kissed the top of his head, then slipped out the door, guilt riding on her shoulder. Poor Tiny. He felt the unhappy vibes in the house. In his doggy heart did he wonder what he'd done to deserve getting adopted into a broken home? If she'd known this was going to happen she'd never have visited that rescue site.

There was nothing she could do about that now. She'd make it up to him, somehow. How, exactly, she didn't know. She hoped she could find someplace to rent that allowed big dogs that drooled and had a tendency to shed. *Oh, dear.*

Her Black Friday was getting blacker by the minute. She left the house, punching in Cecily Sterling's phone number on her cell as she walked.

Ella and Cecily had been friends since high school. In fact, it was Cecily who had gotten Ella and Jake together. They'd lost touch when Cecily moved to L.A. but had reconnected when she returned to Icicle Falls earlier in the year. Cecily had been shocked to hear about the divorce but she'd been sympathetic and supportive. She had men interested in her, two to be exact, but she was done with men (or so she claimed), which made her the ideal dinner companion.

"Have you eaten yet?" Ella asked.

"Nope," Cecily answered. "I just got in the door."

"I don't suppose you'd like to go back out the door, would you?"

"Maybe. What did you have in mind?"

"I need a place to hang out for a couple of hours. Dinner at Zelda's?" Even though it was Friday night and the town was packed with tourists gearing up for Saturday shopping, Charlene Albach could always find a table for her friends.

"Jake's still home?" Cecily guessed.

"Yeah," Ella admitted. This was silly. She couldn't keep running over to Charley's restaurant every time Jake was home.

"I could go for a huckleberry martini," Cecily said.

Oh, yes, a huckleberry martini sounded good. Or two. Whatever it took to wash away the image of Jake in his boxers.

Jake slammed a pot on the stove and pulled a can of chili from his side of the cupboard. Canned chili. He might as well have been a bachelor again.

Oh, yeah. He was.

He frowned at the can as he secured it to the electric can opener. This sucked. His life sucked. From perfect to puke in less than a year.

Was there a song in there somewhere? Probably not. He emptied the chili into the pot, along with a can of stewed tomatoes and a can of corn, his own secret recipe.

Tiny was in the kitchen now and looking expectantly up at him. "Yeah, I know. You like chili, too," he said to the dog. He opened another can and added that to the pot. "You know this will make you fart."

Tiny wagged his tail.

"Yeah, you're right. Who cares? We're guys, it's what we do." And they also walked around the house in their boxers.

Except not anymore, now that he and Ella weren't together. Walking around in his boxers was no longer allowed. So maybe he should talk to her about leaving her bras hanging out in plain sight when she did the laundry. Did she have any idea how crazy that made him? All it took was one glance at those lacy little cups and he could picture Ella with him in that sleigh bed they'd found at an estate sale, going at it like rabbits.

He heaved a sigh. How had he gone from happily married to miserably divorced so fast?

He and Ella were meant to be together. They should've gone to counseling, worked things out.

Aw, heck, they wouldn't even have needed counseling if he'd explained when she first started singing her version of "Your Cheatin' Heart," accusing him of being unfaithful. He'd tried to, but she'd cut him off. Then she'd thrown those pictures down in front of him and he'd been so shocked that his mother-in-law would do something that outrageous, and so offended and just plain pissed...he'd lost it. Wounded pride and anger had escorted him to the edge of the matrimonial cliff and then pushed him off.

It had been a fast fall and he learned firsthand that once the *D* word's been said, there's nothing else left to say.

So here he was, broken and miserable. The woman who'd once thought he hung the moon now wanted nothing more to do with him.

And his chili was burning. He swore and pulled it off the burner. "You're getting the crusty part," he informed Tiny. "You don't care."

You don't care. Ella had thrown those words at him, insisting he sign the divorce papers.

"I'm not the one who filed for this," he'd shot back.

"Just sign it, Jake. Please."

When he'd seen those tears in her eyes, he should have pulled her to him and kissed her breathless. Then he should've torn up the papers, borrowed some money from Pops and moved them to Nashville. *There* was someplace he was sure her mother would never have followed. And that was probably what they needed. It could've been the two of them rather than the three of them.

He put his culinary creation in a bowl, gave Tiny the rest

and then went back to his room. His room. That sucked, too. This was the guest room. Someday it was supposed to have been the nursery. Now it was his room.

He sat on the single bed that was six inches too short for him (a garage sale find), and sighed. Here he was, a squatter in his own home. Maybe Lily Swan was right. Maybe he was a loser. Maybe he had no talent. If he'd just admitted it, quit the band and taken a job in the warehouse at Sweet Dreams Chocolates, maybe he and Ella would still be together. There'd have been no groupies, no Jen, no reason to be jealous. Instead, he'd had to dream of a songwriting career and stardom. He'd tried to support his habit (and them) by working in the music shop on Fourth, but then the music shop had gone out of business. He still had a few guitar students but he wasn't exactly getting rich. In short, these days he was a loser, unable to hang on to his woman and barely able to hang on to his dreams.

He looked at the dresser and the diamond in Ella's engagement ring winked at him mockingly. He'd made payments on that for a whole year. Then he'd bummed the rest of the money he needed from Pops, paid it off and asked her to marry him that same night. She'd given him back both the engagement and wedding rings the day she'd shoved the divorce papers in front of him. "I can't keep them," she'd said. Just like she couldn't keep him.

"No. I gave them to you. Keep them," he'd insisted.

Ella loved jewelry and she'd especially loved that engagement ring, but she'd shaken her head and backed away.

Jake couldn't bring himself to get rid of either ring. They still meant something to him, even if they didn't to Ella.

Damn, he was a walking country song.

With a growl, he set aside his chili and finished getting dressed. No sense hanging around here any longer. He'd go to the Red Barn. Maybe he'd find some cute chick there who appreciated him and his music.

Even if he did, he'd look at her and see Ella.

And that sucked the most of all.

3

Charlene Albach, Charley to her friends, surveyed her domain with satisfaction. *Six o'clock and all is well.*

Zelda's restaurant was filled with diners, many of them out-of-towners who'd come up to enjoy a Thanksgiving weekend getaway. Charley had been happy to oblige. She'd hated to miss going to her sister's in Portland to be with family, but the restaurant was entirely hers now and she simply couldn't leave. So she'd focused instead on giving other families a spectacular holiday, serving turkey dinner with all the trimmings, including stuffing made from her great-grandmother's recipe. Well, with a few new twists. That was part of the fun of owning a restaurant. You got to create new recipes, dream up taste sensations that would keep customers coming back for more.

They were sure coming tonight. People had obviously

worked up their appetites sledding and spending money in the shops. Tomorrow there'd be more sledding and shopping and more diners crowding into Zelda's. And that meant more money in the cash register, which was bound to make for a very merry Christmas. This year Charley planned to be extravagant when shopping for her friends. They'd been there for her at every painful bump on the road to unexpectedly single, and she intended to show her thanks in a way that would make Santa proud.

She had just seated a fortysomething couple with a texting teen in tow when Ella O'Brien and Cecily Sterling came in. "And I thought my shop was crazy," Ella observed, looking around.

The scene was a feast for the eyes. People of all ages and sizes, dressed in winter garb, consumed house specials such as salmon baked in golden puff pastry, squash seasoned with curry, baked winter vegetables and wild huckleberry cheesecake. There was plenty to occupy the other senses, too. The tantalizing scent of sage drifted out from the kitchen, encouraging diners to try the special turkey lasagna Charley's head chef, Harvey, had created, and the clink of silver and hum of voices reminded her that life was good.

No, better than good. Great. Who needed a man, anyway? Getting free of her louse of a husband had freed up her creativity. The restaurant was better off without him. And so was Charley. Anyway, sex was overrated.

And if she kept telling herself that, she might begin to believe it.

"Can you find us a spot?" Cecily asked.

"I can always find room for a former employee. Are you sure you don't want to come back to work for me?" Charley added as she led them to her last remaining two-top. "Like now?"

"Samantha's keeping me busy enough at Sweet Dreams," Cecily said with a smile. "I think my restaurant days are over."

Just like her matchmaking days, or so Cecily claimed. Sometimes Charley entertained the idea of seeing if Cecily would put on her matchmaker hat one last time and find her a perfect man. But then she remembered there was no such thing, which was probably why Cecily was out of the matchmaking business and helping run her family's chocolate company instead.

And there's a reason you're single, Charley told herself. Men were a liability, and they had no staying power. Richard, her ex, had proved that.

Never mind him. You're having a really successful Black Friday. No need to turn it blue.

"So, business was good today?" she asked Ella as she handed her friends their menus.

"We moved a lot of inventory," Ella said, sounding pleased.

Hardly surprising. Ella had a gift for creating irresistible displays in her shop. Charley had certainly succumbed to temptation often enough. How could a girl not when a hot top paired with a sweater that begged to be touched called her over, whispering, "Just try us on. Oh, and don't you love this amazing scarf that's hanging out with us?"

Ella herself was a walking ad. Tonight she was dolled up in jeans tucked into brown suede winter boots trimmed with a faux fur, along with a cream-colored cashmere sweater. She'd finished the look with a jaunty red jacket and a beret. It took style to pull off a beret. Ella had style in spades. Hardly surprising, considering who her mother was.

"That'll make your mom happy," Cecily predicted.

Did anything make Lily Swan happy? Charley could count on one finger the number of times she'd seen the woman smile. Well, really smile. How had such a snobby sour lemon produced such a nice daughter?

It was one of life's mysteries, right up there with the mystery of how Charley could have been so dumb as to miss the fact that her husband was conducting an affair right under her nose…with the woman who worked as their hostess, for crying out loud. Somehow, Ariel hadn't gotten the memo that her hostess duties applied only to paying customers. They did not extend to making your boss's husband at home in your bed.

That was past history. Charley returned to the present. "So, you here celebrating?" she asked Ella.

"More like avoiding," Cecily suggested, making Ella frown. "Jake's still home," she added for Charley's benefit.

"I can see this house-sharing thing is working out great," Charley cracked.

Ella shrugged. "It won't be for long. Anyway, he can't afford a place on his own and I can't afford my half of the house payment plus rent somewhere else."

"Your mom would probably help you."

"I know, but I wouldn't feel right asking her."

"I'd have kicked his butt to the curb," Charley said in no uncertain terms. "Let him stay with one of his band buddies."

"Their wives and girlfriends would have been all over that," Cecily pointed out with a grin.

"Beggars can't be choosers," Charley said. "Neither can cheaters." Oooh, how she hated men who cheated on their wives!

"I know he looked as innocent as a man going to the bank in a ski mask, but I still have a hard time picturing Jake cheating on you," Cecily said to Ella. "It doesn't seem like him."

Good old Cecily, always trying to see the best in people, even when there was no best to see. Although Charley had to admit, Jake had seemed like a nice guy. He and Ella had been Cecily's first successful match, back when she and Ella were in high school. Going their separate ways for college hadn't quenched Ella and Jake's passion, and after graduation had come the big church wedding. Her mother hadn't approved of Jake, but she gave Ella a wedding fit for a princess. They'd not only been a lovely bride and groom, they'd also seemed like the ideal couple, united for life.

Well, she and Richard had seemed like the ideal couple, too. Things weren't always what they appeared.

"I don't want to talk about it," Ella said stiffly.

"Good idea," Charley approved. "Keep this table a heartbreak-free zone." She caught sight of another couple coming in the door and excused herself to greet them.

They were somewhere in their thirties. The man was going bald and his woman was no beauty, but the way they looked at each other proved that love was blind. She hung on to his arm like she'd never let him go.

Charley could remember when she'd held on to Richard like that. Somewhere along the way she'd released her hold....

She yanked herself back into the present and smiled at the

newcomers. "Hi, how are you doing?" As if she had to ask. They were still happily in love.

"Great," said the man.

"Do you have a reservation?" Charley asked.

He shook his head. "Someone told us this is a good place to eat. How long is the wait?"

"About twenty minutes, but we're worth it." Charley smiled. "If you like, you can wait in the bar and we'll call you when there's a table. Try the chocolate kiss," she told the woman.

"That sounds good," the woman said, and squeezed her man's arm.

"We'll wait," he said, and gave Charley his name.

Watching them go, she wondered if they'd be happy together for the rest of their lives. Yes, she decided, they would be. And on their twenty-fifth wedding anniversary they'd come back to Zelda's to celebrate. On that pleasant thought she went to help a frazzled-looking Maria clear the corner table.

As Ella and Cecily enjoyed huckleberry martinis while waiting for their food to arrive Cecily took another stab at convincing her friend that she might have made a mistake.

It wasn't the first time she'd tried, but Ella had been determined to divorce Jake even though Cecily was sure she was still in love with him. Yes, he wasn't perfect, but he was perfect for Ella—a good guy with a nice family. Easygoing, fun-loving, just what Ella needed to balance the life of perfection her mother expected from her.

"I know it seems too late now that the divorce is final,"

Cecily said, "but I can't help thinking you should reconsider this. It doesn't feel right."

Ella stared into her martini glass. She looked like she was going to drop a few tears into it. "I know you're famous for those hunches of yours, but this time you're wrong, Cec. We just aren't a match. He's irresponsible. And untrustworthy."

"But all you really had were suspicions."

"I had more, believe me," Ella said, and took a giant sip of her martini.

Jake was such a stand-up guy, Cecily found that hard to believe. What the heck had happened to these two? They'd been madly in love when she moved to L.A., yet by the time she'd moved back home they were done.

"Well, he's not really irresponsible," she defended Jake. "I mean, I know he doesn't have a normal nine-to-five job, but he has a dream."

"You can't live on dreams."

That sounded more like Lily Swan than Ella O'Brien. Ella's mother had never liked Jake, probably thought he was too much of a redneck for her elegant daughter. Ella had beautiful taste in clothes and decorating, but when it came right down to it, she was a simple, small-town girl, not a New York jet-setter. That was Lily Swan, though. She'd settled in a small town to raise her daughter but she'd always fancied herself a sophisticated woman. Having a son-in-law who was a country musician and who eked out a living teaching guitar and playing in a band didn't line up with her idea of a successful life.

Had Lily herself been all that successful? Surely if she'd been a top model she'd have wound up living in London or

New York or L.A.—some place other than Icicle Falls. If you asked Cecily, Lily Swan had started believing her own press.

Not that anyone was asking Cecily, and not that she would've said what she thought even if she *was* asked. And she wouldn't be saying anything now, except that Ella was miserable and she hated seeing her friend miserable.

"I don't know," she said. "It seems to me if you don't have dreams you're not really living." She'd dreamed of coming home and carving out a new life for herself, and so far that was working out pretty well.

Her new life didn't include love, though. She'd had enough misery in that department. She had to remind herself of this on a regular basis, every time she saw Luke Goodman, Sweet Dreams' production manager. She also had to remind herself that sexual attraction did not equal love every time she ran into Todd Black, who owned the Man Cave, the seedy bar at the edge of town.

Ella finished off her drink. "It just wasn't meant to be. Mims was right."

Mother knows best? Lily Swan had done a fabulous job of brainwashing her daughter. Of course, she'd brainwashed herself, as well, convincing both of them that Ella could do better than Jake. Maybe she could if she was looking for wealth and status. But that wasn't Ella. Hopefully, she'd realize it before it was too late and some other girl came along, picked up Jake's broken heart and put it in her pocket.

The evening went by in a busy blur for Charley. By nine-thirty her feet hurt. That was nothing new. Her feet always hurt by nine-thirty. A few diners remained, savoring coffee and dessert or an after-dinner drink, but most of the crowd had moved on or relocated to the bar at the back of the restaurant. The dining area was now a burble of soft voices and an occasional clink of silverware on plates.

Sore feet aside, this was Charley's favorite time of the night. The dinner rush over, she could bask in the satisfaction of having delivered a memorable dining experience to people celebrating and connecting over food.

Food. It was the centerpiece of life. From dinners of state to family gatherings, sharing food was an essential part of human connection. And it was the spice of love. How could you *not* fall in love when you were gazing across the table at someone? And when your sense of taste came alive over a Chocolate Decadence dessert or a crab soufflé the other senses joined the party. There was a reason lovers went out to dinner.

Some might say she simply owned a restaurant. Charley knew better. She owned a slice of people's lives.

Tonight she'd had a great slice. She smiled, remembering how the texting teen had actually stopped on the way out to tell her she loved the wild blackberry pie. Her smile grew with the memory of the couple in love strolling out the door hand in hand. Oh, yes, a very successful night, she concluded as she loaded dirty dishes onto a tray.

She had just lifted it up to haul off to the kitchen when a cold gust of wind blew in the door. She looked up to see who the latecomer was and received a shock that made her heart jump and the tray slip from her hands, sending dishes and glasses to shatter on the floor. Oh, no. It couldn't be.

But it was. The Ghost of Christmas Past. Her ex.

4

Charley stood gaping at her former husband. Random thoughts circled her brain like so many spinning plates. *What's he doing here? Am I hallucinating? Let's test that theory by throwing a broken plate at him.*

Maria hurried over to help her clean up, saw Richard and managed a shocked "Oh."

Okay, now Charley knew she wasn't hallucinating.

He stepped into the dining area. "Hello, Charley. You look good."

So did he. Richard wasn't a tall man, coming in at around five foot eight, but what there was of him was yummy. Yes, he'd added some gray strands to his dark hair—she hoped the new girlfriend had given him every one—but other than that he was sailing pleasantly into his forties with only a hint of lines around those gray eyes. He still had that full mouth and the misleadingly strong jaw. Anyone would mistake him for a movie hero. Movies, yes. Hero? Definitely not.

He stood there in his jeans and winter jacket, looking at her—how? Hopefully? No, that couldn't be it. She had nothing he wanted. He'd made that abundantly clear when he chose another woman.

"What are you doing here?" she asked, her voice flat.

"I wanted to see you."

"Well, I don't want to see you. Ever again." Charley bent next to Maria and began to pick up some of the bigger pieces of dishware.

Richard joined them, loading a chunk of broken glass onto the tray.

"I don't need your help," Charley growled. "Anyway, you might cut yourself and sue me." She was already giving him enough money. Talk about adding insult to injury. As part of the divorce settlement she'd had to buy out his share of the restaurant. *Her* restaurant!

Oh, yes, he'd worked it with her, but it had been hers—her vision, her creation. She'd sunk her entire inheritance from her grandmother into the place when it was a dying dump, and with imagination and hard work she'd built it into a popular community gathering spot. Richard had only come along for the ride.

And then taken her for a ride.

He laid a hand on hers. "I really need to talk to you."

Maria gave a disgusted snort before hauling the tray full of breakage off to the kitchen.

Charley's sentiments exactly. She sat back on her heels and regarded her ex. "You can't want more money. God knows you've taken enough from me."

He looked at her as if she'd stabbed him with a steak knife. "Charley…listen, we can't talk here."

"I don't want to talk at all."

"I know I don't deserve so much as the time of day from you, but please, can we go back to the house?"

"*My* house," she reminded him. She was buying out his share of that, too.

"Please?"

Maybe she was curious, or maybe the desperation in his voice gave her an appetite for more of the same. She could feel herself weakening.

Still she hedged. "I'm not done here."

"I'm staying at Gerhardt's. Call me on my cell when you're finished."

The same cell phone he'd used to text messages to Ariel, setting up stolen quickies in the bar before the employees arrived. Before Charley arrived.

"Charley, please. I know I don't deserve it but please."

"I'll think about it," she said. "And that's the most I can promise."

He managed an awkward nod. "I'll be waiting," he said, and then walked out the door.

Charley stood slowly. She was only thirty-nine but she suddenly felt ninety and weary right down to her soul.

Maria was back with a whisk broom and dustpan, frowning. "What did that *bastardo* want?"

"I'm not sure." And she wasn't sure she wanted to find out. "But he wants to see me later."

"Don't do it," Maria cautioned. "He already hurt you once."

"Don't worry, I won't let him do it again," Charley assured her.

But when she finally got home she found herself calling him. He probably wouldn't leave until she gave in, so the sooner she saw him, the sooner he'd go.

He was at her door ten minutes later.

"Make this fast," she said as he stepped in. "I'm tired and I want to go to bed." *Alone, like I've been doing ever since you left.*

He motioned to the living room. "Can we sit down?"

The last thing she wanted was Richard back in her living room. Bad enough that almost everything in it held a memory of their life together, from the brown microfiber sofa where they'd cuddled watching football or the Food Network to the Tiffany-style lamp he'd bought for her birthday three years ago. She should have gotten rid of that lamp. Heck, she should've gotten rid of everything. "I don't understand why you're here," she said bitterly, leading the way to the couch. She sat down, crossed her arms over her chest and scowled at him.

He sat close to her—too close—and looked at her earnestly. "I'm here to ask you to take me back."

This was the biggest shock she'd had since, well, since she'd discovered him cheating on her. "What?"

"I don't know what I was thinking."

"I don't either, but I know what you were thinking with," she retorted.

His face flushed, but he held her gaze. "If I had it to do over…"

"You wouldn't have done her?" Charley finished for him. "What's the matter, Richard, did she dump you for a younger man?"

The flush deepened. Bingo! "I was a fool."

"Yes, you were," Charley agreed, "and for all I know you still are. Why should I take you back?"

"Because I love you."

That produced a bitter laugh. "Oh, please. Don't make me sick."

"I do," he insisted. "I always have. Ariel was a mistake."

"A mistake you were happy enough to make," Charley said. "You had a chance to give her up and you didn't."

"I wasn't thinking clearly."

"Well, I am." She stood, signaling that this ridiculous conversation was over.

He stood, too. He was barely taller than she was. Why had she picked such a small man?

"All I'm asking is that you give me a chance to prove I've changed. Twelve years together, Charley—that has to count for something."

"It should have counted for something when you were looking around for a side dish."

He sighed. "You're right."

"You know where the door is."

His eyes filled with regret. "What would it take to convince you I've changed?"

She studied him. "You know..."

He regarded her hopefully.

"I can't think of a thing." She walked to the door and opened it. "Good night, Richard."

He took the hint and walked out the door, but as he passed her he said, "I'm not giving up. You're worth fighting for."

He hadn't thought that a year ago. She slammed the door after him and locked it.

★ ★ ★

The Gingerbread Haus opened at ten but Cass was always in by six, baking cookies and, at this time of year, assembling gingerbread houses, many of which would be shipped all over the country.

She got plenty of appreciation in her hometown, too, and Olivia Wallace arrived at eleven to pick up the creation Cass had made for the lobby of the Icicle Creek Lodge. A perfect replica of Olivia's B and B styled after a Bavarian hunting lodge, it even sported a blue-frosting creek running past it.

"It's lovely as usual," Olivia said. "I don't know how I'll be able to resist nibbling at it."

Olivia's well-rounded figure testified to her lack of willpower. But Olivia was a widow and, as far as Cass was concerned that gave her unlimited nibbling rights. Anyway, Cass was in no position to say anything. She was a nibbler, too.

"Here's a little something extra for when you get the urge," she said, and handed Olivia a box containing a baker's dozen frosted gingerbread cookies cut in the shape of Christmas trees.

"Oh, thank you," Olivia said. "How much do I owe you for these?"

"Nothing. They're on the house. The gingerbread house," Cass added with a wink.

Dani came in from sending off the day's shipment of gingerbread creations. "Here's our bride-to-be," Olivia greeted her.

Dani's cheeks flushed with pleasure and she smiled at Olivia.

She's going to be a beautiful bride, Cass thought. If only they had more time to plan this wedding.

"I just gave your grandmother and aunt our last room," Olivia said to Dani. "It's a good thing you called when you did, or that one would've been gone," she added. "I've had three calls since."

"One of them was probably my stepmother," Dani said, and now the pink in her cheeks wasn't from pleasure.

Babette. Cass could feel her mouth slipping down at the corners. *Bimbette* was more like it. Cass hadn't met her, but she'd seen pictures. The woman was nothing more than arm candy. Cass had it on good authority (her son's) that she couldn't cook.

Not that Mason had married Babette for her culinary skills. She'd been a professional cheerleader for the Seattle Seahawks, a Sea Gal, and she had the body to prove it. Of course, once she snagged Mason at the ripe old age of thirty, she gave that up. Now she was all of what, thirty-one? And stepmother to a twenty-year-old. What a joke.

Olivia looked distinctly uncomfortable. "I wish I'd known earlier. I'd have reserved a block of rooms for you."

"If any of us had known earlier we would've been more organized," Cass said. She'd meant that as an explanation, not an accusation of her daughter. Judging from the deep rose shade blooming on Dani's cheeks, she'd taken the remark to heart. "But Mike got a job in Spokane and he starts in January and they want to be together."

"Of course you do," Olivia said to Dani. "I sure hope the rest of your guests find someplace. I know Annemarie is full up and so is Gerhardt."

No room at the inn. What a shame. Mason and Bimbette might have to miss the wedding. Not a very gracious thought, Cass scolded herself.

"Oh," Dani said, a world of worry in her voice.

"Mountain Springs over by Cashmere might have something," Olivia suggested. "That wouldn't be too far away."

Dani nodded and whipped her cell phone out of her jeans.

As she stepped away to make the call, Olivia lowered her voice. "I imagine this is all a little awkward."

There was an understatement. "A little," Cass said.

"I almost felt like a traitor saving a room but Dani asked."

"It's okay. In fact, I really appreciate it. Otherwise, they might have had to stay with me."

The very thought of that was enough to make Cass shudder. Her judgmental ex-mother-in-law and her gossipy ex-sister-in-law staying with *her?* Ugh.

Two middle-aged women had come in and were waiting patiently in front of the glass display case. Olivia, like everyone else in Icicle Falls, knew the value of a tourist dollar. "Well, I'd better be going," she said. "I've got to get to the grocery store or my guests won't have breakfast tomorrow." To the newcomers she said, "The gingerbread boys are delicious, but make sure you get a couple of those cream puff swans, too. They're to die for."

The women took her advice, purchasing gingerbread boys and girls and a couple of cream puffs. One of them bought a gingerbread house, as well.

Meanwhile, more customers had come into the bakery. Normally Dani would be helping Cass, but right now she and her cell phone were in the kitchen looking for lodging for Mason and Bimbette.

Let them find their own place to stay. Cass moved to the kitchen area. "I could use some help out here."

Dani turned her back and held up a hand, which meant—what? Trying to hear? Be there in a minute?

"Now," Cass added in her stern mama-bear voice.

"Okay, thanks," Dani said, and ended the call.

"Honey, you're going to have to do that later," Cass said. "We've got customers."

"We've always got customers," Dani muttered grumpily.

Which was how they paid the bills. This had never bothered her daughter before.

But then she'd never been engaged.

Twenty minutes rushed past before they had a lull. Cass knew it was temporary. Once the lunch hour was finished, the customers would return.

She turned the sign on the door to Closed. "We'll Be Back by One," said the clock below. That gave them time for lunch, and in Dani's case, time to go back to calling every motel and B and B within a twenty-mile radius.

Cass sat down at a corner table with her cup of coffee and watched as Dani became increasingly desperate with every conversation. That desperation began to make Cass's coffee churn in her stomach. If her daughter didn't succeed in her mission it boded ill—not for Dani, and not for Mason and Bimbette, but for Cass.

Sure enough. At a quarter to one Dani plopped onto the chair next to her and tossed her smartphone on the table.

Tell me we're out of eggs, tell me someone's order never arrived, tell me anything but what you're about to tell me.

"There's no vacancy anywhere," Dani announced miserably.

Cass spoke before her daughter could say the dreaded

words. "It'll be okay. Seattle's not that far. Your dad can drive over the day of the wedding."

Dani looked at her, eyes wide in horror. "But what about the rehearsal dinner the night before? And what if something happens? What if they close the pass?"

Then we can get on our knees and thank God.

Okay, that was truly rotten. This was her daughter's big day and she wanted her father there. "I'm sure he'll figure it out," Cass said, trying to sound as if she cared.

"Mom, how can he when there's no place anywhere?"

Surely that was a rhetorical question. She kept her mouth shut.

"Can they stay with us for a couple of days?"

There it was, what she'd known was coming all along. Just what she wanted for Christmas, her ex and his bimbo bride staying with her. "We have no place to put them," she argued.

"They can have my room. I can sleep with Amber."

"I was going to give your room to Grandma Nordby." Cass would jump into boiling oil before she'd turn her mother out in favor of Mason and Bimbette.

"Then give them Willie's room and put him on the sleeper sofa. Or put them on the sleeper sofa."

That was what Cass wanted, to come out and find her ex and his second wife curled up together in her living room.

"We could find a place for them for just one night, couldn't we?" Dani begged. "Two at the most."

There had to be some other way they could work this out. Cass stalled for time. "Let me think about it, okay?"

Dani made a face like she'd just eaten baking soda. "I know what that means."

So did Cass, and she felt like the world's meanest mother.

A woman with two little girls had come to the door, and the girls were peering inside.

"Go unlock the door," Cass said wearily.

"Sure. Fine," Dani said in a tone of voice that showed how un-fine everything was.

"It would be nice if you could greet our customers with a smile instead of a frown," Cass called after her.

"I'm smiling," Dani called back. Smiling on the outside, seething on the inside.

They'll find someplace to stay, Cass told herself. Now, if she could only believe that.

5

It was Sunday evening, time for Cass's weekly chick flick night. The friends had decided to watch Christmas movies during the month of December and Cass's pal Samantha Sterling had picked the one for tonight—*The Family Man*.

"I love that movie," she'd said. "Love how the hero changed from a Scrooge to a great husband and dad."

"I never knew you were so sentimental," Cass had teased.

"I'm not," Samantha had retorted, "but I know what's important."

Cass would give her that. Samantha Sterling had fought hard to save her family's chocolate company. In the process she'd resuscitated the town of Icicle Falls, which had been in an economic slump, by sponsoring a chocolate festival. Spurred on by that success, the town leaders had caught festival fever. October had seen Oktoberfest, December's tree-lighting event had been expanded from one weekend to every weekend and there was talk of a wine festival in the early summer.

Samantha and her sister Cecily were the first to arrive, rosy-cheeked and smiling, stomping snow off their boots. Blue-eyed, blond-haired Cecily was the beauty of the family, but with her red hair and freckles, Samantha wasn't exactly a troll. She'd married Blake Preston, the bank's manager, in August and still sported a newlywed glow. That would wear off eventually.

Listen to you, Cass scolded herself. *Queen of the cynics.*

"We brought vitamin C," Samantha said, handing over a holiday box of Sweet Dreams Chocolates.

Chocolate, the other Vitamin C, and a girl's best friend. "This takes care of me. I don't know what the rest of you are having," Cass joked. "Did you bring the movie?"

Cecily held up the DVD with Nicolas Cage on the cover. "We're set."

Ella was the next to arrive. She wasn't as beautiful as her glamorous mother, Lily Swan, but she was cute and she knew how to dress. Tonight she looked ready for a magazine shoot in skinny jeans paired with a crisp white shirt, a black leather vest and a long, metallic red scarf, and bearing a bowl of parmesan popcorn, her specialty. Ella even did popcorn with flair.

Cass decided that flair was something you either soaked up in the gene pool or you didn't. She could create works of art in her bakery, but when it came to personal style she couldn't seem to get beyond unimpressionist. Oh, well. What did she care? She didn't have anyone she needed to impress.

Not even your ex-in-laws?

No, she told herself firmly. Living well was the best revenge and she was living quite well, thank you. She didn't
need to look like a cover model to prove it.

She pushed aside the thought of Babette, who would, of
course, show up for the wedding with her hair perfectly
highlighted and her skinny little bod draped in something
flattering. Maybe Cass would pass on the chocolate and
popcorn tonight.

Charley was the last to arrive. She came bearing wine
and looked frazzled enough to consume the entire bottle
single-handed.

"Okay, what's wrong?" Cass asked once the women were
settled in the living room with their drinks and goodies.

"Richard's back." Charley took one of Cass's gingerbread
boys and bit off his head.

Cass nearly dropped her wineglass. "What?"

Charley nodded. More of the gingerbread boy disappeared.

"Why is he back?" Cass asked. "What does he want?"

"Me," Charley said.

"You? He left you for another woman! Tell him to take
a hike off the mountain," Samantha advised.

Cass couldn't have said it better herself. "I'll second that."

"So he's left Ariel?" Cecily asked.

"He says it was all a mistake."

Men always said that when they got caught with their
pants down. Cass frowned. "Not as big a mistake as taking
him back would be."

"You're not going to, are you?" asked Samantha.

"Absolutely not," Charley shook her head vigorously.

"Good for you," Cass said. Charley had the kind of never-ending legs that made men drool and gorgeous long hair and plenty of personality. She didn't have to settle for letting a loser back in her life.

"Did you tell him that?" Samantha asked.

"Of course I did."

"Then why is he still here?" Samantha persisted.

Charley was on her second gingerbread boy now. "He says he's not giving up."

"Oh, brother," Ella said, rolling her eyes.

"Why is it men only want you when you don't want them?" Charley grumbled.

"Because they're bums," Cass said.

"Not all of them," Samantha murmured.

"Blake is the exception to the rule," Cass told her.

"There are other exceptions out there," Cecily added.

"Like Luke Goodman?" her sister teased.

"Like Luke," Cecily agreed, her voice neutral.

Ella sighed. "So why do we always like the bad boys?"

Charley sighed, too. "Because we're masochists?"

"There's something about bad boys," Cecily said, then seeing her sister's frown, got busy inspecting a lock of hair for split ends.

"Yeah, something bad," her sister said firmly. "Men like Richard and Todd Black are nothing but heartbreak on two legs."

"I wasn't talking about Todd," Cecily said, her cheeks pink.

"I was," Samantha said.

Cecily grabbed a handful of popcorn. "I don't know about the rest of you, but I'm ready to watch the movie."

With Samantha in bossy older sister mode that was understandable. Cass started the movie.

As the plot unfolded, chronicling the life of the fictional Jack Campbell, she couldn't help thinking of her own choices, of Mason. What if they'd been given a glimpse of a better future, one where they stayed united and lived as best friends instead of combatants? What would her life look like now?

What did it matter? She and Mason had made their choices and no hip angel was going to drop into their lives to give them a second chance. The best glimpse she could get was one of her daughter's wedding going smoothly, of herself managing to be civil. If she could pull that off, it would be a miracle.

What a wonderful movie. And what a wonderful way to start the holidays. Ella was teary-eyed by the end of it. She always cried at movies. She cried over movies with sad endings because she felt so bad for the poor people. A movie with a happy ending, especially a romantic movie, brought her to tears because, well, it was all so overwhelmingly hopeful. Somewhere out there in the real world a man could be coming to his senses, realizing that he didn't need to go off in search of El Dorado, that there was gold right in his own backyard. Maybe like the Jack Campbell character, Charley's husband had figured that out.

Jake had insisted he had, that Ella was all he needed.

What big fat lies! Thank God her mother had opened her eyes to the truth. Otherwise, she'd have wasted the best years of her life, keeping the home fires burning on a shoestring budget while he carried on with other women.

"Well." Cass raised her glass. "Here's to the Jack Campbells of the world, wherever they're hiding."

"I'll drink to that. I found mine," Samantha said.

"And here's to Christmas," Cecily toasted.

"And Christmas weddings," Samantha added. "Do these guys know Dani's engaged?"

"That's wonderful! Why didn't you tell us?" Ella asked Cass.

"You've been anticipating this for months. I'm surprised you haven't been crowing from the rooftops," Charley said.

"I was going to tell you all." Cass shrugged. "I got distracted."

When Ella and Jake had gotten engaged, she'd told everyone. How did a woman get distracted from sharing such big news? "That's so exciting. Tell us now."

"She's getting married the weekend before Christmas at Olivia's."

"Oh, that'll be gorgeous," Cecily said. "Olivia always has the place decorated like something out of a magazine."

Especially at Christmas. The outside of the lodge would be awash with white twinkle lights, and inside cedar swags and red bows would adorn the banisters. But the best decoration of all was the vintage sleigh, decked out with swags and ribbons, surrounded by decorative gift boxes. Ella could envision Dani and Mike in that sleigh, posing for pictures in their wedding day finery.

"But wow, it doesn't give you much time," she said. It had taken her nine months to plan her wedding.

"And I thought we had a challenge putting together our chocolate festival in six weeks," Cecily joked.

"Why so quick?" asked Ella, and then blushed as one obvious possibility occurred.

"No, they don't have a baby on the way," Cass said. "Just a move to Spokane in January."

"Are you going to be able to pull it off?" Ella asked after Cass had explained about Mike's new job.

"Are you stressed about getting everything done?" put in Cecily. "We can help, you know."

"Absolutely," said Charley, and Ella nodded her agreement.

"That's not the bug in the soup, is it?" Samantha looked at Cass.

"Then what?" Ella asked. "Are you worried that she's too young?"

"She is young," Cass admitted. "And I was figuring she and Mike would wait a year before getting married. But she's had her life mapped out since she was twelve—baking, husband and babies."

Ella could identify with that. Well, except for the baking part. She'd always wanted a family, complete with husband. "Then what's the bug in the soup?"

Cass frowned. "Dani wants her father to walk her down the aisle."

They all knew how Cass felt about her ex. "Oh," Ella said, at a loss for anything else to say.

"Yeah, *oh*. And it gets better. Guess where my daughter wants him and stepmommy to stay?"

Charley's eyes got so big Ella thought they'd pop out of her head. "Seriously?"

"Pathetically seriously," Cass said.

Cecily picked up the box of chocolates. "You need one of these."

Several chocolates and much commiseration later, the party broke up.

"How are we going to help her get through this?" Cecily asked as the women made their way down Cass's front walk.

"We could beat up Bimbette," Charley cracked. "Or poison the ex." She shook her head. "Cass is nuts if she goes along with this."

"She'll cave," Samantha predicted. "She likes to pretend she's tough, but when it comes to her kids she's softer than a marshmallow. I think we're going to have to be available 24/7 so she's got someone to vent to."

"For sure," Charley agreed. "I can't imagine being stuck in the same house with your ex." She seemed to realize what she'd said and her face turned as red as a poinsettia. "Sorry, Ella."

"It's okay," Ella said. "And I can tell you from experience, it's going to be hard."

"Hopefully your place will sell soon and you can move on," Samantha told her.

Move on. Move. Ella's holiday spirit suddenly moved on without her. "Hopefully," she echoed.

She said goodbye to the others and returned to her empty dream house.

Jake was at an open mike at the Red Barn so the only one home was Tiny. He greeted her with a woof and a wagging tail.

"I know," she said, rubbing the top of his massive head. "You're ready for some exercise, huh, boy?"

Tiny woofed again and danced back and forth. She opened the front door and he darted out into the night.

Ella followed at a more sedate pace, wondering what it was like to be a dog. Did dogs ever worry? Did they ever question whether they'd made the right choice, done the right thing?

Silly thought, of course. All a dog had to do was enjoy being a dog. Someone else made the tough decisions.

If she and Jake had been Saint Bernards...

She shook her head at her own foolishness and whistled for Tiny to heel. Too bad she couldn't have whistled for Jake to heel before he went bounding off.

Jake wasn't the kind of man to heel. Instead of saying how sorry he was and asking her to forgive him after his fling with that keyboard player, he'd gotten combative. "I'm tired of this shit, Ella. If you can't trust me, then we can't be together."

It had been all downhill from there.

"You don't need a man to be happy," Mims had told her.

Except Ella no longer had a man and she wasn't happy.

She stewed over that for twenty minutes while Tiny sniffed and marked his territory. Then it started to snow and she turned them toward the house. By the time they got back she was in need of some bedtime hot chocolate.

She shed her coat and went to the kitchen to get her last packet of instant cocoa. She was pleasantly surprised to see that Jake had actually cleared his dishes from her vintage red Formica table. And then not surprised to find them in the sink. From the sink to the dishwasher was only one more step. How hard was that? He'd probably left them there, figuring she'd do it for him.

She opened the cupboard beneath the sink to get out the dish soap.

What was this? Water. A little pool of water. How had he managed that?

She mopped it up, then loaded the dishes. Now all that was left was a pot crusted with bits of burned chili. It didn't take long to deduce that the chili was welded to the pan, so after a futile attempt to dislodge it, she added more soap and filled it to the brim with water to soak overnight. Then she rinsed out the sponge and the sink and opened the cupboard to put away the dish soap.

Oh, no. Here was a fresh puddle. Just what they needed right now, a leaky sink. She'd have to call a plumber first thing in the morning. Another bill to split down the middle.

She picked up the phone and called Jake's cell. He was probably up on the bandstand singing about love with that man-stealing keyboard player or sitting at a table nursing a Coke and flirting with some cowgirl poured into tight jeans. That was his life—fun, glamorous and irresponsible. And while he flirted and played his guitar she dealt with leaky faucets.

She was well rid of this relationship. Next time she'd be smart when it came to choosing a man. Maybe she'd even find herself a plumber.

She'd expected her call to roll over to Jake's voice mail but he answered on the second ring. "Everything okay?"

Why did he immediately think something was wrong? Oh, yeah. She was calling him. "The pipe under the kitchen sink is leaking. I just wanted to let you know so you wouldn't use it when you got ho—back." *Home,* that would've been the wrong word to use. This house wasn't a home anymore.

"I'll call the plumber tomorrow." Maybe he could squeeze her in that same day. It would make life simpler, since the shop was closed on Mondays.

"Don't do that," Jake said.

"We can't leave it." No one would want to buy a house that was falling apart.

"I know. I'll fix it."

Jake wasn't the world's best handyman. Last summer he'd gone through a pile of two-by-fours trying to fix one broken front-porch step. "I don't think that's a good idea."

"Hey, any guy can fix a leaky pipe," he said. "I'm not paying a plumber."

She sure wasn't going to foot the entire bill. "Okay," she said. "But you'll fix it first thing tomorrow, right?" Their Realtor, Axel Fuchs, had cautioned her to always have the house in tip-top shape. You never knew when a potential buyer would want to look at it.

"I'll do it tomorrow," Jake said. "Don't worry."

Don't worry? That would be possible only if she were a Saint Bernard.

6

Richard was history. He needed to stay history, and that was exactly what Charley was going to tell him next time he popped up like the Ghost of Christmas Past. It wasn't right to come back into a girl's life after she'd worked through her anger (well, most of it) and gotten on with things. And she'd tell him that, she decided as she put on her makeup.

It was Monday and the restaurant was closed. She never bothered with makeup on Mondays.

She glared at her reflection. *Why are you doing this?*

Pride. She wanted Richard to see her at her best when she told him to set his boxers on fire and get lost.

"You liar," she scolded herself. "You just want him to see you looking your best, period."

Charley tossed her mascara in her makeup basket and left the bathroom.

She always stayed home on Monday mornings. She did her laundry in the morning and fooled around on Facebook. After lunch she'd read or watch the Food Network and then she'd take a run to Bruisers for a quick workout on the treadmill. Or go to the bakery for a little something—always more fun than the treadmill.

No hanging around the house this morning, she told herself. If Richard tried a surprise attack he'd find the fort deserted. She could finish her Christmas shopping. She'd hang out in Gilded Lily's, Hearth and Home and Mountain Treasures. Oooh, and for lunch she'd indulge in a bratwurst at Big Brats. Then maybe she'd stop in at Sweet Dreams and say hi to Samantha. Or wander over to Gingerbread Haus and treat herself to a gingerbread boy.

She donned the knitted hat Ella had made for her and grabbed her winter coat.

And opened the door just in time to see Richard coming up the front steps, bundled up for winter in a parka and ski cap and carrying a thermos. She didn't know which irritated her more, the fact that he'd ignored her command to bug off or that at the sight of him her heart lost its groove and gave a nervous skip. "What are you doing here?"

"Kidnapping you."

"That's against the law. Anyway, you're not big enough to overpower me," she added, and hoped that hurt. She shut the door after herself and started past him.

"Kidnapping you to go on a sleigh ride," he said, ignoring her barb.

She stopped in her tracks. A sleigh ride. Other than chocolate, there was nothing more tempting. Sleigh rides were becoming a popular tourist activity in Icicle Falls. Ever since she and Richard had moved to town, Charley had wanted to take one, but somehow she'd never found time. There was something so romantic about a sleigh ride.

There would be nothing romantic about taking one with her ex. "Currier's doesn't offer sleigh rides on weekdays."

"They do this week. I made special arrangements with Kirk Jones."

Special arrangements. What strings had Richard pulled to get the owner of the Christmas tree farm to harness up his horses on a Monday?

Richard held up the thermos. "Hot chocolate with peppermint schnapps."

"I don't care if it's champagne."

"That's for brunch. At the Firs."

The Firs was an exclusive resort compound that extended for acres and included everything from hiking trails to outdoor hot tubs and pools surrounded by mountain rock. Cabins were outfitted with luxury furnishings and the dining hall provided feasts prepared by the kind of top chefs Charley only dreamed of hiring.

Now she was doubly tempted.

Don't do it.

"All I'm asking for is a chance. Just give me today."

One day, that was all he was asking.

She sighed. "Why did you have to come back?"

"Because I need you."

"You didn't need me a year ago when you were boinking Ariel in the bar."

Richard grimaced. "Charley, I've changed. Let me prove it."

Eating at the Firs was the equivalent of eating at Canlis in Seattle. She had no intention of getting back together with Richard, but that didn't mean she couldn't use him. Just deserts, she concluded. She'd use him like he'd once used her. Then he could see how it felt.

"Okay, I'll go," she said. "It's not going to do you any good, but I'll go."

He grinned like she'd just offered to sleep with him. "It's a beginning."

Currier's Tree Farm was rustic and picturesque. The snow-frosted split rail fence along the property was draped with cedar swags and red bows. The big tree in the yard was adorned with lights and huge colored balls and a shawl of snow. Behind the house, the tree farm stretched out with every imaginable kind of holiday tree. Off to the left she saw a stand where visitors could enjoy complimentary hot cider and to the right sat a big, red barn. There, in front of it, stood an old-fashioned sleigh decked out in cedar swags and ribbon. The chestnut draft horses looked equally festive, with jingle bells in their harnesses, their manes and tails braided with red ribbons. One of them stamped a foot. Another let out a soft nicker.

A lean, gray-haired man in winter garb came out of the barn and waved at them. "You're right on time," he called to Richard, and motioned for them to join him. "Got a perfect day for a sleigh ride," he greeted Charley.

"It was nice of you to open for us," Charley said.

He grinned, a big, broad smile that filled his face. "Anything for lovers."

Lovers! Was that what Richard had told him? "Not exactly," Charley said, frowning. "We're exes."

That made Kirk Jones's bushy gray eyebrows shoot up and Richard's mouth turn down.

"Oh, well," Kirk said, and then cleared his throat. "It's a great day for a sleigh ride."

"No matter who it's with," Charley said, ignoring Richard's helping hand and climbing into the sleigh.

Kirk had provided a plaid wool blanket and Richard spread it across her legs.

"Thanks. Lover," she said with some asperity.

"You can't blame me because people jump to conclusions," he said.

"Did you give him a little push?"

"No. I told him the truth."

Charley cocked an eyebrow. "Oh? And what was that?"

"That this is for a special lady. No lie." He uncorked the thermos and pulled two disposable cups from his coat pocket.

As he poured she remembered how good he'd always been at romantic gestures—creating a dish and naming it after her, taking her over the mountains to Seattle one year to look at Christmas lights and then spending the night in a downtown hotel, hiding a bit of anniversary bling under her pillow.

What romantic things had he done for Ariel?

He handed over her hot chocolate. Then he poured himself a cup and capped the thermos. "To new beginnings," he said, and raised his cup to her.

She said nothing in return, just took a sip and looked away.

"Or the hope of new beginnings," Richard amended.

In your dreams, Charley thought, and downed some more.

Kirk was up in the sleigh now. He clicked his tongue and gave the horses' rumps a gentle slap with the reins and they lurched forward.

Good thing her cocoa was half-gone, or she'd have been wearing it. And that would have been a shame because it was delicious. This was no instant stuff, she could tell. It had been made with cream and fine Dutch chocolate. Chocolate, the way to a girl's heart.

But not this girl's. Richard would never find his way back to hers, not even with a GPS made of solid Sweet Dreams dark.

Still, she decided, she might as well enjoy the ride.

There was plenty to enjoy. The sleigh ride was everything it should be. They wooshed past fir and pine trees clad in frosty white and open fields that beckoned them to come play in the snow, and all the while the sleigh bells on the horses' harnesses jingled. The air was crisp and Charley could see her breath but the cocoa and the blanket kept her warm. Meanwhile, Richard was looking at her like he was a starving man and she a six-course meal. The best salve in the world for wounded pride.

Except it had been Richard who'd wounded her pride in the first place. Starvation was too good for him.

"This is perfect, isn't it?" he said, and placed an arm around her shoulders.

She slid out from under it. "Almost."

He was smart enough not to ask what kept it from being perfect.

They turned onto a path that led down a small incline and took them under a canopy of snowy tree boughs. This was magical. Charley sighed and leaned back against the seat cushions.

Up front Kirk was crooning a song about lovely weather for a sleigh ride.

"With you," Richard whispered. "Aw, Charley, there's no one like you."

"You're right," she agreed.

"I'm just sorry I had to learn that the hard way."

"Yes, you are a sorry man," she said, making him frown. And that made her snicker.

After a brunch that involved several glasses of champagne she'd switched from snickering to giggling.

"I drank too much," she realized as he drove her home.

"Maybe a little," he said.

"Why did you let me drink so much champagne?" She groaned. "I'm going to have the mother of all headaches later."

"Well, we can fix that," he said. "You just need some water, and lucky for you I've got Perrier."

She eyed him. "You thought of everything, didn't you?"

"And then some," he replied with a smile.

She shivered, but not because of what his smile did to her. She'd gotten chilled on the sleigh ride, that was the problem.

"How about I build you a fire?" he offered as they pulled up in front of the house that used to be theirs.

All she needed was him in her house building a fire. "I don't think so. I have things to do." Except after their gargantuan meal and those glasses of champagne, all she wanted to do was take a nap. She got out of the car before he could come around and let her out. "Thanks, Richard," she said, and shut the door.

He got out, too, and held up the green bottle. "Water. Remember?"

"I think I can manage to turn on the faucet."

"This tastes better," he said, and followed her up the walk. Like a bad smell.

She opened the door and before she could tell him good-bye and close it in his face he'd slipped in.

Ella returned home from running errands to find a village of dishes in the sink and the water still turned off. Jake's voice and the sound of his guitar strumming drifted down to her. Great. He'd forgotten to fix the sink.

She marched up the stairs and into his room. There he sat on the bed, wearing jeans and T-shirt, his feet bare—a gorgeous country balladeer with tousled dark hair, looking good enough for a CD cover and completely oblivious to the rest of the world. Once upon a time Ella had thought that was so cute. Now she just thought it was irresponsible.

Tiny, who'd been lying at his feet, enthralled, bounded up at the sight of her and came over, tail wagging. Jake's singing stopped and his hands froze on the guitar strings. He turned his head, his expression both guilty and surprised. "You're home already?"

"It's 5:20," she informed him. "You said you were going to fix the sink today."

"I was. I am."

"Well, it's not fixed. I'm going to call a plumber."

He set the guitar on the bed. "I'll get the stuff right now and have it fixed in an hour."

"The hardware store closes in ten minutes."

"I can make it."

She frowned but said nothing. She knew she shouldn't have trusted him to take care of this. Thank God no one was coming to see the house tonight.

By the time he returned from the hardware store she'd changed into her jeans and a sweater and was heating up leftover chicken soup.

"That smells good," he said.

He'd always loved her chicken soup. These days, though, they didn't share food.

"Fix the sink and I'll give you some."

He grinned and spread his tools on the floor—a wrench, a flashlight, some sort of hose and a bowl he'd gotten from the cupboard.

"That's all you need?" she asked.

"It's a simple job. All I gotta do is replace the flex hose for the cold-water line. I'll need you to hold the flashlight, though."

Assuming she'd be there (like he'd always assumed), he opened the doors below the sink, got on his knees and crawled in, taking the bowl with him. She turned off the soup and picked up the flashlight.

"What's the bowl for?" she asked, trying to ignore the sight of his finely crafted behind.

"To catch whatever water is left in the line. Hey, where are you?"

"I'm here." She got down on her knees, too, and aimed the flashlight at the pipe.

"I need you to come in here farther. Shine the light on the hose. Right there."

She came in farther. And now there they were, side by side under the sink, closer than they'd been in a year. His spicy aftershave reached out to her, bringing back memories of his kisses. She could see the play of his muscles as he worked the wrench. She'd never realized how quickly it got hot under a kitchen sink.

Now the old hose was off. "Hand me the other hose," he said.

Feeling a little like a nurse in an operating room, she handed it over. "Scalpel, doctor," she cracked.

"That's me. Dr. Fix-it."

Too bad he couldn't have fixed what was wrong with them.

It didn't take long to connect the new flex hose, but that was long enough for her to entertain all kinds of ridiculous thoughts that a divorced woman shouldn't invite into her mind, at least not about her ex.

He gave the wrench one final twist. "There, just like new." Now he turned to her and his easy smile gave way to something else, a look she knew well, one that always led straight to the bedroom. "Anyone ever tell you that you look good under a sink?"

The gift of blarney. Jake O'Brien had it in spades.

"Anyone ever tell you you're full of it?" she replied, and backed out.

Tiny, who had been sitting there watching the proceedings, gave a woof. Then they heard the front door opening and the sound of voices drifted into the kitchen. With another woof, Tiny was off down the hall.

"Anyone here?" called Axel Fuchs, their Realtor. "Tiny, down!"

Ella stared at Jake in wide-eyed panic. "Axel!" She scrambled to her feet and hurried down the hall.

Sure enough, there he was, suave as usual in his business clothes and camel-hair overcoat. Axel was a tall, slim man with blond hair and strong Germanic features. He always dressed to the nines and could have posed for the cover of *Gentleman's Quarterly*. Ella was very aware of her grubby jeans and messy hair. Even more so looking at the well-dressed couple he had in tow. They appeared to be in their late forties and practically smelled of money. A potential sale.

And there was Jake in the messy kitchen with tools on the floor and a dead kitchen hose. She'd get him to ditch all that while the couple was looking around upstairs. She thought of the rumpled, unmade bed Jake had been sitting on. Ugh. Still, it was better than letting them see the kitchen mess.

Tiny was doing his best to welcome the newcomers. Ella grabbed him by the collar. "No, Tiny. Down. Don't worry, he won't bite," she assured the woman, who had ducked behind her husband.

"But does he chew?" the man asked, looking around suspiciously, as if checking for damage.

"No, he's a well-behaved dog," Ella said.

The woman was relaxing now. "Something smells good."

"Oh, I was just heating up some soup," Ella said, smoothing her hair. *And repairing our leaky faucet.*

It was so embarrassing getting caught like this. Normally she wouldn't have even been here. Neither of them would. Axel preferred the owners to be gone when he showed a house. Why hadn't he let them know he was coming?

"I love to cook," the woman volunteered. "Let's see the

kitchen first." And before Ella could stop her, she was off down the hall.

Once they were in the kitchen, Ms. Potential Buyer came to a halt at the sight of Jake gathering up his tools and the dead flex hose. "Oh."

Oh…no. "Just a little leak," Ella said, willing Jake to take his hose and scram.

The man, who'd said nothing so far, grunted. Ella didn't know much about real estate but she did know that grunts were not good.

"Let's go see the rest of the house," Axel said smoothly. "It really is in excellent condition."

"Yeah, I can tell," the man said, and that was worse than the grunt.

They went down the hall and Ella shot an angry look at Jake.

"What?"

"You had all day to fix that sink," she hissed.

"I was working on a song."

"Well, I hope it was a good one because it might have cost us a sale."

"There'll be other buyers," he said.

"When? Darn it, Jake! That was the only thing I asked you to do. Why couldn't you have done it?"

"I did. Just now."

There was no point in talking to him. He was hopeless. She hurried after Axel and the couple. They were in the living room now, looking around. "We recently painted in here," she said.

"Mmm," the woman murmured.

"We've taken excellent care of the house," Ella continued.

The husband responded with another grunt and Axel quickly said, "Let me show you the bedrooms." His clients started up the stairs and Ella got ready to follow them. "Why don't you wait down here," he suggested.

"Oh." Feeling frustrated and foolish, Ella sat on the couch with an issue of *Martha Stewart Living* and hoped against hope that the couple would forget what they'd seen in the kitchen. They probably wouldn't, though, thanks to Jake. At this rate they were going to be here forever, stuck in limbo.

Axel and the buyers came back downstairs and took another trip out to the kitchen. The woman was smiling politely, but her husband looked like he'd had a close encounter with the Grinch. Another five minutes and they were out the door.

"I'll be right with you," Axel called after them.

Ella was at his side in a minute. "Did they like it?"

"Most of it. I'm afraid the leaky sink didn't make a good impression. Neither did Jake's bedroom. Ella, everyone wants to buy something that looks like a picture from a magazine. You two have to keep on top of things."

That stung. She was *trying* to keep on top of things. It was that ball and chain she was no longer married to who was messing up her perfect house. "I have been," she protested. "I had no way of knowing the sink was going to break. And I didn't know you were coming."

"I told Jake I was, this afternoon," Axel said.

"You did?" Jake had known all afternoon and he hadn't gotten the sink fixed? She was going to strangle him with a string of Christmas lights.

"He didn't tell you?"

Ella shook her head.

Axel frowned. "That guy is a disaster."

Ella sighed. "He is."

"What did you ever see in him?" Axel wondered, and then before she could say anything, added, "I'll see what I can do with Mr. and Mrs. Winters and get back to you."

She thanked him and shut the door with a weary sigh.

Now Jake was coming down the hallway. "Well, did they like it?"

"They might have, if they hadn't seen the leaky sink," Ella said frostily.

"Hey, sinks leak."

"Yes, they do. And Realtors call."

His cheeks took on a ruddy tinge.

Ella pointed a finger at him. "You knew we had people coming to look at the house. Axel called you this afternoon."

"It was late afternoon."

"That is beside the point," Ella said, throwing up her hands in frustration.

"No, it's not. It must've been four when he called. I was right in the middle of working on a song. I didn't want to lose it."

She was about to lose it. "So you just played on. What did you think, Jake, that the fairies were going to come and fix the sink and wash the pots and pans?"

"I was going to get to it," he said sullenly.

"But you didn't, and that probably cost us a sale." Ella marched back to the kitchen and Jake followed, with Tiny bringing up the rear, whining.

Ella pulled her pan of soup off the stove. "Here, you can eat all of this. I'm not hungry anymore."

Now Jake was beside her, "El, I'm sorry. I should have fixed the sink right away."

He should have done a lot of things. Ella kept her back to him.

"I really did lose track of time."

"Oh, and that makes it okay? If you'd just fixed the sink this morning it would've been done. Were you writing this morning, too?"

"No."

Ha!

"I was working on arrangements for the band."

"The band," she growled. Of course, the band and his home-wrecking keyboard player came first. It was all Ella could do not to dump the pan of chicken soup over his head.

Her cell phone called to her from the table in the entry-way where she'd dumped her purse and she hurried to dig it out. "I'll bet that's Axel. Maybe he's talked that couple into making an offer." She picked up just before the call could go to voice mail and said a breathless hello.

"Sorry, Ella, it's a no-go."

She was going to cry. She went back to the living room and fell onto the couch. "I thought they liked it. At least the woman did."

"They did, but not enough to make a offer. Don't worry, we'll find you a buyer."

At the rate they were going, that could be years from now. She scowled at the copy of Jake's favorite book sitting on the coffee table. *Do What You Love and the Money Will Follow.* How about do what you promised and a sale will follow?

If she stayed here with Jake much longer she was going to

kill him. They had to get the house sold and move on with their lives. "What can I do to make this place sell?"

"Keep it looking good."

"I will," she promised. "Anything else?"

"Have dinner with me tomorrow and we'll brainstorm," Axel suggested. "You need to get out, get away from that loser."

Now Jake was in the living room. He was a loser. It would make her life so much easier if he looked like one.

"Dinner sounds good," she said.

"Dinner?" Jake echoed. "With who?"

"I'll make reservations at Schwangau for Wednesday," Axel said.

"Schwangau sounds great."

Jake frowned. "You're not going out with that fatheaded wuss, are you?"

"Fine. I'll pick you up at seven."

"Perfect," Ella said.

"That guy is as far from perfect as a man can get," Jake muttered.

"See you tomorrow," Ella said, and Jake made a disgusting noise as she hung up. "Oh, very mature," she said.

"Yeah, as mature as you going out with that twit just because you're mad about the sink."

"Yes, I am mad about the sink but that has nothing to do with why I'm going out with Axel."

"Then why are you going out with him?" Jake demanded.

"None of your business," she told him. "We're not married anymore and I can do what I want. And at least I waited until we were divorced to do what I want."

"So did I! But I'm still not getting to do what I want,

'cause what I want is— Oh, never mind," he ended grumpily, and stomped off upstairs.

What had he been about to say? *What* did he want?

What did it matter? Ella picked up her magazine and
stared unseeingly at it.

Tiny came over, sat on the floor and laid his big head in
her lap. "I know," she said as she petted him. "It makes you
sad when we fight."

Tiny belched and licked his chops. The belch smelled suspiciously like chili.

"Has Daddy been feeding you chili again?" Ella asked.

Tiny whined and thumped his tail.

She frowned. Tiny had been gaining weight. There could
be only one person responsible for that and it wasn't her.
"He's not supposed to give you people food. I'll bet he's been
sneaking you cookies, too."

Tiny wisely kept his doggy mouth shut. Instead, he just
looked at her with his big brown eyes.

"Don't worry, you're not in trouble," she told him. "I
know whose fault it is."

The same man whose fault it was that their potential buyers had decided to take their money elsewhere. Jake O'Brien
was a thorn in her side.

A sudden memory of the two of them picnicking up at
Lost Bride Falls the day he proposed made tears sting her
eyes. She'd thought she'd seen the ghost of the lost bride,
who was a local legend. It was an experience everyone in
Icicle Falls knew portended engagement. And Jake had been
ready with her ring in his pocket.

"Marry me, El. Make my day, make my life. Say yes."

She'd said, "Yes, yes, yes!" and they'd sealed the deal with a kiss. That had been the happiest day of her life.

Now it seemed like a million years ago. Jake O'Brien wasn't a thorn in her side. He was a thorn in her heart, and the sooner she pulled him out, the better.

Jake kicked his pile of dirty clothes across the floor. He'd meant to get that sink fixed before Ella got home and before Axel the twit came over, but he really had been absorbed in a new song. Ella knew how he got when he was busy song-writing. Why hadn't she believed him? Hell, why didn't she *ever* believe him?

The answer to that could be summed up in two words. Her mother. Lily Swan had never liked him from the start. His family were simple people who hunted and fished and cleaned their own houses, and that didn't make them cool enough for old Ms. America's Top-Model-Who-Never-Was. She'd obviously wanted her daughter to marry some jet-setter and not a country boy from Eastern Washington, so she'd immediately set out to break them up.

And that was a downright sin because he and Ella had been happy together. They were meant to be together. He would've made it as a country singer in time and Ella could have lived that fancy life. He'd have been able to buy her anything she wanted.

She'd believed that once. She obviously didn't anymore. Now, in her eyes, he was nothing but a skirt-chasing, lazy loser. Thanks, mother-in-law, for poisoning the waters. Thanks for ruining our lives. Thanks for putting that stuck-up nose of yours where it didn't belong.

Too bad he hadn't hit the big time yet. He'd have sent

good old Mom on a nice long trip—to the edge of the world. And then pushed her off.

The thought made him smile. Then it made him think. Then it made him chuckle as he picked up his guitar. "Mama, I'm about to write you a song for Christmas."

7

Dani still hadn't found lodging for Mason and his child bride, and Cass was feeling the pressure. Every sigh, every accusing you–could–fix–this look from her daughter sent guilt and anger racing through her veins. She finally did what any sensible woman would do. She called her mother.

"And now Dani wants me to find room for them at our place," she finished miserably.

"Well," her mother said, "I think you have two choices. You can refuse, which will make you feel better...for about two minutes, or you can squeeze us all in and make your daughter happy."

Cass sighed. "This is not what I envisioned when I thought of Dani getting married."

"He would have been at the wedding, Cassie," her mother said reasonably.

"I never dreamed she'd want him to walk her down the aisle!"

"Not want her father to walk her down the aisle?"

"Her mostly absent father."

"Her father all the same."

"Sad but true. So, okay, somewhere in the back of my mind I might have known that was a possibility, but I never figured I'd have Father of the Year and Bimbette staying in my house."

"Life rarely goes according to plan," said Mom.

Maybe that was why Cass had become a baker. Baking was easy. You followed the recipe and everything came out just as it should. Perfect.

There was no recipe for a perfect family, though. Unlike flour, sugar, butter and eggs, people were unpredictable and often uncooperative. Rather like she was being right now.

"It's only for a couple of days," her mother said. "If I were you I'd play nice."

Play nice. Ugh. Cass ended the call and went back inside the bakery, where Dani was in the kitchen, putting the finishing touches on a special-order gingerbread house. They'd been working together in strained silence since 7:00 a.m. Heck, they'd been working together in strained silence since Saturday. It was almost ten now, and in another few minutes, they'd open and be busy with customers for the rest of the day. Now was the time to settle this.

Cass's heart began to race. She didn't want to do this. She *so* didn't want to do this.

She took a deep breath and plunged in. "Okay, I give. Call your father and tell him Hotel Wilkes has a vacancy."

Dani's expression went from glum to thrilled in a millisecond. "Really?"

Cass frowned. "Really. God knows where we'll put them, but we'll find a place somewhere." Maybe at the bakery, in the walk-in fridge.

Dani dropped her icing bag and rushed across the kitchen to hug Cass. "Thank you! You're the best mother in the whole world."

Or the stupidest.

Dani grabbed her smartphone and made a call. It didn't take a genius to guess who she was calling. Sure enough. "Daddy? I've got great news!"

For someone, but not for Cass. Oh, well. Onward and upward. "Now we can start planning," she said after Dani ended her conversation with her father.

"That'll be fun," Dani said.

Yes, it would, and the fun of planning this big event with her daughter would make up for the irritation of having to host her former husband. "To start, we'll need to get invitations out as of yesterday. I'm thinking we should close a little early and run over to Wenatchee."

"Oh, we're not going to do invitations," Dani said breezily.

"No invitations?" How did you have a wedding with no invitations?

"We're doing evites."

"Email invitations?" Was that tacky or was Cass just getting old? No, forty-two was not old. So that left tacky.

"It's quicker," Dani said. "Anyway, most everyone already knows."

"Well, one less thing to do. Good idea," Cass said, going with the flow. "There's still the flowers, though, and the cake and of course—"

Before she could even mention the gown Dani said, "I was thinking cupcakes."

"Cupcakes," Cass repeated. Her daughter wanted cupcakes for a wedding in three and a half weeks. At their busiest time of the year. A cake Cass could do in her sleep, but cupcakes, the little devils, were much more labor-intensive. At least they would be for her, because she'd want to make each one special. And where one slice of cake was sufficient for the average wedding guest, cupcakes went down fast and easy and few people would eat just one, which meant she'd need to bake and decorate a lot of them. "Dani girl, you know what things are like around here right now."

Dani bit her lip. "I really wanted cupcakes."

She hated to disappoint her daughter, but… "I'm just not sure," Cass began.

"Okay, fine," Dani snapped, and marched off to unlock the door for their customers. "It's my wedding, but do what you want."

If Cass was doing what she wanted, Mason and his child bride would be off the guest list. Cass frowned, grabbed the icing bag and went to work finishing the trim on the gingerbread house.

Where had that outburst come from, anyway? She'd bent over backward for her daughter, practically turning herself into a human pretzel, but that hadn't been enough.

Cass knew about the bridezilla phenomenon, but she'd

never expected to experience it. Dani was a sweet-tempered (well, usually) cooperative, responsible girl. Correction: Dani used to be a sweet-tempered, cooperative, responsible girl. It looked like that was about to change. And they hadn't even started talking about food, flowers or the bridal gown. Or the budget, which—due to the unexpected early advent of this wedding—wasn't exactly going to be huge. What fireworks lay in store if they clashed over the budget?

The gingerbread house was now complete, temptingly decorated with icing and a lavish variety of candy. The stained-glass sugar windows gave the illusion of a cozy fire within. For a moment, Cass imagined herself safely huddled inside it, nibbling at its walls in peace and quiet.

Then the door of her gingerbread sanctuary opened and in came a gingerbread man who looked suspiciously like Mason, with a lady in tow. And here came a girl, stamping her little gingerbread foot and demanding her mother bake enough cupcakes to feed all of Icicle Falls.

Cass shook her head to dislodge the horrible vision. Ugh. Where were those sugarplums when you wanted them?

Wednesday morning Ella was just finishing her remerchandizing, putting back the blouses her last customer had left in the dressing room, when Charley came into Gilded Lily's to browse.

"Are you shopping for any special occasion?" Ella asked.

Ella loved helping women look their best, and Charley, with her long legs and size-eight figure made that fun, rather like playing dolls on a large scale. Ella couldn't say the same for all her customers. Some of them were a real fashion challenge. Still, she tried hard to help everyone find colors and styles that would flatter them, and women who entered Gilded Lily's left feeling good about themselves.

"Not really," Charley said. "I'm just looking. Maybe a sweater. Or a new blouse to wear with my black pencil skirt when I'm at the restaurant."

Only a couple of weeks ago Charley was saying she didn't need any new clothes. "Who's there around here to impress?" she'd joked.

Who, indeed? "Um, you haven't seen Richard, have you?" Ella ventured. Okay, that was none of her business.

But...she and Charley had become good friends since Ella joined Cass's chick-flick nights. Didn't friends watch out for one another?

Charley suddenly became busy inspecting a white silk blouse. "He took me to the Firs."

"Oh."

"He claims he's sorry. He wants to try again."

If Jake asked to try again, Ella wondered, would she give him a second chance?

"Of course I'm not going to."

"That's probably a good idea," Ella said. "If he cheated once he'd cheat again."

Charley took the blouse off the rack. "Do you think people can change?"

If they could, wouldn't Jake have dismantled his flirt mechanism? Wouldn't he have been able to stay true to her? And wouldn't he have proved he was serious about settling down by getting a real job somewhere when the music store closed instead of teaching a handful of students in the afternoons and playing in his band? Teaching teenage boys with dreams of getting on *American Idol* was barely letting him make a living, and in ten years he'd probably be doing the same thing—playing his guitar and helping his father in the family orchard during apple harvest season. By sixty he'd be playing on street corners in Seattle.

Or Nashville. He was still determined to write a hit song and get to Music City. Once upon a time they'd both dreamed of going there. He would make it big. They'd buy an old house somewhere in town that she'd decorate to the hilt, and when he went on tour she'd come along.

But then she'd grown up.

"Some people change," she said. They put away their little-girl dreams and got practical.

Charley nodded thoughtfully. "I think I'll try this on."

It would look lovely on her, especially if she put up her hair and showed off her long Audrey Hepburn neck. Ella handed her a necklace of freshwater gray pearls. "This would accessorize nicely. Add that black skirt and some heels and you'll be good to go."

Charley took the necklace. "Why not?"

A couple of minutes later, she stepped out of the changing room to model for Ella. "Oh, yes," Ella approved.

"That's what I thought," Charley said with a smile. "Sold. I'll wear this to work tonight."

Where Richard was sure to put in an appearance. *Oh, Charley, be careful.* Should she say that? Maybe not. But she wanted to. She bit her lip as she rang up the sale.

"I know what you're thinking," Charley said.

"That I don't want to see you get hurt?"

"Don't worry. I have no intention of getting hurt."

Ella nodded. Charley was a strong woman, and once she made up her mind it stayed made up. But the best of intentions could easily get lost in a romantic fog. She hoped Charley's didn't.

She left with her fashion finds and the store fell quiet. Ella treated herself to a ten-minute break and pulled a Vanessa Valentine romance novel out from under the counter.

She should've been able to jump right into the story because when she'd stopped reading she'd left Ophelia and the duke caught in a compromising situation. But the words on the page refused to register. Instead, Charley's question kept repeating itself over and over in her mind. *Do you think people can change?*

She finally gave up on the book and decided she needed to make a new window display.

She'd just finished when her mother stopped by. Mims ran the shop on Sundays, so Ella could have the day off, but she also came in a couple of times during the week. Today she was all in black, except for the brown cashmere coat she wore over her V-neck sweater and wool pants. She'd accented the outfit with an Hermès scarf and gold jewelry. Between the outfit and her perfectly highlighted blond hair, she looked like a modern-day Grace Kelly.

"Nice display." She nodded at Ella's handiwork. "When did you do that?"

"Just now. It's been quiet."

"The calm before the weekend tourist storm," Mims said. "I see someone bought the pearl necklace." Mims saw everything. "You might want to put out another one so we don't have a bare space."

Of course, she should've done that right away. Good as she was, she always managed to forget something. She hurried to the back room to get another necklace out of their stock.

This time she chose a multibead red one that was ideal for the holidays and bound to sell in a hurry.

Mims followed her. "I thought you might like to go to Schwangau tonight. I hear they have a new vegetarian menu."

"I can't tonight," Ella said.

Her mother frowned. "Why not? You certainly don't want to stay in the house with…that person."

Her mother had had trouble remembering Jake's name for the first six months they were together. He was James, Jack and sometimes even George. Now Mims seemed to take delight in not having to say his name at all. Ella wasn't sure why, but it bugged her.

"I'm not going to be in the house with Jake," she said, emphasizing his name. "But I do have plans for dinner."

"Oh?" Now Mims's eyes had an inquisitive glint. "Who?"

"Axel Fuchs."

"Axel." Mims gave this information great consideration. "He's not bad-looking." The way Mims said this made it sound as if, for once, her daughter had managed to show good taste. "I hear he might run for mayor next year." That, along with Axel's more metrosexual style, would be a winning combination as far as Mims was concerned.

Was it a winning combination for Ella? She wasn't sure. But he was nice-looking, and going out beat staying home and feeling frustrated with her current state of affairs.

"He drives a Lexus," Mims continued.

Well, that settled it. Axel was the catch of the year. Ella couldn't hide her disgust as she hung up the necklace.

"There's nothing wrong with dating a man who's going somewhere," Mims said.

"I don't know if this is a date. We're going out to talk about ways I can make the house more appealing so it'll sell."

"What a flimsy excuse," Mims scoffed. "Of course it's a date. What are you wearing? Not that outfit, I hope. You look like a shopgirl."

She *was* a shopgirl. Ella shrugged but didn't bother to comment.

"Where's he taking you?"

"Schwangau."

Mims nodded approvingly. "You can try the wild mushroom lasagna and tell me how it is. And wear the ABS trapeze necklace dress I got you for Christmas."

"I was thinking of something more casual," Ella said.

"Not too casual. It only inspires men to pinch pennies."

"I don't need a man to spend a fortune on me," Ella protested.

Her mother gave her a long-suffering look. "And that is exactly what got you into the mess you're in now. Be a little wiser this time around, baby."

And marry a millionaire. Or a prince from some small European country.

Ella sighed inwardly. Her mother still had hopes that some of her glamour would rub off on Ella, but it was too late. If Mims had wanted to turn her into a jet-setter, she should never have settled in a small town.

When Mims had inherited the house in Icicle Falls, she'd expected to use it as a mere way station in life while she recovered from what she'd referred to as a slight career setback (translation: aging), but she'd stayed too long and Ella had become too attached to the town. She'd tried to rectify her mistake (and find her footing in the world of glam once more) by hauling Ella to New York for fashion week on a regular basis, but New York had been too big and too crowded for Ella. Mims finally realized her daughter wasn't enjoying those trips and abandoned the effort, taking her buying trips alone or with her fashionista sidekick, Gregory.

"Ella, where are you?"

Ella dragged herself back to the present with a blink. "I'm here."

"That boy will be a millionaire by the time he's fifty," Mims predicted. "You could still land on your feet."

"I don't even know if I like him...that way."

"At least give it a chance. This isn't New York, baby. Your options are limited."

Rather like Mims's had become since settling here. Why on earth didn't her mother move to New York or Paris or... someplace?

Ella knew the answer to that. It was because of her. Mims had her faults, but she took her mothering seriously, and living far from her daughter had never been a consideration. If Ella wanted to live in a small town, then Lily Swan would live in a small town. And make regular trips to Seattle, the East Coast and Europe. The only downside to all of that was, every time she returned, she became less enchanted with Icicle Falls. She had a condo in Seattle. She could live there. Ella had once pointed this out.

"Not until I see you well established," Mims had said. "What kind of mother would I be if I just ran off and lived for myself?"

The answer to that was easy—a happy one.

"I know you'll have a fabulous time tonight," Mims said. "And I can hardly wait to hear about it." She kissed her daughter on the cheek and left, the fragrance of her perfume lingering like a nosy ghost.

"I *will* have a fabulous time," Ella decided. And she wouldn't think about Jake even once.

Could a person change?

8

J ake saw the silver Lexus pull up in front of the house and frowned. Axel Fuchs was a predator in a silk tie, and it wasn't hard to guess who his prey was. So he drove a Lexus, so what? He had to be at least ten years older than Ella and he looked like a Viking reject—blond and blue-eyed, but too skinny and wimpy to be allowed to go pillaging with the big boys. What would any woman see in him? Oh, yeah, the silk tie and Lexus.

Naturally, he was taking her to Schwangau. It wasn't as hip or fun as Zelda's but it was the most expensive restaurant in town. Overpriced, if you asked Jake, especially the beer. Who cared if it was imported?

He had taken Ella there for their anniversary once and she'd raved over it like it was Disneyland. White linen tablecloths on the tables, soft lighting provided by little candles that made it hard to read the menu.

"You're paying for the atmosphere," Ella had said, taking in the dark wood paneling and the paintings on the walls.

Atmosphere. Why was that a big deal to women? Jake had never understood. He was more a burger-and-fries kind of guy. Or a picnic kind of guy. On sunny Sunday afternoons they used to pack sandwiches and chips and a couple of apples and find a spot on Icicle Creek. They'd spend the day on the bank, dangling their feet in the water and talking. Sometimes he'd throw his guitar over his shoulder and take it along and sing to her. She'd loved that. Or so she'd said.

Axel was coming up the walk now. How much had he paid for that suit? Ella would be able to guess right down to the penny. She loved nice clothes and knew how to dress, but she never got that it wasn't the clothes that caught a man's eye. It was the woman wearing them.

Clothes make the man—whoever said that was wrong.

The doorbell rang and Jake considered letting Axel stand out there in the cold and keep ringing. Maybe his finger would freeze off. Maybe he'd give up and go away. Not likely, though.

Jake was halfway to the door when Ella came running down the stairs, Tiny racing behind her. "I'll get it."

Scowling, Jake went back into the living room and picked up his guitar.

He started strumming. Loudly.

He could still hear Axel say, "Ella, you look incredible."

Like that was unusual? Ella never looked anything *but* incredible. Tonight she'd taken extra care—had her hair down (all that gorgeous long hair he loved to play with) and wore what women called a little black dress along with black heels. How women could run or even walk in those was a mystery. But man, a chick in heels—what a turn-on.

And she was wearing them for Axel. Jake strummed harder. But he still heard Ella say, "Thanks, Axel. It's always nice when a man notices how you dress."

Jake always noticed how she dressed. And then he thought about undressing her. He'd lay odds that Fuchs was thinking the same thing, the bastard.

The door shut and they were gone. Tiny lumbered into the room and sat down at Jake's feet. Actually, sat on one of them. That foot would be numb in a matter of minutes. If only Jake could numb his heart as quickly.

He strummed a C 2 chord. "Wish my heart was ice." Followed by an A minor seventh. "Then I couldn't feel." The chords flowed and the words poured out. "How long will this hurt go on? How long before I heal?" Dumb question. He would never heal.

He shoved his guitar back in its case with enough force to make the strings twang in protest.

Ella studied the menu. Everything here at Schwangau was expensive, even the schnitzel. Of all the restaurants in town, this was Mims's favorite. Ella's, too, although on the rare occasion she went out to eat she usually went to Zelda's—partly because she enjoyed the food but mostly because Charley was a friend and she liked to support her friends. So, this was a rare treat.

Axel was making a great show of selecting their wine. "Since we're in a German restaurant we should start with a Rhine wine, don't you think?" he asked her.

"That sounds fine," she agreed, although it would probably be wasted on her.

She was no connoisseur. Other than an occasional huckleberry martini at Zelda's or some rum-spiked eggnog at Christmas, she drank soda pop or juice. She supposed it would come across as unsophisticated if she confessed that to Axel. And if he wanted to spend money on an expensive bottle of wine, she'd let him. In fact, if he was going to spend that much on wine, then she certainly wasn't going to look for the cheapest meal on the menu.

Once the wine was ordered, he leaned back in his chair with a satisfied smile. "I think you'll love this. It's unpretentious but tasty, and a good way to begin the evening."

"I'm sure I will," she lied.

"It's a favorite of mine. There's nothing better after a long day than relaxing to some jazz with a glass of wine."

Jazz. Ick. Ella was more of a country music girl.

"Jazz is the true American music," Axel said.

"So is country," she added, trying to keep up her end of the conversation.

"Not very sophisticated," he said with a shake of his head. "Twang, beat-up trucks and beer. Oh, that's right. Jake plays in a country band, doesn't he?"

Jake had a beat-up truck, but he sang hip country and he drank organic fruit juice. Even at the clubs he played he stuck to soft drinks. "Booze and music don't go together well," he said. "Makes you sloppy. Anyway, if a guy can't get high on the music, he shouldn't be in the business."

Why was she remembering things Jake said? Who cared what he had to say about anything? She was here with Axel, who was rich and sophisticated—everything Jake wasn't.

"Let's not talk about Jake."

"Excellent idea," Axel said. "So, what kind of music do you like?"

"Oh, just about everything." It was always good to keep an open mind, expand your horizons.

"What do you listen to when you get home from work?"

Jake, playing his guitar. She'd miss that once the house was sold and they'd divided the money and split. The final split. "Well, right now it's hard to listen to anything. Jake is either giving guitar lessons or working on a song."

Axel frowned. "A bad situation. You need to get out of there." He sounded like her mother.

"There must be something I can do to make the house more appealing," she said.

"It's already a nice house. The Craftsman style works well here."

"I'd so hoped that couple was going to buy it," she said with a sigh. "Would it help if we had some Christmas decorations, a tree maybe? Make it feel more homey?"

"Possibly. If you don't go overboard. These days it's all about staging."

"I was thinking it looks a little, I don't know, bare."

"A tree might be a nice touch."

So she'd put up a Christmas tree. And maybe string some cedar boughs along the mantel and put out a few candles. Cinnamon. People were drawn to a house with good smells; she'd known that even before Axel told her. Anyway, she liked decorating her home for the holidays. She pushed aside the thought that this would be her last Christmas there with a new thought—next year she'd have a new place to fix up. A new place and a new beginning.

Their wine arrived and the waiter poured the obligatory
sip for Axel to sample. He sniffed, swirled and swilled, then
nodded his approval and the waiter poured. They placed their
food orders—sauerbraten for her, rolladen for him and an
appetizer for both that promised plenty of lobster—and then
Axel raised his glass to her. "Here's to a sale and freedom."

"To freedom," she said. The house was a millstone around
her neck. She couldn't move on until it was sold and Jake
was out of her life completely. She raised her glass and drank
deeply, then caught sight of Axel's raised eyebrows. "It's
been a long day."

"I can imagine," he said.

They talked about the house some more and how hard
Axel was working to get her out of there. After that, the conversation moved on to a new topic, which was really more of
a move back to a topic they'd already touched on—Axel. He
liked to travel. He had a condo in Seattle that he'd acquired
in a short sale. He loved going into the city to see plays at
ACT or musicals at the Fifth Avenue. TV, other than the
offerings on PBS, was for morons, and why would anyone
bother with those dumb reality shows and sitcoms when he
(or she) could be enjoying a James Joyce novel?

Maybe this wasn't the moment to confess that her TV
viewing consisted of shows like *The Bachelor* and her favorite read was always a good romance novel.

"What do you like to read?" Axel asked.

"Vanessa Valentine," she blurted.

"Who?"

"She writes about...relationships."

Axel nodded slowly, unimpressed and trying to hide it.

"I like to read all kinds of authors."

He smiled approvingly and took another sip of his wine. "Your mother was right. You and I have a lot in common."

Her mother! "You were talking to my mother?"

"A while back," he said with a shrug. "You know it's not that easy to find a woman with class in a small town."

Maybe he needed to move to New York. There was a reality show about Realtors in New York. He could be on it, drinking Rhine wine.

"Of course, I knew *you* had class the minute I saw you," Axel continued.

"Did you?" It was hard not to be flattered. It was hard not to be impressed. Axel had it all—success, money, nice looks. And he liked jazz. Well, no man was perfect.

Now he began to wax eloquent. "I've got to tell you, a man can have all the success in the world, but without the right woman to share it, it doesn't mean much. I mean, where's the fun in taking a gondola ride down a Venice canal by yourself or strolling the banks of the Seine alone?" He smiled at Ella. "A beautiful woman completes the experience."

He thought she was beautiful. With her snub nose and round face she'd never thought of herself that way. Who could when comparing herself to the incomparable Lily Swan? Even Jake had never told her she was beautiful. Cute, yes. Hot. But beautiful?

She could learn to like jazz.

Jake was in a foul mood when he got to band practice.

"What's eating you?" asked Tim the drummer.

"Nothing," Jake lied. Even though these guys were all his pals, he wasn't ready to tell them that his ex was on a date.

Jen offered him mock comfort, playing the chorus of Elton John's "Sorry Seems to Be the Hardest Word" on her keyboard. "You need some comfort, Jake," she said silkily.

"Got some Southern Comfort in the cupboard," offered Larry, who played lead guitar. Larry had agreed to the no-drinking-on-the-job rule, but during practice everyone was allowed a beer or a shot of booze. Jake was the only one who never indulged.

"Nah, he needs to start jamming," said Guy, his bass player. "Did you bring the new song you told us about?"

Oh, yeah, and Jake was in just the mood to play it.

By the end of the first chorus everyone was guffawing, proof that, as Jake suspected, this was a kick-ass country song. His ex-mother-in-law had her uses, after all. The others joined in with the instruments on the second verse and chorus and, great players that they were, had the song sounding good within only a few measures.

Once they'd finished the last chorus Larry said, "That rocks, man. We should do it this weekend, kick off the holidays."

"Hell, it could kick off more than the holidays. This could be a hit," Guy said. "There hasn't been a mother-in-law song on the charts since the sixties. Has there?"

"I dunno," Larry said, "but there should be. Every guy on the planet could relate."

Guy shook his head. "Not me," he said. "My mother-in-law rocks. She bakes my favorite cookies at Christmas and makes a steak dinner for my birthday every year."

"That ain't normal," Larry said.

"Well," Jake said, "I know guys who like their mamasin-law." Too bad a man couldn't mix and match. *I'll take this woman and her best friend's mother.*

Larry made a face. "They're probably lying. Chrissie's mom drives me bonkers."

"She don't count as a mother-in-law," Guy told him. "You and Chrissie ain't married."

"And we're not gonna be until she gets a new mother," Larry said.

Guy turned to Jake. "All I can say is that if your ex's mom inspired this, it was worth all the pain."

"Not really," Jake muttered.

He forced himself to set aside all further thoughts of his ex-wife and concentrate solely on arranging the song. They worked on that, then ran over a couple more Christmas songs and the new Brad Paisley hit. After an hour and a half, he began wondering if Ella was still out with Axel. Maybe he'd taken her home by now. Had he dropped her off and left, or had she invited him in? If she'd invited him in, was he still there? What were they doing?

"Let's pack it in for the night," he said.

"This early?" Jen protested, looking disappointed. "Come on, Jake, I'm ready to make a night of it." Jen was always ready to make a night of it.

Guy looked at him like he was nuts. "We never quit this early. Are you sick?"

He had to be sick in the head to be obsessing over the woman he was no longer married to. "Yeah, I feel like shit." He'd felt like shit for a long time but that was beside the point.

"Okay, fine with me," Larry said. "We'll kick back and

have a beer in your honor. Just make sure you're well by
Friday."

"I've never missed a gig," Jake assured him, and loaded
his guitar in its case.

He pulled up in front of the house fifteen minutes later,
just as Ella and the slime in a suit were arriving. Jake got
out of his truck and eyed the Lexus with disfavor. What a
wussy car.

They didn't seem to be in any hurry to get out so he took
his time going up the walk. They kept sitting in the wuss-
mobile. Jake ditched his guitar and let Tiny out for some air.
Tiny was happy to see him and equally happy to trot around
the front yard, sniffing the bushes. Jake stood on the porch
and watched…Ella and Axel.

Finally Fuchs got the hint and vacated the car, going
around and opening the door for her. She slid out and flashed
a well-curved leg from under her winter coat. Ella had great
legs. Heck, Ella had great everything.

Here they came up the walk together, both frowning.

Three's a crowd, huh? Too bad. He stood in the open doorway, leaning on the door frame. "Hey, kids, how was the
dance?"

Ella glared at him, but Axel refused to rise to the bait,
merely smiling pleasantly. Always the good businessman.

Now they were on the porch. "Were you going in?" Ella
asked pointedly.

"Tiny's not done."

"I can watch him," Ella said.

"I don't mind."

Axel gave up. "Well, I guess I'll be going."

"I had a great time," Ella told him.

Great? Really? It was just dinner. Oh, but dinner with fancy tablecloths. That made all the difference.

"We'll do it again," Axel said.

Not if Jake had anything to say about it. Oh, yeah. He didn't.

Axel went back down the walkway and Ella marched past Jake into the house. He called Tiny and followed her in, wearing a smirk.

But once inside she wiped the smirk off his face. "That was mature," she said as she slipped off her heels.

He played dumb. "What?"

"You know what. You're such a hypocrite."

"What!"

"You can have other women but I can't have other men? Is that it?"

"I never—" he began.

She cut him off. "You always. I'm going to see Axel again and I'm going to have a life. And I'm going to get a Christmas tree and get this place sold!"

He wasn't sure what a Christmas tree had to do with anything, but he got the general gist of that tirade. He was out of the picture. And once they sold the house, he'd be out of her life for good. Now would be the time to say, "Baby, we've been so wrong. Let's sit down and talk, really talk. Let's lose the suspicion and the anger. Let me make love to you." Instead, he just stood there in the hallway, glaring as she went upstairs.

His life was like a bad country song. All he needed now was for his truck to break down and his dog to die.

As if reading his thoughts, Tiny whimpered.

"I didn't mean it, boy," he said. "Come on. We'll go out to the kitchen and get us some chili."

Ella threw her shoes in the closet and fell on her bed. She could hardly wait to sell this house and get away from Jake O'Brien. Him and his immature behavior and his tacky country songs. He was probably downstairs right now, messing up the kitchen, just like he was trying to mess up her life.

Well, she wasn't going to let him. And she was going to learn to appreciate jazz if it killed her.

9

Ella was getting ready to go to the shop on Friday when Axel called. "I just wanted to give you a heads-up that I've got a couple arriving in town who are looking for a second home. I think they might like your place."

"That's great," Ella said. If these people were looking for a second home they obviously had money. They might even be willing to pay the asking price.

"We'll be over this afternoon, so if there's anything you need to do…"

Like have Jake pick up his underwear and clean the sink? Very diplomatic. "I'll make sure the place looks good," Ella promised.

As soon as she ended the call, she went searching for Jake. It wasn't hard to find him. She just had to follow her nose to the kitchen, where he was frying an egg, spatter-ing grease all over the stove. Everywhere he went he was a mess in progress.

"Axel's bringing over some people to see the house this afternoon," she said.

His only response was a grunt.

He'd been downright hostile since her dinner out with Axel, which meant it was difficult to make any kind of rea-sonable request. She made hers, anyway. "So, you will clean up the kitchen, right?"

"Yeah," he said, obviously insulted.

"Thanks," she said and left the kitchen. She didn't have time to stand around and exchange rude looks. She had to get to work. But first, she'd run up to the attic and get a few decorations, Christmas the house up a little. Staging was important.

So was getting to the shop on time. Mims was a stickler for that. Ella picked up her pace, opening the door to the attic and hurrying up the narrow stairs.

The closed door kept it nippy. She rubbed her arms and did a quick scan of the odds and ends lying around, pieces of their life together. There was the picnic basket Cecily had given them for a wedding present. Off in the corner lay Jake's old catcher's mitt. She'd gone to all his softball games back when they were a happy couple. There sat the old trunk they'd gotten at a garage sale. And over in the corner, care-fully preserved and bagged, hung her wedding gown. She quickly averted her gaze.

Jake had put the decorations away last Christmas and the boxes were shoved in a corner every which way. Fortunately, she recognized the one with her candles and the Fitz and

Floyd snow globe. Those would be perfect on the mantelpiece. Just the right touch until she could get a tree.

Maybe she wouldn't even need a tree. Maybe the couple
Axel was bringing by would fall in love with the house and
make an offer today.

Conscious of the ticking clock, Ella took the box and hurried down from the attic.

After arranging her decorations, she ditched the box in
the coat closet and left for the shop. Hopefully, before the
day was over, the house would be sold. History. Like her
and Jake.

Jake had just finished some song charts and was recharging
with a cup of coffee when he saw the silver Lexus pull up
in front of the house. The wuss was here. And he wouldn't
be happy to see Jake. Well, Jake wasn't going to be happy to
see him, either, so that made them even. Anyway, this was
still half his house and he had every right to stay.

He stood by the window, watching as Axel and his clients
got out of the car and started up the front walk. The couple
was older, maybe in their fifties. He looked like a model
for The North Face. She was wearing a coat trimmed with
some kind of fake fur over slacks and heels. Her hair was as
phony as the trim on her coat, a youthful blond chin-length
and carefully coiffed. Everything about her said, "My man
has money." Yuck. *This* was going to buy his house?

Axel spotted him at the front window and his smile stiffened.

*Yeah, I know. You were hoping I'd be gone. You've been hop-
ing that ever since you started drooling over Ella.* Jake saluted him
with his coffee mug and chuckled to see the smile slip into a

frown. But then Axel put his salesman's game face back on and began talking to the two fish he had on the line as he ushered them up the steps and onto the porch.

Suddenly, Jake heard a noise that didn't bode well for Axel and the fish. It was a great thundering woosh that sounded like Santa and a million reindeer were using the metal roof as a slip 'n' slide. Uh-oh. Ella had been in the attic getting Christmas decorations before she left for work. She must've left the door open—not a good thing because that meant a lot of heat had been rising up to the attic for a long time, enough to melt the snow accumulation and send it sledding down onto—

He heard the scream, saw the avalanche and then watched in horror as one of the icicles he'd forgotten to knock down hurled itself like a sword at the feet of three snow people, making them all jump back. The woman's shriek was enough to break off all the other icicles that hadn't already been dislodged.

Jake ran to the door and pulled it open. "You guys okay?"

"What do you think?" Axel said through gritted teeth.

The couple was in shock. They both looked like the abominable snowman's cousins. The woman blinked out at Jake from behind a snowy mask. She whimpered as she brushed at her face and then raked the cap of snow from her hair, leaving it plastered to her head. "Oooh, my hair." That wasn't her only problem. Her eye makeup had run and she looked like Barnabas Collins in drag. Her husband, who was sweeping the snow from his shoulders, appeared ready to murder someone.

So did Axel. Jake was sorry his clients got dumped on, but Axel—that was another story. It was somehow satisfying to see the guy drenched in snow from the top of his smarmy head to the tip of his expensive shoes. Jake almost laughed, but the realization that Ella was not going to be happy about this kept him sober.

"What was that?" the man demanded.

"This happens sometimes with metal roofs," Axel said smoothly. "Nothing to be concerned about."

"Nothing to be concerned about?" the man echoed, his voice rising. "One step closer and that icicle would have gone through Annabel's skull."

There probably wasn't much in there, anyway, Jake thought. "Come on in and get dry," he offered.

The woman took a step back. "I don't think so."

Now Tiny was at the door and let out a bark of greeting.

"Eeep!" cried Annabel.

Another icicle stabbed the front porch. "Eeee!" Annabel turned and fled down the steps.

"Show us a condo," her husband said, and hurried down the walk after her.

"You blew that sale," Axel told Jake, glaring at him.

"Hey, I'm not responsible for snow sliding off my roof," Jake snapped. "That was an act of God."

Axel looked as if he'd like to say more, but instead, he brushed the last of the snow from his expensive overcoat and stalked off down the walk after his clients.

"Good riddance," Jake said, and slammed the door after him.

Ella wasn't going to think that.

Sure enough. An hour later Jake's cell phone rang. Figuring the best defense was a good offense, he didn't give her a chance to say anything. "El, that was not my fault."

SHEILA ROBERTS

"You didn't knock down the icicles and I asked you to. How is that not your fault?"

"Okay, that part is," he admitted. "But not the snow thing. I went up and checked. You left the door to the attic open. All that warm air drifting up there all day warmed the roof and loosened the snow."

That shut her up. But a moment later he could hear sniffling. "Oh, come on, El, don't cry. Someone will buy the house."

"Not if we try to kill them with snow and icicles."

"Look, the icicles are all gone and I shoveled the snow off the porch. So next time…"

"I don't even know if there'll be a next time. Axel was really mad."

"Well, Axel can go—" Jake bit off the rest of the sentence, realizing it would hardly be productive.

"Oh, why am I talking to you, anyway?" she said miserably.

Then she hung up before he could say, "Because I'm the one you come to when you're upset, because you still love me." He looked down at Tiny, who was watching him, head cocked to one side. "Let me tell you, being a guy is a lot easier for you than it is for me." Love shouldn't be this hard.

Now, there was a good title for a song. Too bad it was also the story of his life.

Cass closed the bakery an hour early on Friday so she and Dani could pop over to Lupine Floral and pick out flowers for the wedding. It was December 1, and the town was buzzing with shoppers.

About this time the following day the town square would

be packed with visitors, watching the tree-lighting ceremony. This included a carol sing, an appearance by Santa and an invocation from one of the local pastors. Then there'd be a countdown and the hundreds of lights on the giant fir in town square would burst into glorious colored bloom and the handbell choir would play "Joy to the World." The week before Christmas there'd be something going on every night, including performances by choirs and the local folk-dancing club. In addition to all that, bonfires would blaze by the skating rink every evening so families could enjoy roasting hot dogs and toasting marshmallows. Icicle Falls knew how to celebrate the holidays.

And bring on the visitors. They'd had a rough winter the year before with little snow for the skiers and winter sports enthusiasts, but they'd learned from that. The town was now holiday party central. Besides Christmas, they'd found a festival to celebrate something every season. And more were in the works. Their little town was quickly becoming a destination.

Even Lupine Floral had come up with a way to lure in holiday visitors, offering special Christmas corsages featuring red carnations and small candy canes that women could pin on their winter coats and hats. Cass counted half a dozen as she and Dani hurried through the Friday afternoon crowd toward the florist's.

The shop window was a winter work of art, a study in white and silver, with a river of silver ribbon running among arrangements of white roses and carnations in silver mercury-glass vases. A small forest of baby's breath stood tall in milk-glass vases linked by faux-pearl swags. A table-size flocked tree sported silver balls and shiny blue ribbons.

"I could go for that," Dani said as they walked in.

"Which part of it?" Cass asked.

"All of it."

Cass could see the money flying away. She nodded gamely and followed her daughter inside, wishing she'd saved more.

Even if Dani had given her a year, she wouldn't have been able to sock away the kind of money she suspected they'd end up spending on this "small" wedding. She should have started saving long ago. *Cheer up. By the time you've paid for this Amber will be engaged and you can start all over.* Thank God one of her children was a boy.

Kevin Carlyle, looking spiffy in designer jeans and a gray cashmere sweater, was just saying goodbye to a customer when they walked in. "Here's the bride-to-be!" he greeted them. "Congratulations, Dani. We're so happy for you."

"Thank you," Dani said.

"There's nothing more beautiful than a Christmas wedding," Kevin went on.

Or more expensive, Cass thought. If Dani and Mike had been getting married in the summer they could have culled flowers from all their friends' gardens and saved a bundle. But that would have been tacky, she scolded herself. It was important to support local businesses, and heaven knew Heinrich and Kevin had bought enough goodies from her bakery.

Heinrich emerged from the back of the shop where he'd probably been working on a floral arrangement. Kevin was barely into his forties, but Heinrich was pushing fifty. His brown hair had begun to thin and he was edging toward fashion's dark side—a Donald Trump comb-over. He, too, wore expensive jeans topped with a black mock-turtleneck sweater.

"Ladies," he greeted them, "this is going to be so much fun. I haven't done a December wedding in ages."

"I hope you can do one on a budget," Cass said, earning her a dirty look from her daughter.

Heinrich laughed. "We'll make it work. Come sit down and let's talk." He took a slim laptop from under the counter and led the way to a white ironwork table and chairs in the corner. Like everything else in the shop, this little meeting spot was a delight for the eyes, the table covered with a white cloth and, on top of that, a square glass vase bearing a holiday floral arrangement.

Kevin brought them bottles of Perrier, and Heinrich opened the laptop. "What's your color scheme, darling?"

"Gosh, I thought I wanted red and white," Dani said. "My gown's white with white faux-fur trim."

"Your gown?" Dani had already picked out a gown?

"I was going to show it to you," Dani said to Cass. "I saw it last month when I was visiting Daddy in Seattle."

"You went to a bridal shop with your father?" The green-eyed monster landed on Cass's shoulder, and began breathing down her neck, souring the moment.

"No," Dani said. "I just…went."

"All by yourself?" Where was the fun in that?

"Babette and I were out shopping."

Babette! The child bride, Mason's trophy wife? Her daughter had been looking at wedding gowns with Babette?

"We happened to walk by the shop and I saw it," Dani said. "I didn't buy it or anything, Mom. I was waiting for you to come with me."

But she'd already tried it on. Babette had seen it. *So what,* she told herself. *So what, so what, so what!*

It didn't help. She could feel tears pricking her eyes.

Heinrich cleared his throat. "Well, red and white are perfect for Christmas."

Cass jerked her petty self out of that Seattle bridal shop and back to the present. "I think Dani might be leaning toward something else now."

She must have succeeded in straining the hurt from her voice because the pink in Dani's cheeks faded and her shoulders relaxed. "I really like the white and silver combination you have in the window."

"That would go with almost anything," Heinrich said. "What color are your bridesmaids' dresses?"

"We haven't decided yet," Dani said, "but Ella has some great dresses at Gilded Lily's. There was a really pretty gray one that my bridesmaids liked."

"That would go well with silver and white. And we could accent with red, maybe in your bouquet." Heinrich smiled at Cass. "And your mother could design an amazing cake using silver and white, maybe a little red."

Good old Heinrich, trying to use flattery as a salve for wounded motherly pride.

"I like that," said Dani.

"And where are we holding the wedding and reception?" he asked.

"All at Olivia's," Dani said. "The wedding will be in that big conference room and the reception in the dining hall."

"Ah, perfect. And the view from the dining hall." Heinrich kissed his fingers. "We can bring the outdoors inside."

With that they were off.

"It's all gorgeous," Cass said finally. "What are we looking at costwise?"

"What's your budget?" Heinrich asked.

Not much probably wasn't a helpful answer. Cass had been doing some rough calculations in her head, which had given her a headache. She threw out a figure she hoped wouldn't make her sound like the cheapskate of Icicle Falls.

Her daughter looked at her like she *was* the cheapskate of Icicle Falls.

Heinrich had been taking notes as they talked. Now he said, "Let me run some figures," and disappeared into the back room, taking Kevin with him.

"Jeez, Mom. That won't buy much more than my bridal bouquet and boutonnieres."

"We still have to pay for food and your gown and a DJ, and we have to pay Olivia."

"I have some money saved up," Dani said. "I can pay for the flowers."

"No, I'll do it. You need to keep your money for the move," Cass said quickly. Dani had asked for little enough growing up. She deserved the wedding she wanted. And the flowers she wanted. Cass would just have to load up her credit card, that was all. How much was that wedding gown going to cost?

Don't think about it.

Now Heinrich was back, with a smiling Kevin right behind him. "Okay, we're good to go."

"So you can do the flowers for that amount?" Cass asked. Surely not.

"Not quite," Heinrich said.

"Well, then," Cass began, ready to drain her account.

"But we're picking up the difference," Kevin added before she could finish. "As a wedding present."

"Oh, thank you," breathed Dani.

Cass felt those pesky tears burning her eyes again. "Thanks, you two. Anything you want from the bakery, anytime."

Kevin grinned. "I'll remember that when we throw our New Year's Eve party."

So there it was, the first wedding hurdle safely jumped. Now all she had to worry about was…everything else.

Mason could pay for half of this, she told herself. But the idea of asking him galled her. He'd been little more than a child-support check when the kids were growing up, and obviously he didn't want to be involved now or he would have offered. No, she'd find a way to get whatever her daughter needed all on her own. Like she always had.

Dani slipped her arms through Cass's. "Thanks, Mom. It's going to be beautiful."

Yes, it was. No matter what it cost.

Richard strolled into Zelda's toward the end of the evening. Charley was visiting with Ed York and Pat Wilder as they enjoyed their pie and coffee. The sight of him whipped up more than one emotion in her. When he'd first reentered her life she'd felt anger and resentment. But tonight's mix bore something new—yearning. *What if?*

What was she thinking? This was not a good ingredient to add to the stew.

She tried to keep her easy smile but it must have faltered because now Pat was looking at the door. "Oh, my," she murmured.

There was an understatement. Charley found herself wishing she'd hired a hostess for weekday evenings. Yes, she was the general manager, but she didn't need to live here 24/7 as if she had no life. If she hadn't been on duty tonight she could have hidden in her house, kept the door locked. Pretended she had a life.

Why wouldn't he give up? She made her way up to the front, stopping to check with a diner here and there en route. *Let him wait.*

He seemed to have no problem waiting and greeted her with a smile when she finally got to him. "Looks nice in here," he observed, taking in the red bows she'd put up at the windows and the small tree in the lobby done in red and gold.

"Glad you approve." *Now, scram.*

"You look nice, too. In fact, you look good enough to eat," he said, taking in the black pencil skirt and the new blouse and necklace she'd gotten at Gilded Lily's. What, did he think she'd worn it for him?

If not him, then who did you wear it for?

She pleaded the fifth.

"Is it too late to get a table?"

"You know it's not," she said, and led him to a corner table by the kitchen. Not the best seat in the house by any means, but he didn't deserve the best seat. He didn't deserve any seat.

"Perfect," he said. "Now I can observe the new chef in action. Is he as good as me?"

"There are lots of men who are as good as you. Better even." She handed him his menu, then walked away.

"Take your time getting to him," she told Ginny, his waitress.

Ginny looked at her wide-eyed, and no wonder, since

she had only one other occupied table in her station, but she nodded.

Richard didn't seem to mind. Every time Charley glanced at him, he was sitting there smiling contentedly, observing everything. As if he still had a stake in this place. The old anger fired up. How dared he! She avoided him for the rest of the night, even when he was the last person sitting at a table.

Finally, at ten, she told him, "The restaurant is closing. You need to go."

"I'm not done." He held up the glass of wine he'd been nursing for the past half hour. It had one sip left in it.

She took the glass and downed the wine. "Now you are."

He leaned back in his chair. "I didn't see your car outside. How about I walk you home?"

"How about you don't."

"It's only a walk home, Charley."

It would be too long a walk. She shook her head. "No, thanks."

"Please."

He looked so contrite. And so handsome. Oh, jeez. What was wrong with her?

"Charley, I want to make up for how I hurt you."

The very mention of what he'd done strengthened her resolve. "You can't," she said, her face stony.

"I can try, if you let me."

After several more minutes of contrition wrapped in flattery she gave in. *Fool. What are you thinking?* She had a suspicion, and it left her feeling uneasy.

Charley exchanged her shoes for the boots she'd worn to work and they walked home in a wintry wonderland, the houses along her street looking like frosted gingerbread.

Many had their Christmas lights up already and they glowed like giant gumdrops. Charley huddled inside her long coat, trying to fight off the shivers. She should've worn pants.

"You're cold," Richard said, and put an arm around her.

"Not that cold," she lied, and removed it, then hunched inside her coat collar like a giant turtle.

"Won't even let me fight off the cold, huh?"

"I can do my own fighting."

He acknowledged that with a nod.

They walked the rest of the way in silence, and when they got to the front porch, she turned and said, "See? I didn't need you to walk me home."

"You've never needed me."

Was that some sort of accusation? "Is that why you found Ariel so attractive? She needed you?"

He shrugged.

"How convenient to have an excuse." Charley turned her back on him and unlocked the front door.

She tried to shut it in his face but he blocked the move and slipped inside, just like last time. Well, he was going to get nowhere now, just like last time.

"One nightcap, then I'll go. I promise."

She should tell him to go now. *So, tell him.* "One nightcap," she said. She hung up her coat and then went to the dining room sideboard where she kept the liquor. She didn't need to ask what he wanted. She knew. Jack Daniel's, straight up.

She handed him the glass.

"You're not having anything?"

"No."

"No peppermint schnapps?" he coaxed.

"No." Charley liked a glass of wine now and then, and this time of year she enjoyed cocoa laced with peppermint schnapps. But she preferred companionable drinking. There was no companionship here. There was something else, though, and that was giving her shivers worse than she'd had on the walk over.

"Well," he said, raising the glass to her, "here's looking at you, kid."

Casablanca, their favorite movie. "Did you make the same toast to Ariel?"

He gave a snort. "Like she would even have known where it came from?"

"Everyone knows where that comes from." Yet it had sounded so special when Richard said it to her.

She should have left her coat on. The house was cold. She didn't usually bother to heat it though, not when she came straight home from work every night and went to bed. Alone. The shivers returned full force.

"Let me build a fire," Richard offered, and moved to the fireplace.

"No!" Her voice was sharper than necessary, certainly sharper than she'd intended. "I'm not planning on staying up that long." She sat on the couch and pulled an afghan around her shoulders.

"Or having me here that long?"

"What would be the point?"

"To talk, and remember why we got together in the first place."

"Temporary insanity?"

"We had something good. Until I blew it," he added

quickly, probably before she could. "And I'm not sure you can call twelve years temporary."

"I thought it was going to be for a lifetime." Charley found an inconvenient sob rising to choke her.

"It should have been." Now he was next to her on the couch, his drink forgotten on the coffee table. "Oh, baby. I'm sorry. I blew it."

She pulled away. "Yeah, you did. And now I'm supposed to simply forget that and welcome you back with open arms?"

"No. I wouldn't expect you to do that. All I'm asking is that you think about starting again. Remember how good we had it?"

She remembered. Maybe that was why his betrayal hurt so much. She stood. "It's late, Richard, and I'm tired."

He nodded and stood, too. "Walk me to the door."

She remained where she was. "You know where it is."

He nodded, took her hand and led her toward the entryway.

In only a few nervous heartbeats they were standing in the archway that separated the entryhall from the living room, right where Charley had always hung a satin ball decorated with mistletoe.

He pointed to the spot. "The mistletoe isn't there this year."

"No, it's not," she agreed. "I haven't exactly been in a kissing mood." Now she wished she'd hung it there, found some great-looking guy to kiss her under it. She could have taken a picture, posted it on her Facebook page, sent a copy to Richard with a note that said, "See what you're missing?"

"Let's pretend it is," he murmured, and then, before she

could stop him, he kissed her. Oooh, how long had it been since she'd been kissed? Richard had always known how to turn her to mush. He hadn't lost his touch.

He'd had plenty of practice. With another woman. She pulled away and yanked the front door open. "Good night, Richard."

He grabbed his coat from the coat tree where he'd tossed it. "I like that."

She couldn't resist asking, "What?"

"You said good-night. You could have said goodbye." He turned and ran down the steps.

"Goodbye!" she called after him. But it was belated and halfhearted and they both knew it.

10

Charley was enjoying a leisurely Saturday morning with her December issue of *Bon Appétit* when Richard showed up on her doorstep bearing eggnog lattes from Bavarian Brews.

She scowled at him. "Would you like me to tell you what you can do with those?"

He held up a cup, letting the aroma of coffee and nutmeg drift her way. "It would be a shame to waste this."

She snatched the cup from him. "Lattes for life couldn't atone for what you did."

"Charley, I'm trying. Please, let me come in."

She hated him for the pleading expression on his face, hated how it almost made her feel sorry for him. She opened the door wider and he stepped inside.

Great. You've let the snake slither back in your house in ex-

change for an eggnog latte. Smart, Charley. She turned her back
on him and took a sip. The latte was better than her judg-
ment. "What do you want, Richard?"

"I want you to go out to breakfast with me."

"I don't think so."

"You have time. It's only ten."

"Just because I have time doesn't mean I have the inclina-
tion." Her phone rang. Saved by the ringtone. Whoever it
was, whatever that person wanted, it would make the perfect excuse to ditch her ex.

"Uh, Charley, it's Bruno."

Why was her grill chef calling her at ten in the morning?
Why was he calling her at all? If there was a problem she
should've been hearing from Harvey, her head chef.

Dread dropped in to wish her happy holidays. "Where's
Harvey?"

"I don't know. That's why I'm calling you."

"What?" She fell onto the nearest chair. Her chef should
have been in at seven. By now he should have had all the
orders put away, the goose portioned and the kitchen crew
prepping the night's set menu. Instead, there was...Bruno.
Good old Bruno, who never operated on all four burners.
And who'd waited three hours to call her.

"He's not here," Bruno said. "And there's nothing in the
walk-in. The meat guy hasn't shown up and Sysco hasn't
brought the produce order. I don't know what I'm supposed
to be prepping for the set menu."

The mayor's holiday dinner—thirty movers and shakers,
politicians, even the representative for their district would
be present. "I know you'll come up with a wonderful meal
for us, Charley," Mayor Stone had said.

"Oh, yes," she'd assured him.

"Oh, yes," her head chef had assured her. "We can give him goose, roasted winter vegetables, a traditional figgy pudding for dessert."

Now Bruno was telling her they had nothing, and *her* goose was cooked. "I'll be right there," she said. She ended the call and raced for the door, both her latte and her ex forgotten.

Richard hurried after her. "Charley, what's going on?"

Hell's kitchen, that was what. "My head chef didn't show up." Richard said something but she didn't listen. She was too busy panicking. This was a disaster. Her life was flambéed, all thanks to Harvey's disappearing act. She raced to her car, putting in a call to Harvey as she went. His phone rang. And rang. And rang some more. Finally his voice mail kicked in. "Harvey, where are you?"

As if she had to ask. She knew. Harvey had broken his promise to go to AA. Harvey was out with his best friend, José Cuervo. Harvey, the worm in the bottle. They'd had this conversation only two weeks ago when she'd caught him helping himself from the bar. For his sauce, he'd claimed. But she'd smelled his breath. His kitchen creations weren't the only things getting sauced. She'd given him another chance; now she wanted to give him a black eye. Oh, she was going to murder the little weasel! How good it would feel to be able to break a plate over his head.

Except who had been the fool who gave him a second chance? No, she was the one who deserved to have a plate broken over her head.

The kitchen at Zelda's was normally a beehive of busyness on a Saturday morning, with staff cutting tomatoes and tearing lettuce leaves into big bins, pulling desserts out of the oven, cutting and weighing steak. Instead, Charley found Bruno, leaning against the counter, a block of cement with a head, wearing a white chef's jacket and a befuddled expression. Next to him stood Andy, her salad and dessert man, a short, skinny guy, also in a white jacket. "There's no produce," he informed her.

She marched to the walk-in cooler and threw open the door. All she saw was bare metal shelving, giant Sysco containers of mayonnaise, mustards, garlic, shallots, pan racks with vacant metal trays, plastic inserts filled with sauces and dressings, but no produce or meat to be dressed. Bruno had told her but she hadn't wanted to believe him.

She stood for a moment, staring at shelves full of empty, then she left the cooler. There, in the middle of the kitchen, stood Tweedledum and Tweedledumber, looking at her, waiting for their orders.

She went back into the walk-in, shut the door after her and, woman of action that she was, grabbed two fists full of hair and screamed. Then she marched to the door. She was going to bang her head on it until her brains fell out. Brains for dinner, hahahaha.

She was just about to whang her head on the door when it opened.

There stood Richard.

"Excuse me, but I have to go stick my head in the oven," she said, and started past him.

He caught her arm and pulled her back inside the walk-in, shutting the door. Not exactly the warmest place for a cozy conversation but Charley had worked up enough of a sweat having her meltdown that she was barely aware of the cold.

"You have to get a grip," he said.

"I intend to get a grip—around Harvey's neck."

"Harvey's history. Right now we have to make a list of what you need."

What she needed? She needed all her deliveries. And a head chef, pulling together the set menu for the evening. "I need—" she threw up her hands "—everything! I need a miracle. I need to murder Harvey, and serve his head on a platter. The mayor's dinner party is tonight and there's *nothing!*"

Richard grasped both her arms. "Charley, calm down. This isn't like you."

"This *is* like me," she growled. "This is like the new me."

"Well, get in touch with the old you and calm down," he said firmly. "Let's come up with a game plan."

She ran a hand through her hair. "Right. You're right."

"Okay. You calm now?"

She nodded. "I'm cool. Call me cucumber." How was she going to fix this mess?

"Good. Now, first of all, what's the set menu for the mayor's dinner?"

She told him, trying not to sound as hysterical as she felt.

When she'd finished, he said, "Okay, we'll have to alter the menu."

"Wait a minute," she said. "You don't have to help. This isn't your problem."

"I know. I want to."

"Then I'll pay you." The last thing she wanted was to be indebted to her ex.

"Don't be ridiculous." He picked up a clipboard and disappeared into the walk-in to do inventory. Of course, there was little enough to inventory and he was back out in a couple of minutes. Oooh, she was going to get hauled away in a straitjacket before this day was over.

Richard was unfazed, however. While Charley fantasized about hunting down Harvey and flogging him with a frozen salmon, Richard went on a wild-goose hunt, putting in a couple of calls to fellow chefs at other restaurants. Once more he was the head chef at Zelda's, throwing together a special menu on the fly, compiling a shopping list, calling their suppliers and barking out orders to Bruno and Andy, sending them scurrying to the grocery store for food to tide them over.

Charley was scurrying, too, getting the new menu printed, then helping Richard and the rest of the crew prep the food. Lunch was crazy, with a ton of tourists, hungry from a morning of shopping and exploring town, but they made it through. Then they had to gear up for the dinner service. By the time that was done, she had less than an hour to run home, freshen up and change into an evening outfit suitable for greeting diners. She made it back just in time to open, and when the mayor's party arrived everything at Zelda's was running as it should—smoothly.

"We're looking forward to this dinner, Charley," Mayor Stone said to her when he entered the restaurant, a pudgy blonde on one arm and his sister, Darla, on the other.

"I know you'll love it," Charley said.

And they would. Richard had managed to find a goose— not enough to serve thirty, but enough to make a goose soufflé. In addition to that, he'd produced a prime rib, the roasted winter vegetables Harvey had promised, a crab-artichoke salad and bread pudding (faster to make than figgy pudding), complete with rum sauce.

Like the Lone Ranger, Richard had ridden in and saved the day. Who knew? Ex-husbands were good for something, after all.

Jake was coming out of the kitchen with a hot dog when Ella came downstairs. He glanced disapprovingly at her short skirt and clingy black sweater. She'd accessorized with suede boots, gold earrings and bracelet and a nice Hermès knock-off scarf.

"You look like a hooker," he informed her. "Are you going out with that wuss again?"

Oh, he had his nerve! "Just because Axel doesn't wear cowboy boots and run around shooting helpless deer—"

"For food," Jake cut in.

"Whatever. It doesn't make him a wuss. And I don't look like a hooker."

"Could've fooled me. What do you think is gonna go through that man's mind when he sees you like that?"

"Maybe every other man doesn't have the same kind of dirty mind you have," Ella retorted.

"Trust me. They do."

"Axel is a gentleman, and unlike some people he actually has self-control."

"I have self-control!"

Yes, she could tell by the way his voice was now bordering on a roar. "Anyway, I can dress how I want and see who I want. And at least I waited until I was divorced," she couldn't help adding.

"I never did anything with anyone!"

Oh, please. "Well, you're free to do whatever you want now, and so am I," she said. Saying those words should have made her happy but it didn't.

"Fine." He threw up his hands. "Go out with that turkey, but he's only after one thing."

She refused to dignify his remark with a response. And she refused to stay in the living room with Jake while she waited for Axel, so she marched out to the kitchen. She'd probably find it a mess.

She looked around in surprise. There was no mustard jar on the table, which had been wiped down. She walked to the sink. No dishes. He'd even cleaned it.

"I'm not a total slob, you know."

She turned to see Jake leaning in the doorway, Tiny by his side. Tiny seemed to like him best these days. Of course, why wouldn't he? Jake was home all the time, feeding him treats, making him fat.

Jake had always been the messy one. You'd never know it now to look at the kitchen. He obviously wanted to sell the house and get out of there as much as she did. That should've made her happy, too, but it didn't. Maybe she was never going to feel happy again.

You're happy now, she told herself, and decided to believe it.

The doorbell rang and she brushed past Jake and hurried down the hall. She shrugged into her coat and met Axel at the door, not even giving him a chance to come in. The last thing she needed was Jake standing there in the background, an unwanted third party.

"A woman who's ready on time? Now, that's impressive," Axel said. He took in her outfit. "You're impressive in so many ways, Ella."

She could read in his eyes what he was thinking. Jake was right.

Well, so what if he was? It was nice to be desired.

Once in the car she felt the need to apologize for the last disastrous showing—or, rather, nonshowing—of the house.

"Don't worry," Axel said. "I'll find the right buyers, I promise. Tonight I want you just to relax and have fun."

Fun was a local artists' show at D'Vine Wines. Modern art. She almost lost her appetite for the brie cheese she was nibbling.

What was she supposed to make of that picture of a path lined with crazy-colored trees that could've been painted by a third-grader? At the end of the path stood a naked woman with a tulip for a head. And here was a painting of a red couch spread out over four panels. It was hard to see the couch for the random black-and-white squiggles all over it. To Ella it looked as if someone had vandalized the painting.

"Striking, isn't it?" Axel said by her side.

"Striking," she repeated. It struck her as stupid.

The artist was approaching now, a fortysomething man with carefully cut shaggy hair, wearing an old gray sweater thrown on over jeans. She supposed he thought his outfit made him look like an artist. She thought it made him look dowdy.

"Dorian," Axel greeted him. "Great show."

"I'm pleased with it," the man said. Easy to tell from the self-satisfied expression on his face.

Ella couldn't help comparing him to Jake. When Jake had written a song, he was all excitement. And humility. "Do you really think it's good?" She'd be willing to bet this man never asked anyone that. Just as well. It spared people from having to choose between lying and answering honestly.

"This is Ella," Axel said.

Dorian looked her up and down. "Now, here's a work of art."

"Thanks," Ella murmured.

"You should model for me sometime," he suggested.

So she could end up naked with a tulip for a head? Anyway, she wasn't her mother. "I'm not into modeling."

He shrugged. "Shame." Then he turned his attention to Axel. "I have the perfect painting for you. Have you seen *New Day?*"

"No, show us," Axel said. He looked so eager, like a man about to be shown buried treasure.

Wineglasses in hand, they followed Dorian to a corner of the room to… Oh, that one? Seriously? Ella gaped at the primitive painting of a bloodred sun rising from a river of chartreuse toxic waste.

"That makes a statement," Axel said.

It made a statement, all right: *take Pepto-Bismol before looking at me.*

Axel was nodding at it. "Yes, I think I might have to get that."

Oh, he had to be joking. Ella glanced at the price. Rather an expensive joke.

"Do I know your taste or what?" Dorian asked.

"Tell Bridget to save it for me. I'll be by for it tomorrow," Axel promised.

Dorian sauntered off in search of a new victim and Ella turned to Axel. "You really like that?"

"Absolutely. Don't you?"

She could learn to like jazz. She could get into reading the classics, but this? She shook her head.

"Modern art grows on you once you understand the symbolism," Axel told her. Was that true or was he simply repeating something he'd heard from some other sucker who'd purchased an overpriced painting?"

"Trust me, this man's work is going to be hanging in MOMA someday."

"Who?"

"The Museum of Modern Art, in New York."

Oh, that museum. All right, maybe she *was* ignorant. Maybe she could learn to like modern art.

"I've got some great pieces at my place. Why don't we go over there? I'll show them to you, give you an art lesson."

Ella was sure he had more in mind than an art lesson.

"Okay," she said. Why not? She wasn't married anymore. She was ready for art lessons.

Axel's house was a huge, modern number with glass windows everywhere. The great room had hardwood floors covered with expensive Persian rugs and sleek, modern furniture that suggested you admire it rather than get comfy in it. And there over the equally uncomfy fireplace hung a huge painting of…nothing. Only white space.

"Um, is it waiting for inspiration?" she asked.

He chuckled. "It's called *Vacuum,*" he said, and launched into a detailed explanation.

She sighed. "To me, it just looks like a canvas waiting for someone to do something with it." She wondered if Axel thought of her that way. Was he trying to make her more polished?

"Well," he said, "art is subjective." He sat on the uninviting couch and patted the space next to him. "If you sit and study it, you'll be surprised by what you see."

She sat, she studied, she saw nothing. And she wasn't at all surprised when Axel decided to kiss her.

The kiss was as good as any a certain ex-husband could manage and it stirred up interest in all the right places. But it stirred up something else, too, something that protested, *What are you doing?*

She pulled away. "Axel, I'm sorry. I can't."

"Oh, of course. You're still angry over your divorce, but you need to know that not every man is a bum like your ex-husband. You can trust me."

That was what Jake used to say. Maybe a woman couldn't trust any man. "I think I need more time," she said. That was the problem.

"Understandable," Axel agreed, but he kept his arm around her shoulders.

They sat a moment and contemplated the painting of nothing hanging over his sterile fireplace.

"It grows on you, doesn't it?" he finally said.

She hoped so.

Charley's day had rushed past in a blur, and by the time the last diner left Zelda's she was a zombie. She and Richard had run on adrenaline for the past sixteen hours. She fetched a bottle of wine from the bar, along with two glasses, and invited him to join her at the little table in the back of the kitchen where the staff took their breaks.

She kicked off her shoes and he did the same, watching as she filled the glasses. She handed him one, saying, "You saved the day."

"No, *we* saved the day," he corrected, and raised his glass in salute. He took a drink, then leaned back in his chair and regarded her. "What are you going to do tomorrow?"

She shrugged. "See if I can haul Harvey out of whatever bottle he crawled into."

"So he can do this to you again?"

"Oh, believe me, I'll be looking for his replacement." Harvey should be thanking his lucky stars that she wasn't looking for a hit man. "I should never have believed him when he promised he'd go to AA."

Richard shook his head. "You're too softhearted, Charley. Don't keep him another day. Eighty-six his ass."

"And be both general manager *and* head chef?"

"I'll help you."

"You have your own restaurant," she reminded him.

"I know. But I can stay here a little longer."

Long enough to help her find a decent chef? That was easier said than done. "You don't want to be away from your place, though."

"Let me worry about that. Okay? Right now there's only one place I want to be and that's here," he added with a smile.

She felt his stockinged foot creep up her leg. A day ago she would have not only moved her leg out of range, she'd have tossed her wine in his face. Tonight, well, she was just too tired. And too grateful.

"Let's do the new song," Jake's bass player said.

Good idea. Jake had left the house ready to punch something and his mood hadn't improved as the night went on. He had to keep reminding himself to smile. Then he'd think about Ella out with that prissy Axel Fuchs and want to smash his guitar, preferably over Axel's head.

Of course he would never do that. It would be a waste of a fine instrument.

A cute little number with hair like honey, wearing skin-tight jeans, came up to the bandstand. "Can you play a Christmas song?"

"Sure," Jake said. "We've got just the song." To the dancers on the floor, he said, "We've got a song for all you married men out there. It's called 'Merry Christmas, Mama.'" He turned to Tim, the drummer. "Count us in."

And with that they were off. The cute little number frowned as her man shuffled them along the floor in a slow two-step but he was grinning. So were a lot of men in the room. The brotherhood of the sons-in-law. Once the song ended, there was much hooting and clapping.

"Looks like we got ourselves a hit," Larry said.

The cute little number was back at the bandstand now. "Can't you play something a little nicer?"

"How about 'Grandma Got Run Over by a Reindeer'?" Jake asked. Take out mother-in-law and Grandma in one fell swoop.

"I love my grandma," she informed him, and stomped off.

"Yeah? Well, I love my grandma, too," he called after her.

"Dude," Guy said, "what the hell's eating you?"

"Nothing," Jake growled. "Let's do 'Santa's Flying a 747 Tonight.'"

It was an old country song, but a great dance number and people loved it.

Not nearly as much as they loved Jake's song, though. Lots of guys gave him a thumbs-up or slapped him on the back as he made his way to the band's table when they went on break.

Yeah, he'd nailed it. If all the mothers-in-law in the U.S. could be rounded up and sent out to sea, the divorce rate would plummet, Jake was sure of it. Well, okay, not Guy's, whose mama-in-law baked him cookies and served steak dinners in honor of his birthday. She could stay.

"You guys were great," said Larry's girlfriend, Chrissie. She held up her smartphone. "I recorded it."

"Sweet," Larry said. "Let's put it up on YouTube and see what happens."

Jake shrugged. "Why not?" *Payback's a bitch…kinda like my ex-mother-in-law.* He grinned and downed his Coke.

By the time he got home Ella was in bed, her door firmly shut against him. As he passed her bedroom, a tiny germ of a thought two-stepped across the back of his mind. Maybe putting that song up wasn't such a good idea. Maybe writing it hadn't been such a good idea. Maybe he should tell Larry to hold off.

But then he asked himself, why? What did it matter now? Ella was moving on. He should, too. Like a gambler in Vegas, he said to himself, "Let it ride."

11

Sunday afternoon found Ella at Santa's tree lot, along with half the residents of Icicle Falls, who were all bundled up in winter coats and hats. She spotted Cass and her kids and went over to say hi. "Looks like you're getting a tree early, too."

"Busy as we are with the wedding, we decided we'd better do it now," Cass said.

"How are the plans coming?" Ella asked.

"We picked out the flowers yesterday," Dani said.

And that launched a discussion about colors and bridesmaids' dresses. "I can stay open a little later on Tuesday if you want to bring Mikaila and Vanessa in after they're done with work," Ella offered.

"That'll be great since Mom and I are going over to Seattle tomorrow to check out bridal gowns."

"Oh, fun!" Ella could still remember standing in front of the mirror at the bridal shop, looking at herself in that elegant white gown and envisioning her perfect life with Jake. Parts of it *had* been perfect. "Sure. Anytime that works for them. Just let me know."

Willie was busy inspecting trees one row over. "Hey, Mom, how about this one?"

"Guess I should get back to business. See you tonight," Cass said, and went to join her son. Ella could hear her. "That's a good one, but it's out of our price range."

"Come on, Mom," Willie wheedled. "It's Christmas. Don't be a Grinch."

Ella couldn't help smiling. Cass would cave. When it came to her children, she was a softy.

Ella had thought that by now she'd be looking at trees with a little one in tow, maybe a girl dressed in pink Baby Gap. Life never turned out the way you planned. Why was that?

She wandered down the rows, inspecting trees, searching for one that would say Home, Sweet Home to potential buyers. Finally she found it. This tree would look lovely in the window. Anyone entering the house would think a happy family lived there. Well, until they saw the his-and-hers bedrooms.

"You've picked out a beaut," approved Al, Mr. Santa himself. He looked around, making his Santa hat wag like a tail. "Where's Jake?"

Last year Jake had been with her. They'd bought a small tree, taken it home and decorated it with strung popcorn. Jake had eaten more popcorn than he'd strung and she'd given him a hard time about not doing his fair share. It had

all been in fun, but come February, when Mims was sitting
her down for a serious talk, she'd realized how true those
words had been.

"We're not together anymore," Ella said, and the merry
smile disappeared from Al's face. She hated having to tell
people, hated seeing the embarrassment and pity on their
faces. *Poor kid. She couldn't make her marriage work.*

"Oh. Well, that's too bad," Al said. "So, uh, let me get
this tree over to your car. Got some rope to tie it on?"

"I've got some in the trunk."

With the help of his son, Al hoisted the giant tree onto
the roof of her car. It promptly swallowed the vehicle.

"Good thing you don't have far to drive," Al said. "That's
a traffic ticket waiting to happen."

"Better hope Tilda's not on the road," his son added.
"She'll give you one for sure."

Ella thanked them, then got in her car and drove home,
peering through the fir fringe. She parked in front of the
house in time to see Jake and Tiny strolling up the street.
At the sight of her Tiny raced over to the car and greeted
her as she got out.

"Hey, boy," she said. "Did you have a good walk?"

Now Jake was at the car. "You didn't tell me you were
getting a tree."

Why should she have? It wasn't like they were going to
spend a cozy afternoon together trimming it. "I didn't think
you'd be interested."

He scowled at it. "I don't see the point."

"Maybe that's why I didn't tell you."

"How much did it cost?"

She'd spent more than she should have, but she didn't need

him pitching in. She could handle it on her own. She was going to be handling things on her own from now on, and that included Christmas trees. "Never mind," she said, and began fumbling with the rope.

"Here, let me," he said, stepping in and taking over. "I don't know why the hell you bought a tree."

"To make the house look nice."

"Oh, yeah. That figures."

"What?" she demanded.

"Nothing," he said irritably.

Mims had always hired decorators, so for Ella trimming the tree was still a novelty and a delight. But it was an activity that should be done with smiles. There would be no smiles today. What a dumb idea. What had she been thinking? As if a tree alone would sell her house. It probably wasn't the lack of holiday decor or faulty plumbing that was keeping this house on the market. It was the lack of love inside it. People picked up on things like that.

Jake lifted her purchase down from the car and hauled it up the front walk, rather like a cave man bringing home a dead animal. "Be careful," Ella said as he went up the steps, the tree dragging along behind him.

"Don't worry about it."

She sighed and followed him in. Definitely a dumb idea.

He propped the tree by the front door. "Do we need the tree stand?"

"I need the tree stand," she said. "I'll get it."

He held up a hand. "I can do it. I'll get the ornaments out of the attic, too."

Half an hour later, the tree was planted in its stand by the front window, waiting to get dressed for the holidays. She assumed Jake would leave now, his part in the process over, but instead he opened the storage container with the lights and pulled out a string. "Tell me how you want 'em," he said, and started stringing them around the tree.

That was how they'd done it in the past. He'd string the lights and she'd look on with an artist's eye and direct operations. She swallowed a sudden lump in her throat.

"How's this?" he asked.

"Nice," she managed.

Once the lights were on, he vanished into the kitchen. His job was done.

She opened the container of ornaments they'd collected and felt sadness fly out at her. All the memories in here were good ones. It was so wrong that they didn't mean anything anymore.

Many of the ornaments were simple colored balls, but they had a few special ones, and she felt tears springing to her eyes when she took out one shaped like a miniature Christmas present. Jake had gotten it for her their first Christmas. "Wish I could buy you a box full of designer jewelry," he'd written on the card, "but for now will you settle for all my love?"

She sniffed and hung it up.

"I remember that," he said, and she turned to see him coming back into the room holding two mugs. He handed her one. "Eggnog. We always drink eggnog when we decorate the tree."

She accepted the mug with a murmured thanks and took a sip. "You spiked it."

"I always spike it."

And she always got tipsy and crazy. They weren't married

anymore. There was no point getting tipsy and crazy. She set it on the coffee table and went back to the ornaments. Jake joined her. "You don't have to help," she told him.

"I know. I want to." He took out a porcelain angel in a lacy gown. "Remember this?"

She nodded. He got it for her three years ago at the Kris Kringl Mart on Thanksgiving weekend. They'd shopped at the merchants and artist booths and drank hot chocolate, and then walked home in the snow. Later that evening, they'd built a fire in the fireplace and made love on the couch. She averted her eyes as he hung it up.

"El, I didn't mean to sound like a bastard earlier. I just thought we weren't going to do a tree. And…"

"And what?" she prompted.

He shrugged. "It sucks that we're doing a tree to get rid of this place."

"You wanted to move to Nashville," she reminded him.

He clenched his jaw, a sure sign that he was keeping back something he'd thought the better of saying.

This had been such a stupid idea. Ella took a big gulp of eggnog.

Jake pulled out the little jukebox topped with a black cowboy hat and she downed the last of her eggnog in one long guzzle.

He looked at the ornament. "Remember when you got this for me?"

She'd found that ornament at a kiosk in a mall when they went to Seattle to celebrate their first anniversary. The company personalized the ornaments and the banner across this one read "I Do and I Will." It was the title of the song he'd written and sung to her at their wedding.

"I need more eggnog," she muttered, going to the kitchen, Tiny trotting after her hopefully. "This wouldn't be good for you," she said as she poured the eggnog. Heck, all those calories wouldn't be good for her, either. She'd be sorry when she stepped on the scale tomorrow but tonight she needed comfort food.

She heard footsteps and a moment later Jake was at her side. "I could use a refill, too," he said, taking the carton from her. He filled his mug, then picked up the bottle of rum he'd left on the counter and added a generous splash. Before she could protest he'd added some to hers, as well. "'Tis the season."

Not to be jolly. She went back to the tree. Enough with the special ornaments, she decided, and dug out a box of plain gold balls. Even those made her want to cry.

Jake gave the jukebox a flick with his finger. "I still think that song could be a hit." He began to sing, painting a musical picture of their wedding.

She grabbed her eggnog and downed more. "Stop."

He frowned. "What happened to us, El? Why didn't we try harder to work things out?"

"What was the point? You're never going to change."

"You liked me just the way I was when we were first together," he said softly.

She didn't say anything to that and they worked in silence for a while, decorating and, every time a new memory came out of the ornament box, drinking. Her mug emptied, he filled it back up. And then it emptied again. How fast the eggnog disappeared when you were trying to wash away memories!

At last the tree was done. "Looks good," Jake said. "There's something missing, though."

She glanced at the stack of boxes. "I don't think so."

He grabbed some old newspaper and started crumpling it. "We always have a fire in the fireplace when we put up the tree."

Had. They always *had.* Ella didn't say anything. Instead, she cleared away the empty boxes while Jake piled on the kindling. By the time she returned, the kindling had caught and he was adding a couple of logs. The fragrance of burning pine began to fill the room. A decorated tree, a husband building a roaring fire—this was a scene fit for a magazine ad selling…what? Happiness.

No, this wasn't *true* happiness, just an alcohol-induced buzz.

Buzzing was good, though.

Jake fetched more rum and joined her on the couch. "Remember the first time we lit a fire in that fireplace?" he asked as he freshened her mug.

She took another sip. How could she forget? He'd thought he was opening the damper and instead had closed it. She smiled. "You've gotten pretty good at building fires since then." He'd gotten good at a lot of things, especially making love to her. He knew every inch of her, exactly what turned her on.

She felt his fingers caressing the back of her neck, right below her hairline. That was one of the things.

"This is our last Christmas," he whispered, then began singing again, the chorus of that first song he'd written for her.

Tell him to stop, she commanded herself, but she couldn't.

She'd always loved it when he sang to her. It had made her feel special. She wanted to feel special one last time.

He took her mug and set it on the coffee table. Then he took her face in his hands and looked at her with longing in those gorgeous dark eyes of his.

He still loves you.

It was the rum talking. She wouldn't listen.

Be honest. You still love him, said the rum. *And you want him.*

The rum was right. She let Jake kiss her. And kiss her again. And then she let him slide his hand up her midriff. Every nerve ending along the way did the Wave. *Woooh!* Oh, this wasn't leading anywhere good.

No, said the rum. *It's leading somewhere great.*

Cecily looked at the clock in Cass's living room. "I wonder what's going on with Ella. It's not like her to be this late."

Cass had the DVD of *Miracle on Thirty-Fourth Street* in the player, waiting for their last movie buff to arrive. Ella loved these movie nights. Where was she?

"I say give her ten more minutes and then we start without her," Samantha said, popping a chocolate mint truffle in her mouth.

"I saw her at Santa's tree lot today." Cass helped herself to another Christmas cookie from the platter on her coffee table. "Maybe she got busy decorating and forgot."

"Kind of early to put up a tree, isn't it?" Samantha asked. "We used to wait until mid-December to put ours up so it wouldn't dry out."

"Al claims his trees are so fresh you don't need to wait," Cass said. "Although, come to think of it, the one we got from him last year was practically a fire hazard by Christmas Eve."

"So when are you putting up your tree?" Charley asked her.

"Good question," Cass said. "Somewhere in between the wedding dress and the DJ."

Samantha shook her head. "Pulling this wedding together so fast is—well, I don't know how you're doing it."

"Piece of cake," Cass said.

"Spoken like a true baker." Samantha grinned. "Have you picked a caterer yet?"

"It's on the to-do list. I need to find someone Dani will like and I can afford."

"Well," Samantha said slowly, "Bailey's planning on coming up for the holidays. She's the queen of caterers and I bet she could be persuaded to come up early. She'd give you a deal."

"Now, there's a good idea," Cass said. "I wouldn't have to worry with Bailey in charge."

"Well, other than worrying about her tripping and falling into the wedding cake," Samantha joked.

Cecily couldn't help smiling. Bailey wasn't the most graceful girl on the planet. But of the three of them, she was the bubbliest. A girl could get away with a lot of klutziness when she was adorable.

Cass poured herself a glass of wine. "Well, I say we start the movie. I have to get up with the birds."

The life of a baker. Ugh. But Cass was right. They couldn't wait indefinitely. "Let me just call her," Cecily said. She picked up her cell phone and called Ella's house.

Jake answered on the third ring.

Now that they were divorced, Cecily never knew quite what to say to him. It was so awkward when friends broke up. Heck, it was more than that. It was heartbreaking. "Oh, Jake. Hi. Sorry to bother you, but we're getting ready to watch our movie and we're wondering where Ella is. Do you know if she left?"

"She's not gonna make it tonight," Jake said. "She had too much eggnog and she can't drive."

It was a fifteen-minute walk from their place to Cass's. "Too much eggnog?"

"We were decorating the tree," Jake said, as if that explained it.

Before Cecily could say anything more, he added, "I'll tell her you called, Cec." And then he hung up. Cecily stared at her phone, trying to figure out what was odd about that conversation.

"So, is she coming?" Samantha asked.

"No," Cecily said. "She had too much eggnog."

"Too much eggnog," her sister repeated.

"Eggnog and tree-trimming. Something is going on over there," Cecily said.

"You think they're getting back together?" Charley asked.

"Bad plan if you ask me," Samantha said, choosing another chocolate.

"Not necessarily," Cecily argued. "Maybe they've come to some sort of compromise." She hoped so.

Cass shook her head. "I don't know. Getting back together with her ex? It doesn't sound smart to me."

"People can change," Charley said.

Cecily hadn't been a matchmaker for nothing. She could

read between the lines, and Charley's statement read like a potential horror story. "Not all people," she cautioned.

Charley pretended not to see her friend's warning look. Instead, she loaded a bowl with popcorn and said, "So, let's start the movie."

Okay, *there* was a heart destined for the heartbreak trail. Charley was going to do what she was going to do, and there'd be no stopping her. Just like there'd been no stopping Ella when she let her mother convince her that she needed to dump Jake. Cecily was the resident love expert here. Why didn't her friends ever listen to her?

Maybe because you've gone through two fiancés? Well, there was that. She filled another bowl with popcorn and sat back to watch the movie. What was going on over at Ella's?

12

Ella stumbled out of a deep sleep Monday morning to find she had three arms. One was under her pillow and another was stretched out in front of her. Over that arm lay the third, a muscular one with dark hair. She blinked herself the rest of the way into consciousness to see that the third arm was attached to a second body tucked up against hers, a body that didn't belong in her bed. Jake.

With a yelp she hurled herself out of bed. This sudden movement didn't do wonders for her head, which was throbbing.

He was awake now and looking confused. "El?"

"What are you doing in my bed?" *Someone's been sleeping in my bed. And doing other things, too.*

"I was sleeping," he said, sitting up.

"Before that?" *Why was she asking? She knew.*

He grinned.

"But we're divorced." She ran a hand through her hair. How had this happened? Of course, that was a stupid question. She'd gotten sloppy sentimental and tipsy.

"We can fix that," he said easily. He slid from under the covers and started toward her.

"Where are your clothes?" For that matter, where were *her* clothes? Naked. She was naked. She grabbed the bedspread and held it in front of her like a shield.

"Scattered all over the living room, along with yours. And it's a little late for that, isn't it?" he teased, pointing at her makeshift covering. He tried to hug her but she jerked away, tripping over the bedspread in the process. "This was wrong. You seduced me!"

"Oh, yeah? Well, you seemed pretty anxious to be seduced. Come on, Ella, quit pretending you didn't want that as much as I did."

"I…" She had. "This doesn't mean anything."

"It means a lot. It means we belong together."

"No, we don't." Jake had been a mistake. Last night had been a mistake. She was done making mistakes. "I'm not doing that again. Ever." At least not with him.

A new thought occurred to her. What if she'd gotten pregnant? It only took once and she wasn't on the Pill anymore. "Did you use protection?"

"Uh, no."

One time, it was just one time. What were the chances? "Ooooh. I feel sick," she moaned. Morning sickness? Already?

"I'll make us some coffee," he said.

Exactly what she wanted, a cozy cup of coffee with her

ex-husband. *You didn't have any objections to sharing a cozy mug of eggnog with him last night.* Actually, several.

She hurried to the shower, determined to wash away the fuzzy memory of his touch and any latent traces of longing.

By the time he came out of the kitchen with her coffee, she was on her way out the door.

"Where are you going? It's only eight."

"I need to get to the shop."

"It's not open on Mondays. Don't run away, El."

"I'm not running away," she said haughtily. "I'm just... not staying. I have extra work to do." She'd come up with something.

He frowned. "What a little chicken you are."

"I'm not a chicken."

"Yeah, you are. By the way..."

"What?"

He nodded at her chest. "Your sweater's on backward."

She looked down. He was right. She was so upset she couldn't even dress herself properly. "Thank you," she said, trying for some dignity. Then she shut the door and ran down the walk.

It wasn't until she got to the shop that she realized she'd also put on one black pump and one brown one and she had a black sock on one foot and a navy blue one on the other. Great. Now she looked as messed up on the outside as she was on the inside. Gilded Lily's didn't carry shoes so she was stuck. Unless, of course, she wanted to run back home and change. And see Jake. Which, she insisted sternly, she didn't want to do. It was a good thing they weren't open on Mondays. No one would see her messed-up feet and ask what the heck she'd been thinking when she got dressed this morning.

She spent the next hour updating the store's website and Facebook page, trying to ignore her mismatched shoes and her mixed-up feelings, then got busy ordering merchandise. There was always plenty to do in a small shop. Sadly, nothing she did was enough to take her mind off Jake. She could still remember the touch of his lips on hers, the feel of his arms around her.... *Oh, stop,* she scolded herself, *you sound like one of your romance novels.*

And what was wrong with that?

Plenty, when you were romancing the wrong man.

Sigh.

Jake had finished cleaning up the kitchen. Not so much as a speck of dirt anywhere. That would make Ella happy. He'd done the laundry, too. He could never fold clothes right, but he hoped she'd be pleased that he'd tried. And now the house stuff was finished, or at least all that he could see. He had several hours until Curt Whalen came for his after-school guitar lesson. Jake wished he could pop on over to the shop and take Ella out to lunch. He used to do that when he was working at the music store. They'd go to Big Brats and grab something. Sometimes they'd eaten sandwiches at the shop while she was between customers. Those had been good times, living simply and loving it while they waited for him to catch a break, sell a song.

Last night it was like it had been when they were first married—no worries, no disagreements, no mother-in-law telling lies about him. Why couldn't they go back in time?

Back in time. Was there an idea in there? He went in search of his guitar. Two hours later he'd poured his heart into a kick-ass song, perfect for Lady Antebellum. He went to the spare room downstairs, where he'd set up a small re-cording studio with secondhand equipment, and got to work on a song demo. Any day now a publisher would pick up one of his songs. He was getting closer all the time. Little Big Town Publishing had been encouraging. A song picked up by a Nashville publisher—maybe that would be enough to win Ella back. A guy could dream.

Cecily called Ella's cell shortly before lunch. "Want to get a salad at Zelda's?"

No way was Ella going out in public dressed like this. 'Um, I'm working at the shop."

"On a Monday?"

"I had a lot to do." *And a lot to run away from.*

"Oh. Well, how about I pick up something and come by?" Before Ella could think up some excuse to keep her away, Cecily said a breezy, "See you in a bit," and ended the call.

Ella looked at her mismatched shoes and frowned. She should've told Cecily she didn't have time for lunch. The last thing she needed was her friend the matchmaker com-ing by. Cecily could be unnervingly astute, and Ella was al-ready unnerved enough.

Half an hour later Cecily was tapping on the shop door. Ella opened it and she walked in bearing a big take-out bag, the aroma of chicken dancing in with her. "I got a couple of hot chicken salads," she said just in case Ella's nose wasn't working.

"That sounds good." Ella hurried back to the other side of the counter to hide her feet.

Cecily allowed her a moment to savor her first bite, then said, "We missed you last night."

Ella could feel her face catching fire. "We got busy putting up a tree. I thought it might help sell the house."

"Uh-huh," Cecily said diplomatically. She took a bite of salad, then picked up the multibead red necklace Ella had put on the counter earlier. "This would be cute for the holidays." She checked the price tag. "I think I'll get it for Mom. Even though you're not open, you wouldn't mind ringing it up, would you?"

Ella could feel her friend's assessing gaze on her. Oh, this was awkward. She gnawed her bottom lip as she rang up the sale.

"Everything okay?" Cecily asked.

Ella slipped the necklace in a gift bag. "I think I made a mistake."

"Which time? When you got divorced or when you slept with Jake last night?"

Ella stared at her friend in wide-eyed shock. "Are you psychic?"

"When we called and Jake said you'd been drinking eggnog and couldn't drive, it wasn't too hard to figure out something was up."

Ella groaned. "I was stupid. I don't know what I was thinking."

"I guess you weren't thinking of Axel."

Axel. She'd forgotten all about him. "Oh, if he found out…"

"Don't worry," Cecily said. "Nobody's going to tell him."

Except maybe Jake. "I should never have slept with him," Ella said. "And I'm sure not going to do it again."

"Never say never." Cecily leaned over the counter and

looked at Ella's feet. "By the way, am I hallucinating or are you wearing two different shoes?"

"You're hallucinating."

"Uh-huh," Cecily said, and left it at that.

The bakery was closed on Mondays, so after Willie was out the door for school, Cass and Dani and Amber (who'd been allowed to miss school so she could be part of the all-important mission) had made the trek to Special Day Bridal in Seattle. Now Cass and Amber waited in the seating area for Dani to model the dress of her dreams.

The shop was a feast for the eyes, with celebrity-worthy bridesmaids' dresses and white gowns fit for a princess hanging everywhere. Lace, organza, satin—money, money, money. The velveteen chair Cass was sitting on probably cost more than all her living room furniture put together. She wouldn't be surprised if this dress cost more than all the furniture in her house. *And* the appliances.

Amber hadn't stopped prowling the place since they arrived. "Look at this one, Mom." She pulled out a tiered organza number.

"It's beautiful," Cass acknowledged. Everything here was.

Dani came out of the dressing area, followed by the shop owner, who'd had been hustling in and out with goodies.

"Oh, my," Cass breathed. A montage of scenes flashed through her mind: Dani as a smiling baby, jumping up and down in her crib with excitement, waiting for Cass to lift her out; five-year-old Dani blowing out the candles on the doll-shaped birthday cake Cass had made her; Dani at seventeen, wearing her first prom dress. Her daughter had grown up overnight. Now, here she stood, a beautiful woman in her bridal gown, every mother's dream come true. She wore an off-the-shoulder long-sleeved white silk taffeta dress with a formfitting bodice and sweeping, full skirt. The cuff, neckline and hem were trimmed with white angora to match the white angora hat. Scalloped layers of tulle trimmed with lace and silver sequins added bling. Cass could see why her daughter had fallen in love with the dress.

Dani looked at her hopefully. "Well, what do you think?"

"Wow," Amber said.

"It's stunning," Cass said.

Dani beamed. "I love it so much."

Cass swallowed and asked, "How much is it?"

Dani brushed a hand along the soft trim. "Twelve hundred and sixty dollars for the dress."

"It's on sale, thirty percent off," the store's owner threw in. "And we won't have to do any alteration, which is unusual."

"And the hat?" Cass asked weakly.

"Two hundred dollars."

So, fourteen hundred and sixty dollars. Plus tax. She'd pay it, though. It was worth every penny to see that radiant smile on her daughter's face.

"Don't worry, Mom," Dani said. "Daddy's going to pay for it."

He was? "Oh."

"I talked to him yesterday."

Without telling her. *Be glad he's picking up the tab,* Cass advised herself. *Be glad he wants to be involved.*

"That's...great," she said, injecting goodwill into her voice.

"He said to call him and he'll give you his Visa number," Dani told the woman.

"That was really cool of Daddy," Amber said.

"Yes, it was." In spite of the pep talk she'd just given herself, Cass found it difficult to get the words past the jealous bone caught in her throat. She'd worked so hard, done everything for her kids, and now she felt like she was being displaced. Bought out and squeezed out.

"I know it's not rational," she said to Dot later that day when she was back in Icicle Falls. "But, damn, it bugs me that he gets to ride in on his white horse after being such an absent father. And it's so…passive-aggressive. He doesn't talk to me at all, discuss what he will and won't pay for. He just cherry-picks and coughs up the money for the big, high-drama items."

Dot's bunion surgery had been a success and now she sat enthroned on her couch, her foot propped up on a pillow. The coffee table in front of her hosted a get-well box of Sweet Dreams chocolates from Dot's friend Muriel Sterling, a glass of water, a crossword puzzle book and the TV remote. And now a bowl of the chicken stew Cass had brought.

"Come on, kiddo," Dot said. "Everything's a high-drama item when you're planning a wedding. You know that. And if your ex is like most men, he's clueless. He wouldn't think to offer—he just waits around with his checkbook. Your daughter's got his number, in more ways than one. She calls and says, 'Daddy, I need money,' and he forks it over. The silver lining is that you don't have to pay."

And Dani had the gown of her dreams. Still… "I feel like I'm paying in other ways."

"Everything has a cost. I know it's hard to share when you've pulled most of the load and had the kids all to yourself for so long, but it looks like that's changing and there's nothing you can do about it. It's all part of the for-better-or-worse thing."

"Well, it shouldn't be, since we're not married anymore," Cass said grumpily.

"Divorce doesn't cancel out for better or worse, not when you've got kids."

Dot was right, Cass told herself as she drove home. She had to come to grips with the fact that Mason was in her children's lives (and hers) to stay. Why was that so hard to do?

Because it wasn't fair, that was why.

How many times had the kids said that to her over the years? And how many times had she replied, "Who said life is fair?" Of course, it wasn't, and now she'd have to follow her own advice: make the best of it.

She remembered how happy Dani had looked standing in that bridal shop in her wedding gown. Her daughter was getting married and she got to be a part of it. If she couldn't make the best of *that,* she had something seriously wrong with her.

"I'm not going to keep encouraging Richard," Charley told her reflection. The woman looking back at her was all dressed to party in charcoal slacks, a black sweater and a diamond pendant necklace—the very necklace Richard had given her for Valentine's Day three years ago.

Not going to encourage him, huh? That was why she'd let him play footsie with her on Saturday night. That was why she'd bought mistletoe and hung it up. That was why she was wearing a Victoria's Secret black bra under her sweater. *Planning on removing your sweater later tonight?*

She frowned at her reflection. "You are pathetic." She had to stop being pathetic. Didn't she?

No, she answered herself. Everyone deserved a second chance. Richard really was sorry and he was doing everything he could to prove it. And she was sticking with Victoria.

The doorbell rang, sending butterflies swirling in her stomach. Silly. She felt like a teenager getting ready to go to the prom instead of a woman about to go out to dinner. She opened the door and he stepped in, smelling like Armani cologne.

"You're gorgeous," he said.

"It's just pants and a sweater," she said, feeling ridiculously pleased.

"I wasn't talking about the clothes." He held out a small box.

"What's this?"

"Just a little something I thought you might like."

She opened the box to find a pair of etched silver open teardrop earrings. "They're lovely."

"I thought they'd look good on you."

Pricy earrings, sleigh rides, expensive brunches, pitching in to help during a crisis—no man went to all that trouble unless he was truly sorry for his wicked ways.

And now they were off to the Orchard House Bed and Breakfast several miles outside of town for a five-course dinner sponsored by one of the local wineries. Another pricy bit of penance, and a penance she was happy to let him pay.

Zelda's was closed on Sunday and Monday evenings, and after the crazy weekend they'd had, a spectacular dinner that she didn't have to plan and prepare was exactly what the doctor ordered—although a heart specialist might have suggested she attend with someone else.

The Orchard House's restaurant was a feast for the senses, with a fire burning in the river rock fireplace, sparkling silver and crystal on linen tablecloths and holiday floral arrangements that must have cost an arm and a leg. In addition to a treat for the eyes, diners were given a treat for their ears with a harpist in one corner of the room, playing Christmas carols. Charley took it all in, making mental notes on how she could improve her own place.

The food was incredible, from the first course, which offered caramelized apple with brie and red wine cherry glaze, to the dessert—white chocolate strawberry shortcake paired with a cabernet sauvignon.

"That was fabulous," she said as they drove back.

"Like the woman I'm with." He smiled at her in a way that turned her poor insides to mush.

She was a goner. Tonight she was going to cave. She knew it, Richard knew it. A woman could only hold out for so long. Anyway, it didn't feel right to hold out any longer. Driving home together, sharing this intimate space while Aerosmith serenaded them with "I Don't Want to Miss a Thing" felt like the good old days when they were happy together. They could be happy again, couldn't they? Heck, they were happy right now.

Still, she was going to make him fight for this last bit of ground. When they pulled up in front of the house she didn't invite him inside. She knew she didn't need to, anyway. Just as he'd been doing since he hit town, he'd invite himself in.

Sure enough. "Can I talk you into a nightcap?" he asked softly.

"I'm stuffed."

"How about some conversation, then?"

"Talking is good."

Talking was, indeed, good. They took a stroll down memory lane and then his hand took a stroll along her arm. A minute later he was kissing her. "You are an amazing woman. You know that?" he murmured.

"You're just now realizing?"

"I knew it all along. Take me back."

She pretended to consider. "I might. Depends on whether you're still any good in bed."

He grinned and proceeded to show her.

They'd gotten as far as playing show and tell with her Victoria's Secret bra when she heard sirens. "Do you hear that?"

"Hmm?" he said as he kissed his way down her neck.

"Sirens," she said, stating the obvious.

"Someone probably left a candle burning."

One of her friends or neighbors. She pushed Richard away and sat up, straining to hear. A fire right before Christmas would be a nightmare. She made a mental note to give whoever was dealing with it a gift certificate to Zelda's.

"They're nowhere near us." Richard ran a hand up her back.

She ignored the flutter it caused in her chest. "It sounds like they're somewhere downtown. If that's the case, it's someone's business."

She'd barely finished speaking when her phone rang. Suddenly, she knew who the fire victim was.

13

Charley stood across the street in shock, watching as her baby went up in flames. She'd poured everything into this restaurant—her money, her time, her heart and soul—and now it was dying before her eyes. So was a part of her.

The flames lit the night and the faces of bystanders as firefighters scrambled to put out the blaze. The heat blew in her face, taunting her. It took the chill from the night but Charley couldn't stop shivering. How could this be happening? She stood rooted to the street, hardly noticing Richard's arm around her, watching the place that had hosted so many people, so many events, turn black.

As the fire hoses did their work, the flames evolved into giant plumes of smoke. That was even worse than the flames, a real-life illustration of what was happening to her dreams.

It was difficult to see past the tears, but she became aware of her friends, coming to stand by her. Cass positioned herself on Charley's other side, opposite Richard, and Samantha and Cecily fell in line next to Cass. Finally, Ella slipped behind her and draped a big blanket over her shoulders. They stood around her like palace guards, deflecting inquisitive townspeople and curious tourists alike, wrapping her in love.

Fire Chief Berg came up to her. "I'm sorry, Charley."

"What caused it?" she asked, barely able to speak.

"We won't be able to tell for a while. Once the fire is completely out, we'll do salvage and investigate the area of origination. I'll call you as soon as we know something, I promise."

She nodded and managed to thank him.

"You can't do any good here and tomorrow will be busy," Richard said, attempting to lead her away.

She resisted. "No. I'm going to stay until the fire is out."

"Charley."

"I'm staying," she said through gritted teeth.

He gave up. "Okay."

People began to drift away, but her friends remained until Zelda's restaurant was nothing but a charred shell.

"Now we need to go home," Richard said.

This time she didn't resist. There was nothing more to see.

She didn't cry until she got home. Then she curled up in her bed and sobbed. Richard climbed in behind her. Pulling the blankets over them both, he wrapped her in his arms and let her have at it. She cried until her head throbbed and she was hoarse. Finally, exhausted, she fell into a fitful sleep. But with dawn she was awake and staring at the ceiling while the tears slid down her cheeks.

"I'll make coffee," Richard said.

He brought her coffee in bed, along with a croissant, which she had no interest in eating.

"Try," he urged. "It's going to be a tough day."

That was an understatement. The worst part of her morning was when she got the news about the cause of the fire. It appeared that one of her kitchen workers—probably Bruno—had left a burner on after the Monday lunch shift. A pot on top of the stove, which should have been put away, had eventually ignited and the fire had spread from there. The sprinkler system had failed to activate, and if not for the fire alarm system, the place would have burned to the ground. Charley couldn't help thinking it might as well have for all that remained of it. Renovation would take months. With a heavy heart, she put in a call to the insurance company.

Midafternoon Cecily came into her sister's office at Sweet Dreams Chocolate Company. "We need to take some vitamin C over to Charley." Chocolate was so much better than the other vitamin C when a friend was under stress.

"I'm sure she's buried in paperwork. The last thing she wants right now is visitors," Samantha said.

"We're talking about the woman who threw herself a party when her divorce was final," Cecily argued.

"That was different. She was celebrating then. I don't think she's celebrating today."

"Chocolate is good for celebration *and* commiseration," Cecily said.

Samantha considered this for a moment. "You're right."

Fifteen minutes later they were on their way to Charley's house with a ten-pound box of salted caramels, her favorite.

"You can still smell the smoke from the fire," Cecily said, wrinkling her nose.

"As if it isn't bad enough that she has to see her ruined restaurant," Samantha said, shaking her head, "she has to smell it, too. I can't imagine what I'd do if Sweet Dreams burned down."

"You'd rebuild, of course, just like Charley will. But don't even say things like that. It creeps me out."

"Don't worry, we've already had our share of misery."

"Poor Charley, I hope this is the last misery she has to go through," Cecily said as they walked up her front porch steps.

Samantha rang the doorbell but they didn't hear any sounds of life from inside the house. "I told you this was a bad idea," she said, and turned to go.

Cecily stayed put and rang the bell again. "Give them a minute. She needs this candy, and she needs her friends."

This time they heard approaching footsteps. A moment later Richard opened the door.

"We brought something for Charley," Samantha said, holding out the box.

He took it and nodded solemnly. "That was nice. She could use it."

Cecily expected him to invite them in. After all, they were two of Charley's closest friends. Instead, he said, "Thanks. I'll see that she gets it," and shut the door.

"I don't like that guy," Samantha muttered as they walked down the porch steps.

Cecily frowned and pulled up her coat collar. "I've got a bad feeling about him."

"You should tell Charley."

"I doubt she puts much stock in my hunches."

"She should. They're rarely wrong."

Cecily shrugged. "Even if she did, she wouldn't want to hear this one. Once a woman's made up her mind about a man, it isn't easy to steer her in another direction. When it comes to love, sometimes we have to learn the hard way." Boy, did she know that. Experience was a thorough teacher.

"Someone should invent a spray," Samantha said. "Like bug spray, only for losers."

Cecily chuckled. "Bad-boy spray?"

"Something like that. I'd buy you a bottle."

"Me?" Cecily protested.

"Yeah. Then you could shoot it at Todd Black every time he drops by the gift shop to buy chocolate for his mom. Since when is *he* such a good son?"

Since he'd run into Cecily at the drugstore when she'd returned to Icicle Falls to stay. She'd also encountered him at the gym. Several times. That was a bad place to run into a man you were determined not to be attracted to—T-shirts and muscles and…did sweating release pheromones? Todd Black was a bad boy, a heartbreak waiting to happen. Cecily strongly suspected he was the type of man who'd sleep with her, steal her heart and then steal away, move on to the next conquest. Everything he said was a double entendre, meant to tickle her hormones, and every encounter with him hit her zing-o-meter. It was stupid to let herself be attracted to a man who was so wrong for her. But if he suggested she stop by his seedy tavern to try out his pinball machine one more time, she was afraid she might just give in. If she could go a couple of months without seeing him, it would help, but that was next to impossible in a small town.

But if it wasn't Todd, it would be someone else. Bad boys were her Achilles' heel. And, darn it all, bad boys were everywhere. *It doesn't mean you need to get involved with one,* she reminded herself.

That last thought led her back to Charley and Richard. Hopefully, her intuition was off for once and Charley's bad boy had reformed.

Ella had just sent Pat Wilder out the door with a floating-petals coral top and a new bracelet when Axel Fuchs called.

"I'm bringing some people by to see the house around five-thirty," he said, "so make sure Jake cleans."

"I will," she promised. She could close a little early, run home and pitch in.

"And maybe you'd like to go out with one of your friends for a while after work," Axel added.

He probably didn't trust her to stay out from underfoot. "Okay."

"And get Jake to take Tiny for a walk."

No woman, no man, no dog—make the house look like anything but a home, she thought. Why did that bug her? It already wasn't a home even with them in it.

"These people have driven by and love the place from the outside. And they like the price," Axel continued. "So fingers crossed that we'll have a sale for you this time."

"I hope so," she said fervently. Then she could get Jake gone and move on with her life.

She called his cell. Naturally, he didn't answer. Why did the man have a cell phone when he never bothered to use it? "We might have a sale tonight," she told his voice mail. "Can you see that the kitchen is clean and your bedroom picked up?" She ended the call and frowned. She felt like his mother instead of his wife. Ex-wife, she quickly corrected herself.

An hour later her cell rang. "Got your message," Jake said. "Everything's clean."

Hmm. Jake-clean or really clean?

"I'm running the dishes right now."

"Can you sweep the kitchen floor?"

"Already done."

"Check to be sure the bathrooms—"

"Did it."

This was, indeed, surprising. "Oh. Well."

"Anything else?" he asked shortly.

"Um, Axel wants us both gone when he shows the house."

"When is he bringing them?"

"Around five-thirty."

"Well, I'm not done with my last student until then," Jake said, and his tone of voice added, *And I'm not leaving one minute before.*

"Fine."

Her tone of voice must have added, *Be that way,* because he said, "But Tiny and I will get out of here right after."

"Good."

"Yeah, good," he muttered.

Now she felt bad, like she'd somehow turned him out in the cold. Well, she was out in the cold, too. And anyway, this was for his benefit as well as hers.

She stayed late at the shop, then stopped by Charley's house to see how she was doing. Her friend looked like a zombie, her eyes bloodshot with purple shadows beneath them. She was wearing sweats and her hair was tied up in a sloppy bun.

"Come on in," she said. "Richard's out in the kitchen making dinner. Want to stay?"

"You guys probably don't want company," Ella hedged. She'd really meant to stop by for only a few minutes.

Charley swung the door wide. "I always want company. Anyway, how can you say no to stuffed pork loin?"

It turned out she couldn't. Ella watched as Richard waited on her friend, refilled her wineglass. And the one time Charley grew despondent, he said, "It's okay. We'll go on to do something even better."

How sweet.

"You're right," Charley said. "The kitchen really needed a remodel, anyway, and I'd like to make the bar bigger." She stared at her plate. "I just hope people don't switch loyalties while we're rebuilding."

"Of course they won't," Ella assured her. "Everyone loves Zelda's and everyone loves you."

That made Charley tear up. Richard patted her hand.

"You should rest, babe," he said after they'd finished eating.

Ella got the hint and left, feeling hopeful that things would work out for her friend. And only the slightest bit jealous.

She came home to the smell of Jake's chili. If she'd known he was going to heat that up again, she'd have hurried over and sprayed the house, or lit a scented candle. Except that leaving a candle unattended was never a good idea. Fire hazard.

She thought again of poor Charley's restaurant. Life had

a way of taking turns you never expected. It sure had for her. Who would've guessed she'd be divorced and sharing her dream house with her ex-husband?

She heard Jake's voice and realized he was back home. That meant their potential buyers had come and gone. She slipped off her shoes and padded out to the kitchen, where she caught him feeding Tiny crackers.

"That's why he's getting fat," she accused.

"Hey, it's comfort food. He needs comfort."

Comfort and joy. There was none of that this holiday season. Ella sighed. "Has Axel called? Did the people like the house?"

Jake nodded. "Yeah. He's coming over at seven with their offer."

"Our asking price?"

"Within five thousand."

That was close enough as far as Ella was concerned. "Great. Let's take it."

"May as well," Jake said. He turned his back on her and got busy removing his bowl of chili from the microwave.

She walked out of the kitchen and went to the living room to fidget. There wasn't anything to do here, and she'd read her latest *Martha Stewart Living* from cover to cover. She went upstairs and brushed her teeth. Then she freshened her makeup. Then she was out of things to do once more. She went back downstairs, feeling like a prisoner awaiting sentencing.

What was *that* about? She should be doing a jig. They had an offer on the house. By the new year she'd be done with this ridiculous living arrangement. She'd be a free woman. *You should be celebrating,* she told herself.

Jake came into the living room and sprawled on the couch, staring into the cold fireplace. The sight of him made her feel even less like celebrating.

The doorbell rang and he gave her a stony stare. "You gonna let him in?"

Yes, she was. A moment later Axel was in the living room, brimming with satisfaction. "They want to know if you'll include some of the furniture," he said.

"May as well," Jake said, still stone-faced.

"What furniture?" Ella asked.

"Your bedroom set."

The sleigh bed. They'd shared more than heated encounters in that bed. They'd shared laughter and dreams.

Ella looked over at Jake. He was scowling at the winter darkness outside the window. "Are we cool with that?" she asked.

He shrugged. "We're not gonna use it."

"I guess so, then," Ella said to Axel. Like Jake said, they weren't going to use it.

Within a matter of minutes, the papers were signed and she was seeing Axel to the door.

"I think you got a good deal," he said.

"Yes, we did. Thank you so much."

"Now you can get on with your life."

Exactly what she kept telling herself. "Yes, at last."

"Let's go out Friday night and celebrate. The Icicle Falls chorale is doing their winter concert at Festival Hall. Handel's *Messiah*. We can have dinner before."

Classical music wasn't her favorite, but she certainly liked it better than jazz, and the *Hallelujah Chorus* seemed appropriate, considering that she'd just unloaded her house and her unwanted roommate. "Sure." She had nothing better to do with anyone else. Her thoughts veered to Jake, scowling in the living room.

"Good. The concert's at eight. I'll make dinner reservations at Schwangau for six-thirty."

Just like that, without asking her where she wanted to go. Granted, Zelda's wasn't an option at the moment, but what about Italian Alps or Der Spaniard?

No, not Mexican. That was where she and Jake always went.

Oh, who cared where she and Jake always went. "How about Der Spaniard?"

Axel looked momentarily surprised that some of the planning was being taken out of his hands but he recovered quickly enough. "All right, if that's where you want to go."

"It is." She could eat at that restaurant with anyone and have a good time. Anyone!

With Axel out the door, she turned back toward the living room to find Jake still on the couch where she'd left him, Tiny lying at his feet.

"So, I guess you're going out to celebrate," he greeted her.

"Why not?" she retorted. She sat down on the opposite end of the couch, wishing she could feel more excited by this turn of events. "I mean, this is a relief. We're rid of a house we can't afford." *And a sleigh bed.*

Jake studied her from his end of the couch, those dark eyes of his filled with sadness. "Do you ever ask yourself how we got here, El?"

Suddenly she wanted to cry. She bit her lip and shook her head.

He looked around the living room, taking in everything. "I'm gonna miss this place. We had some great times here."

"Stop." The words came out sharper than she intended.

"You already took away our future, El. Don't take away my past, too."

"Me! Oh, no. Don't make me the bad guy here."

"I wasn't the one who wanted a divorce."

"No, you had a good thing going, didn't you?"

He made no reply to that. Instead, he left the couch and disappeared down the hall. Probably off to the kitchen for more chili. She could hear him out there, opening cupboard doors.

But a moment later he returned with something very different. She saw the Christmas mugs and knew instantly what was in them. "Oh, no. No more eggnog."

He held out a mug. "We were happy once. Let's drink to that. Let's part friends. Can we do that much?"

All right. They could do that much.

She took the mug and he sat down next to her on the couch and clinked his against it. "To new beginnings."

"To new beginnings," she repeated.

Now he was looking around the room again. "I hope the new owners enjoy this house as much as we did. Do you think they'll put their tree in the same place?"

This resigned kindness was unnerving. Ella took a sip of her eggnog. Spiked, of course. "I don't know."

"I hope they don't repaint."

She and Jake had spent an entire weekend painting the living room. She still loved her red accent wall. "Isn't that the color of passion?" Jake had joked, and then proceeded to demonstrate the passion it inspired in him.

She had to stop thinking about all of that. It was in the past. They were done. Through. Finished. That was how she wanted it. She started to cry.

"Aw, babe," he said, his voice anguished.

The next thing she knew he was kissing her. And then she was kissing him. And then they were taking one final ride in the sleigh bed.

14

Jake awoke to discover that he was alone in bed. Dang. He'd been hoping for another round with Ella. He rolled over to check the clock on the bedside table and there sat Tiny looking at him. "Where's, Mom, boy?"

Tiny woofed, doggy encouragement for Jake to get up and find out for himself.

It was only eight-thirty. Ella wouldn't have left for work yet. Maybe she was in the kitchen, making breakfast for them. Now there was a pleasant thought. Except if she was in the kitchen, Tiny wouldn't be up here. He'd have been down there with her, looking hopeful.

Jake threw off the covers and went downstairs to investigate. In his boxers. There'd probably be no more complaining about that now that they were back together. They *were* back together, weren't they?

The kitchen was empty, and clean, with not so much as a dish in the sink. Or a love note on the table. Maybe she'd been in a hurry. Maybe she had to do inventory at the shop. No, inventory didn't happen until January. Maybe someone had an appointment for a private style consult. Ella often did that, and when she did, she always went to the shop early to prepare.

He picked up his cell phone from the coffee table and called her.

She said a wary hello.

Okay, the clues were adding up, making it hard to stay in denial. "Hey, babe. You left before I could kiss you awake."

"Jake, last night was a mistake. We should never have slept together."

Oh, not this again. "Come on, El. You can't believe that. The only mistake we've made was getting divorced."

"I'm sorry, but—"

He cut her off before she could finish. "Let's talk this out. I'll come by the shop and take you to Der Spaniard for dinner." He'd cancel band practice. Or better yet, he'd take Ella with him and she could meet Jen, check out the competition she'd been so jealous of. Ha.

"I can't. I'm going out with Mims."

Her tone of voice guaranteed she wouldn't break that date. And once she'd spent an evening with her mother, it would be all over. *Mims strikes again.* He had to convince Elle to listen to reason before the wicked witch of the Pacific Northwest brainwashed her any more. "Look," he began.

"I'm sorry, Jake, I've got to go," she said and ended the call.

Jake tossed his cell phone on the couch and sat staring at

the dead fireplace. Then he swore. Then he drop-kicked a pillow across the room while Tiny cheered him on with a hearty woof. He drop-kicked another pillow but the second kick didn't help, either, so he marched back upstairs. He threw on sweats and went out the door to Bruisers to work off his anger.

An hour later, most of it was still riding his back. He left the gym, returned home and took Tiny for a long walk. After that he ate a big bowl of sugary cereal, then showered and dressed in his favorite jeans and Washington Huskies sweatshirt. As he stepped out of his pathetic single-guy bedroom, he couldn't help looking into the master where he'd slept last night. The sleigh bed mocked him. *No more rides for you, pal.*

He heaved a sigh. Why was Ella being so stubborn? She had to know deep down that this was all wrong. She couldn't make love like she had the night before and not want to be together. They'd come about as close to heaven as two people could get. Close to heaven. Now there was a good hook. Already humming, he went downstairs in search of his guitar.

Cass was exhausted. Not from work, but from hammering out the food details for the reception with Dani. Dani had sneered at the more affordable suggestions Bailey Sterling had emailed.

"For a wedding? Jeez, Mom."

"There's nothing wrong with Alfredo," Cass had objected, "especially with shrimp in it, and this has shrimp and smoked salmon."

"Probably a teaspoon of each," Dani had said sarcastically.

"Not if Bailey's doing it, and if we add appetizers…"

That had produced an eye roll. "What? More shrimp?"

"In endive, with avocado. And we can add chicken. Everyone loves chicken wings."

"No one loves chicken wings. They're stupid!"

"So is paying a fortune for salmon filets, especially if you want a band."

At that Dani had thrown up her hands. "Fine. Why don't we just make it a potluck?"

Now there was an idea. Before Cass could say anything cheeky, her daughter was crying and threatening to call Mason. Again.

"Go ahead," Cass had snapped. "Let your father pick up the bill for everything. It can make up for all those years he did nothing." Oh, that had been wrong.

"Maybe if you hadn't moved us all the way over here, he would've been able to do more."

"And maybe if I hadn't, you'd never have met Mike."

Their voices got loud enough to break the sound barrier in the kitchen, where Cass had staked out a corner for the family computer. Willie poked his head in the door. "What's going on?"

"Nothing," Cass had growled.

"Yeah, right," he'd scoffed, but neither Cass nor Dani bothered to say anything to that. They had enough to say to each other.

Finally, Cass did something she never did. She cried. Who said brides should have all the fun?

That had ended the fight. Dani knelt in front of her, all remorse and crying, too. "I'm sorry, Mama. I didn't mean all those things I said. It's just…"

"I know. It's your big day. Of course you want it to be special, and so do I." But she couldn't afford to give her daughter a Kardashian-style wedding. Why, oh, why wasn't she rich?

They'd compromised, bagging the salmon and settling for three-cheese-stuffed chicken, fettuccini (minus the shrimp and salmon) and Caesar salad. And no appetizers.

"But we have to have champagne," Dani had insisted. "For the toast."

"How about champagne for the toast and champagne punch for the rest of the meal?"

That, along with a nonalcoholic punch, had been another good compromise.

Now Dani was off with Mike, Willie and Amber were watching a Netflix movie and Cass was going to take a long soak with some peppermint bubble bath from Bubbles, the bath shop that had opened last summer. She did her best to avoid the bathroom mirror as she undressed, but it was hard to ignore the fat woman lurking there.

She was sure she'd put on another five pounds since Dani got engaged. Potato chips and Sweet Dreams chocolates would do that to a woman, particularly when she was stressed.

She didn't care what Dot said. It would've been nice if Mason had called her when Dani got engaged and suggested picking up half the tab for the wedding instead of playing this passive-aggressive game of offering nothing but coming through like a superhero every time Dani called him. Cass would have had twice the money and half the misery.

You could have called him.

She pushed the thought firmly away. She'd hated taking child support money from him when they were divorced, even though they were his kids, too, and it was money she was due. Those monthly checks had felt more like a sop to his conscience than support. It would've felt the same now, too.

In all fairness to Mason, he'd never been a deadbeat dad. He'd occasionally been late with his child support check, but that had been because of his crazy work schedule and forgetfulness rather than deliberate irresponsibility. And he wasn't hurting for money now. So why hadn't he offered up front to fork some over?

The answer was simple. He wasn't merely clueless. He was still the same self-absorbed man he'd always been.

Let him keep his money. She didn't need it. She didn't need him. Hadn't for years. In fact, she didn't need any man. She was fine on her own. Fine.

Were there any potato chips left?

"I'm so glad the house has sold," Mims said as Ella forked into a slice of hazelnut torte.

Once more Ella was eating at Schwangau, the most expensive restaurant in town, and the maître d' was becoming her new best friend. But when they'd walked in and she saw how packed the place was, even on a weeknight, she couldn't help thinking about poor Charley. Would her former customers return once she'd rebuilt her business or would they get in the habit of frequenting other places? Ella sure hoped they'd return. She'd be back.

"The sooner you're out of the house, the better," Mims said as their waiter filled her coffee cup.

"I still have to find a place that will allow Tiny," Ella said.

"Let your former husband have him," Mims said with a dismissive flick of her hand. And that took care of Tiny.

Mims had dismissed Jake just as easily when Ella decided

on a divorce. "Really, baby, you're better off without him. The boy was subpar."

But Tiny wasn't subpar, and Ella had no intention of letting Jake keep him and feed him until he exploded. "He belongs to both of us."

Mims rolled her eyes and took a sip of her coffee. "It was ridiculous to get such a big dog. Really, Ella, I don't know what you were thinking."

She was thinking they'd stay in that house for years, have a child to go along with the dog once they had a little more money. Child. Baby. What were the chances that one of Jake's sperm had succeeded in its egg hunt? She pushed aside the rest of her torte.

"You're not finishing? I'm surprised."

"I'm not hungry." Now she sounded sullen. Well, she felt sullen.

"You shouldn't eat that fattening garbage, anyway."

Mims had raised Ella to believe that sugar was the devil's tool. If a woman had to consume calories they should come floating in a glass of white wine. Well, once in a while, Ella liked to flirt with the devil, especially at Christmas. She'd even tried her hand at baking Christmas cookies the year before last. They weren't as good as Cass's but Jake had liked them.

Him again. She had to stop thinking about Jake. And his sperm. *You made your choice,* she told herself sternly. *Now you have to live with it.* And if that included a baby, fine. She'd wanted a baby.

She'd never wanted to raise a baby by herself, though. If Jake moved to Nashville that was exactly what she'd be doing.

Well, her mother had managed fine on her own and she would, too. She could see it now, Mommy and baby having a little talk. *Sorry your daddy isn't around, but daddies are overrated. Just ask your grandma.*

Mims reached a hand across the table. "Why the glum face? Everything is finally smoothing out in your life."

Smoothing out. Was that what you called it? She'd lost her marriage, her dreams and now her home. Smooth.

"Not again," Larry said.

Jake scowled at him. "What?"

"You've got that same bee up your butt that you had last week. What is bugging you now?"

"Nothing," Jake said, sounding completely bugged.

"I can take away the sting," Jen said. "Did any of you guys check out our song on YouTube?"

The song. With everything else that had been going on, Jake had forgotten about it.

"Oh, yeah," Larry said. "This should make you smile, bro. You wanna guess how many views we're up to already?"

Jake shrugged. "Fifty."

"Try eight hundred," Larry said.

"Eight hundred?" Guy echoed. "I've only got twenty people to my name, including family and friends. Who all is looking at this?"

"People are forwarding the link, dope," Larry told him. "Hell, everyone at the packing plant has sent it to their friends. I knew you were on to something," he said to Jake.

"Yeah, he was," Tim agreed. "Talk about inspired. And what a great way to get back at the mother-in-law from hell for screwing up your life."

"Poetic justice," said Jen.

"Huh?"

"It means she's getting what she deserves," Jen said, and smiled at Jake.

And with all the poisonous crap she was probably still pouring in her daughter's ears, she deserved a lot. Jake found himself smiling for the first time all night. *Yeah, Merry Christmas, Mama.*

By Friday he concluded that his former mother-in-law was deserving of much more than a tacky song. Maybe a nice winter cruise—down Icicle Falls, in an inner tube, buck naked, in the middle of the night. Or a visit to someplace special in one of her favorite cities—a back alley, with hopefully a mugger or two. If not for her, he and Ella would be together again, he was sure of it.

But instead, they were back at square one, sharing the house with an invisible force field between them. Jaw clenched, he watched Ella drive off with Axel Fuchs yet again. God only knew where they were going tonight. Ella hadn't told him. Ella had hardly spoken to him.

The house was sold and she was getting on with her life. He should, too.

He took Tiny for a good, long lope in the snow and then turned back toward home. Not home, he corrected himself. The house. Just a house. Then he got ready to go play his gig at the Red Barn.

"Sorry you're on your own tonight," he told the dog.

Tiny whined and wagged his tail. He'd seen the guitar sitting by the front door and he knew that meant doggy solitary.

Jake gave the dog a goodbye scratch behind the ears. "Maybe she won't stay out too late."

Unless she decided to stay over at Axel's.

Would she do that? Jake frowned. He'd been Ella's one and only. The thought of that slimy wuss having her was enough to make him clench his fists.

She'd do it. Eventually, she'd do it just because she could.

So why was he being a choirboy?

He asked himself again later that night when a cute little groupie named Allison stopped by the band's table to flirt.

"She's hot for you," Larry said.

"Who isn't?" Jen said, and winked at him.

It was obvious Jake could move on with his life, starting tonight if he wanted to.

Well, maybe he did. Maybe he was sick of chasing after Ella like a dumb puppy. He downed the last of his Coke. Maybe he could get laid before the night was over. Why not? Ella always thought he was a player. It was time to live up to the legend.

15

The snoring was loud enough to wake the dead. Jake rolled over and gave his bedmate a shove.

Tiny startled awake and lifted his big head as if to say, "Where's the emergency?"

"You're snoring again," Jake informed him. He glanced at the clock—10:00 a.m. Ella would be long gone.

At least she'd come home the night before. He'd looked in the bedroom when he rolled in around one and found it gratifying to see her slender form under the covers in the sleigh bed—until it occurred to him that she might have had sex with Axel and then come home.

Sex. He'd planned on making a night of it. Until his conscience reminded him that revenge sex wasn't good for anyone, especially the other person. He couldn't do that to someone. He didn't want to be a player. He only wanted to be with Ella.

He sat on the edge of the bed and dragged his hands through his hair, giving it a good pull in the process, hoping to wake up his brain cells. What the hell was he going to do?

Finish that song he'd started for her, that was what.

Cecily was going to meet Luke Goodman, Sweet Dreams' production manager, and his daughter, Serena, at the little downtown skating rink dropping in at Johnson's Drugs first. She'd added mascara to her basket of goodies when Todd Black came strolling down the aisle.

"Hey, there," he greeted her.

Zing went her insides. Why, oh, why did they do that every time he came around? *Cut it out,* she told them, then said a casual hi to Todd.

He stopped next to her and peered into her basket.

She frowned and shifted it away from him.

"You don't need that."

What, the Midol or the mascara?

"Why do women wear makeup, anyway?"

Okay, not the Midol.

"To look nice," she said.

"Guys don't care, you know," he said. "They're not that interested in your eyelashes."

"So you say, but if a woman walked around without makeup you wouldn't even look at her."

"Sure I would," he said. "I'd just be looking somewhere else." He demonstrated, letting his gaze drift down to her chest.

"You're pathetic," she said in disgust.

"No, I'm not. I'm honest."

"Well, thanks for the honesty."

"Just trying to tell it like it is." He threw her a cynical smile. "But you were a matchmaker. You already know how it is. Or did a lot of your clients ask for women with big... eyelashes?"

"No, and maybe that has something to do with why I'm not in that business anymore. And not dating." She started to move down the aisle.

Instead of getting the message to buzz off, he fell in step with her. "Funny how you can be so smart and still not see what's right in front of your face."

She stopped. "Okay, I'll bite. What's right in front of my face?"

He moved to stand in front of her, very *closely* in front of her. "Me."

Zing! All that heat... Her lips were suddenly dry. *Don't lick your lips.*

She couldn't help it, they were dry.

Now the cynical smile had turned much more intimate. He reached up and ran his thumb along her lower lip. "You should get some lip balm, gorgeous. It would be a shame to see those pretty lips get all cracked."

Zing, zing, zing! Her zing-o-meter was going through the roof. She took a step back. "Thanks. I'll do that." She slipped around him and started walking again.

And there he was, still keeping her company. "You know what else is good for fighting off the cold?"

"What?"

"Hot chocolate. I'll buy you some."

She cocked an eyebrow at him. "Have some candy, little girl?"

He chuckled. "Get into my car. Take a ride."

"Sorry, I don't take rides with strange men."

"Come on, Cecily. Quit being such a wimp. You know you want to be with me."

Yes, she did.

And she didn't. The smart part of her didn't.

"One cup of cocoa. What's it going to hurt?"

Probably her heart. "Sorry," she said. "I've got plans."

Not a date. Luke wanted them to be more, but they were just friends, and she was determined to keep it that way. Letting things get serious wouldn't be fair to him. She'd sworn off men, the good, the bad and the...drop-dead gorgeous.

Todd shrugged off her rejection. "One of these days, you're not going to be able to take it anymore. One of these days you'll be knocking on my door, ready for a dance lesson."

She remembered their conversation a few months ago when she'd fainted and wound up in the back room of his tavern. The idea of seeing Todd in action was as tempting now as it had been then. Oh, yes, Todd Black had the moves, and he'd given her a sample of them since she'd come home.

But she wasn't in the market. She wasn't in the market for any man. "I hope you're not holding your breath."

"You'd be surprised how long I can hold my breath. You'd be surprised how long I can do a lot of things."

She rolled her eyes and shook her head and left it at that.

Enough of him. She had better ways to spend her time than sparring with the pirate of Icicle Falls. She made her purchases, then headed for the park.

The ice rink, dotted with skaters clad in colorful winter clothes, would have inspired Norman Rockwell. Around the edges, people sat on park benches and enjoyed hot chocolate or roasted nuts, or stood at fire pits, warming up for the next round. Farther up the hill that led to the highway, a group of boys were having a snowball fight. The scent of cinnamon and vanilla from a nut vendor's booth made Cecily's mouth water.

Luke was already at the edge of the rink, lacing up his daughter's ice skates. Serena, now five, looked adorable in pink leggings and her pink parka, a knitted hat pulled over her curls. The child always appeared ready for a magazine cover, thanks to her grandmother, who'd stepped into the mother role when Luke's wife was killed in a car accident.

Serena saw Cecily approaching and began waving, not a sedate wave, but one that had her bouncing on the bench. Luke turned and waved, too. No bouncing, but the big grin on his face said it all.

She had to stop seeing this man. It wasn't fair.

"Cecily, I have new skates!" Serena called.

"Those are very nice," she said, coming to stand in front of them.

"My feet grew," Serena told her. "Daddy says I'm going to be tall like him and be a lady basketball player."

"Would you like that?" Cecily asked.

Serena wrinkled her forehead. "No. I just want to make cookies with Grandma."

"Maybe you'll grow up to be a baker like Mrs. Wilkes," Cecily suggested.

"And make gingerbread boys!" cried Serena.

"You make 'em and we'll eat 'em," Luke said.

Serena hopped off the bench and began teetering toward the ice. "Let's skate!"

"Wait a minute, kiddo," Luke said, reaching out and grasping her with a big hand. "No going on the ice by yourself. Remember?"

Serena frowned. "Hurry up, Daddy. Get your skates on."

Luke sat on the bench and indicated the spot next to him, and Cecily set to work putting on her own skates.

Serena stood watching the other skaters and Cecily took a moment to watch, too. It seemed half the residents of Icicle Falls were enjoying the fresh air this particular Saturday, with teenagers zipping past more sedate older people. Small children wobbled around, safely tucked between their parents, and one or two advanced skaters practiced jumps at the center of the rink. A little boy in hot pursuit of a squealing girl fell down, blinked in shock at the impact and then scrambled back up and returned to the chase.

Next to Cecily, Luke chuckled. "Maybe by the time they're grown-ups he'll actually catch her." He finished tying his lace, then stood and held out a hand to Cecily. "Ready?"

Ready to be caught? Of course that wasn't what he'd meant. And she wasn't.

But she gave her laces a final tug and let him take her hand. He held out his other hand to his daughter, and the three of them went onto the ice.

Sometimes people forgot what a risky business skating was. A person could fall and break an arm. Or worse. Yet look how many people were out here. There was a thrill in racing over the ice, the wind in your face. And that, of course, was why people took the risk. Wasn't it the same with love?

After this she really had to stop hanging out with Luke. Really.

Ella found herself squirming in church on Sunday as Pastor Jim talked about the importance of self-control. Hers had been sadly lacking of late. Was it wrong to sleep with someone you weren't married to if you'd *been* married to him? Maybe she could get off on a technicality. Right or wrong, it was stupid, and she wasn't going to be stupid again, no matter how much Jake kissed her.

No, no kissing! She let out her breath in a hiss.

"Are you okay?" whispered Cecily, who was sitting next to her.

No, she wasn't. She was...confused. She nodded, though. Heaven forbid a woman should admit that she had problems when she was in church, surrounded by people who cared and would gladly help her.

After the service, she went to lunch with Cecily, Samantha and Samantha's husband, Blake Preston. Anything to avoid being at the house with Jake. They were through. Finished. Done.

He probably wasn't there, anyway. Since the divorce he'd taken to spending Sundays at his parents'.

Sunday dinner with the O'Briens—how she missed that! Pot roast with all the trimmings, homemade biscuits, a rowdy game of cards, maybe even a knitting lesson—those afternoons had felt to Ella as if she'd been dropped right in the middle of some vintage TV family show like *The Brady Bunch*. Now she was in...what? *Desperate Housewives*? *Lost*?

She *felt* lost, and she hadn't touched her yarn and needles in months.

Once you're out of the house everything will be fine, she told herself. Once she didn't have to look at Jake every day. Once she was out of touching range. That was the problem, of course. He was using sentiment like a swizzle stick to stir up her hormones and make her think they— She stopped the thought before it could turn into a sentence and light up inside her mind like a neon sign. But it was still there, anyway. *Make her think they could get back together and be happy.*

Jake was a skirt-chasing loafer. She'd always have to be the one earning the family income and she'd never know if she could trust him. If she got together with someone like Axel she could have it all. The family. The comfortable lifestyle. Venice. Paris.

Nashville.

No, not Nashville!

"Something's off," Cecily said as they all left Herman's Hamburgers.

Ella realized she hadn't been paying attention. Had Cecily been talking? "What?"

"You've been a zombie all morning. Are you sure everything's okay?"

Ella nodded. It was. Well, it would be. Someday.

She was still telling herself that when she showed up at Cass's for their weekly movie night. Cass had her tree up now, and it was decorated with a mishmash of ornaments, many obviously made by small hands, a colorful testament to a happy family. Unlike her tree, which was a sad reminder of family failure. *Oh, yes, you're doing fine.*

The selection for this night was the classic version of *A*

Christmas Carol, with Alastair Sim. The happy ending was very satisfying.

And more than a little thought-provoking. "Do you guys think people can change?" Ella asked. She suddenly realized she was echoing the question Charley had asked her the last time she was in the shop.

"I don't think so," Cass said.

"I didn't used to." Charley helped herself to one of the appetizers she'd brought. "But I think I was wrong, especially after the way Richard jumped in when Harvey went on his bender and left me in the lurch. And he's been so supportive since the fire."

Ella saw Samantha and Cecily exchange looks. "It pays to be cautious," Samantha said.

Charley narrowed her eyes suspiciously. "What do you mean by that?"

"I mean it pays to be cautious."

"Are you talking about Richard?"

Samantha took a deep breath, a clear indication that she was getting ready to dish out something unpleasant. "I don't want to see you rush into anything."

"I'm not rushing," Charley insisted. "Anyway, why are you so suspicious?"

"Because he screwed you over once and he could do it again," Samantha said bluntly.

"She doesn't want to see you hurt," Cecily added. "None of us do."

Now Charley looked ready to smack Samantha. "Just because he made a mistake in the past—"

"Doesn't mean he can't make another," Samantha finished for her.

"That wasn't what I was going to say!"

"I know. Listen," Samantha continued. "It's easy not to notice the red flags when all you're seeing is hearts and flowers. I'm just suggesting you be a little cautious."

"*What* red flags?"

"How about the fact that he can hang around here indefinitely? What businessperson can do that? What restaurant owner can do that?"

"One who has a good general manager," Charley retorted. "You want to come right out and tell me what you're implying?"

"I'm implying that maybe he hasn't been so successful on his own. Maybe he's come back to be with the goose who lays the golden eggs."

"In case you didn't notice, my golden egg got fried," Charley said, her voice icy.

Samantha wasn't deterred. "It's insured. You have insurance money and a valuable piece of property."

A big, ugly silence fell on the room. Ella felt as if each woman was holding her breath.

All except Samantha, who continued on boldly. "He hasn't taken you to Seattle to see his restaurant. Why is that?"

"Because he's been busy helping me," Charley said. "I couldn't just up and leave my place, you know." She glared at them. "Jeez, you guys."

"Wouldn't he want to show you how successful he is?" Samantha persisted.

Even Jake loved playing his songs for her, Ella thought. Men liked to show off to their women, to prove themselves worthy.

That saddened her. Had she failed to give Jake enough appreciation and driven him to look for it from other women?

Meanwhile, Charley and Samantha were still going at it. "Richard doesn't need to prove anything to me," Charley snapped. "Not anymore."

Samantha cocked an eyebrow. "Oh, really?"

Charley was blinking furiously now, obviously fighting back tears. "Yeah, really, and thanks for your support."

"This *is* support." Cass spoke in a quiet, even voice. "Like Cecily said, we don't want to see you hurt again. We want you to be cautious."

"Have you looked up the restaurant on the internet?" Samantha asked.

"I've been busy," Charley said defensively.

"At least check out the website," Samantha urged. "If his place looks like the next best thing to Wolfgang Puck, then you can forget I said anything."

The tears had spilled over now. Cecily handed Charley a tissue and gave her a hug. "He hurt you badly once. Nobody wants to see him do it twice. That's all. We really do care what happens to you, you know."

Charley dabbed at her eyes and nodded. "I know. I'm sorry I'm so bitchy."

"Your restaurant just burned down. You're allowed," Samantha said. "But you can rebuild it and make it even better. It's a lot harder to rebuild a broken heart."

How true.

A few more tears, some hugs, and then Charley was on her way, claiming she still had paperwork to fill out.

"And some research to do," Samantha murmured as their friend hurried out the door. "I hope she does it."

"Do you know something we don't?" her sister asked.

It was plain from Samantha's face that she did.

"Okay, spill," Cass commanded.

"Well, cynic that I am, I looked up this restaurant of his."

"Does he even have a restaurant?" Cass asked, her voice tinged with worry.

"Oh, he has one, all right. But it's not open."

16

Samantha's suspicions burrowed their way into the back of Charley's mind like so many termites and began crunching away.

Richard had moved from Gerhardt's Gasthaus into her bed, and she returned home to find him sprawled on the living room couch, watching the Food Network's *Hidden Surprises,* a show featuring small-town restaurants. After seeing how well getting featured on Mimi LeGrand's *All Things Chocolate* had worked for Samantha, Charley had been toying with contacting this show's producer and inviting him to Icicle Falls. Thanks to her unpleasant surprise, that would be a ways down the road.

She frowned. "You want to turn that off?"

He fired the remote at the TV and the cozy restaurant

scene vanished from the screen. "I was just killing time until you got back home. How was the party?"

Fine until the movie ended. "It was okay."

"Just okay, huh?"

"It's hard to get excited about anything right now." Including Richard. Sometimes a woman shouldn't listen to her friends. Now Charley wished she'd covered her ears and chanted, "La, la, la, la, la."

"Anything?" He patted the cushion next to him on the couch, and she came over and sat down. "There's a new year right around the corner, babe." He put an arm around her and kissed her. "Meanwhile, I bet I can get you excited."

Sort of. Even as Richard was making love to her, the termites kept crunching. *He hasn't taken you to Seattle to see his restaurant. Why is that?*

Any number of reasons. Like maybe he simply wanted to concentrate on winning her back. Maybe he'd figured that bringing up the subject of the restaurant he'd started after he left her would be like pouring salt in a wound. It would.

So there was the reason. And now, with that resolved she could—

Check out Richard's restaurant on the internet the next morning. Masochist that she was, she'd done it when they first split. Try as she had, she'd never been able to forget the name: Piatto Dolce, Sweet Plate. The thought of him serving up sweet plates of anything with his little hostess with the mostest had set her teeth on edge. She'd glared at the webpage, hoped they gave whatever food critic visited them food poisoning and then closed the page, never to look again. She hadn't looked when he returned, either.

She *had* been busy. Really. Maybe she also hadn't wanted to see how successful he'd been without her.

But now she had to get rid of those termites, so she left Richard snoring in bed and slipped downstairs to settle on the couch with her laptop.

Up came the website with the food-magazine-worthy picture of the restaurant's interior on the home page—a sophisticated slice of Italy complete with sexy lighting and linen tablecloths, a tribute to Richard's favorite cuisine. There was something else on the home page, too. A notice saying, "Piatto Dolce is currently closed for renovations. Please check back later. *Grazie*."

Closed for renovations. Richard hadn't said anything about that. But so what? They'd had other, more important things to talk about. Like them. And this explained why he could afford to stay in Icicle Falls....

But wouldn't he want to be on hand to supervise those renovations? She planned to be on site at Zelda's every day, making sure things were getting done. She'd been over to the charred ruins any number of times, picking through things, meeting with the company in charge of cleanup, getting bids from contractors.

Maybe the work on his place hadn't started yet.

That was it. He was here winning her back while he had the time. Once the renovations were done they'd own two restaurants. It would mean double the work, of course, but double the success as long as they could manage both and be together. They'd find a way to work everything out, and he was up here to do just that. He was here for her. Samantha had been wrong. Well-meaning, but wrong.

"Hey, you awake already?"

Charley gave a guilty start and hid the evidence of her snooping with a click before Richard could see what she was up to. "I couldn't sleep anymore."

There he stood, his hair tousled, bare-chested, wearing his favorite black sweats. Dessert with legs. He came over to the couch and looked over her shoulder. "What are you working on?"

She suddenly felt like some kind of traitor. "Just doing some research," she said, and shut the laptop.

"It's going to be another long day. How about some coffee?"

"Please. I think I'll go shower."

"Want company?"

She shook her head. With all the stress of rebuilding her life, it seemed her sex drive had put itself in Park. That was it. The stress. Stress would do that to any girl.

"Like you said, it's going to be another long day," she said. "I'd better get started."

That day didn't turn out to be half as long as the next one. After the last conversation with her insurance agent, Charley finally had an idea of how much money she could expect for rebuilding Zelda's and just how far it would stretch.

"Everything's gone up in price," she lamented as she and Richard worked together on dinner. "There's so much to do. And that darned Ethan Masters is going to drive me nuts."

"He's the best contractor in town," Richard said, slicing apples for their salad.

"And the most infuriating." Charley picked up her wineglass and took a healthy slug of pinot grigio, then moved to help him with the salad, shelling pistachios to go in the bowl with the tossed greens and apples. "He doesn't seem to understand that the longer I stay closed, the more customers I lose."

Richard set down his knife and leaned against the counter. "So run away."

She gave a snort. "Sometimes I'd like to." Lately she'd fantasized about running away from her problems. If it hadn't been for her friends and Richard, she didn't know what she would've done. Samantha could say whatever she wanted, but he really had been there for her, especially since the fire.

"No, I'm serious," he said. "There's nothing tying you here. You don't have to spend the rest of your life in Icicle Falls."

But she wanted to. She loved this town with its friendly people and its gorgeous mountain views. Still, she could keep an open mind. "What were you thinking?"

"Come to Seattle with me."

Maybe they could have two homes, one here and one in Seattle. Still... "It would be hard to run Zelda's from Seattle." How were they going to manage that?

"How about running a restaurant in Seattle instead?" He shrugged. "Don't waste your money rebuilding in this nowhere place."

Wait a minute. The termites began crunching again. "What should I do with it?" *Don't say what I think you're going to.*

"We could put it into my place in Seattle. That's where the action is. Anyway, you're not a small-town girl, Charley."

She wasn't a fool, either. She stopped shelling nuts. "What's going on with your Piatto Dolce, Richard? Do you need a cash infusion?"

The sudden flush on his cheeks answered before his lips even started moving. "A restaurant is a money pit, you know that. But that's beside the point," he added quickly.

"No. It *is* the point. I went to your website. It said you were closed for renovations."

"I'm making some improvements," he said defensively.

And putting them on hold until he had her eating out of his hand and could convince her to take him back. Then he would've returned to live off her or done exactly what he was trying to do now—talk her into sinking *her* money into *his* place.

"And you need money to do that," she said. "My money."

He opened his mouth to speak but the look on his face had already said it all.

"You. Bastard." All the rage she'd felt the first time he left returned with double the force. She whacked the salad bowl and sent it crashing, spilling romaine and spinach leaves and apples across the kitchen floor.

He held up a hand. "Charley, babe, let me explain."

"No, let *me* explain. I can see it all so clearly now. Your restaurant is going toes-up and so you decided to come back to mine. Job security. And then when the place burned, there was all that lovely money to grab for. All I am to you is a cash cow."

"That's not true! I missed you. I told you, I made a mistake."

What a load of crap. He reached out for her and she slapped his hand away. "Well, I didn't miss you," she snarled. "And I must have been insane to even consider taking you back."

"Charley, you're overreacting," he said.

"You come back here to use me and I'm overreacting?" She grabbed the wine bottle with the vague notion of beaning him over the head with it.

"I did not come back here to use you," he protested, taking a step back.

"That's not what it sounded like just now."

"Just now I was being practical."

"Well, now *I'm* being practical. Get out."

"You don't mean that."

"Oh, yeah? You want to stick around and find out how much I do mean it?"

His pleading expression hardened into something uglier. "God, Charley, you're such a selfish bitch."

Her jaw dropped. He'd come back to use her, the ultimate betrayal, and yet she was a selfish bitch?

"You always were," he added.

This from the man who'd left her for another woman and then returned to ride on her gravy train? *Rage* was too small a word for what she felt now. "You—" She hurled the bottle at him and he barely dodged it. It shattered against the wall, leaving white wine running down the wall like tears.

"You're psycho, too," he said as he turned and started for the door.

"Yeah, well you made me that way," she shouted after him.

He kept walking and flipped her off, and she slid down the cupboard amid the violently tossed salad, laid her head on her knees and sobbed.

Samantha and Blake had just sat down to enjoy a pizza from Italian Alps when the phone rang.

Blake groaned. "Do your friends have some kind of radar? Why is it they always call when we're about to eat?"

"How do you know it's for me?" she retorted, getting up to grab it.

"Because I've already talked to everyone I need to talk to."

She looked at the caller ID and frowned. "Go ahead and start." She had a sinking feeling that this call might take some time.

"You were right." The voice on the other end sounded like a zombie version of Charley.

How she wished she hadn't been! "Oh, Charley, I'm so sorry."

"What's wrong?" Blake asked.

She shook her head to signal she'd update him later. "What happened?"

Charley heaved a shaky sigh. "Well, I scattered salad all over the kitchen floor and christened my wall with white wine."

"And Richard?"

"Not to worry. No skunks were harmed in the filming of this farce," Charley said bitterly. "My God, how could I have been so blind?"

"Easily," Samantha said. "You wanted to believe the best." And Richard had, once more, managed to give her the worst.

"His restaurant is closed for renovations," Charley said, scorn dripping from her voice. "More like closed for lack of cash flow. You know what he wanted me to do with my insurance money?"

"I can guess," Samantha said. How different from her man, who'd actually gone into debt to help her save her company. Well, there were men and there were male snakes. And she knew which category Richard fell into. She'd known all along. She didn't say so, though. Instead, she said, "I'm really sorry. He deserves to be roasted over a giant spit."

"That's too good for him," Charley said, and her voice broke on a sob. "And you know what else? He told me I'm a selfish bitch."

"You?"

Now Charley began to cry in earnest.

"You know that's not true," Samantha said.

"Do I?"

"Of course you do," Samantha said. "Your ex is not only bad at business, he's bad at being a human being."

"He broke my heart all over again." The words ended on a sob.

Poor Charley. First her restaurant and now this. The year was not ending well for her. "Come on over and hang with us," Samantha offered. "I'll give you chocolate."

"No. I need to clean up this mess."

"You need your friends," Samantha said sternly.

"I'll be okay," Charley said. "And thanks for opening my eyes. If you hadn't, I might've just drifted along with whatever Richard wanted, never knowing I was being taken."

"You'd have figured it out," Samantha assured her.

"Thanks for being such a good listener."

"That's what friends are for."

They were for a heck of a lot more than that, too. "Charley's in trouble," Samantha told Blake after ending the call.

"I kind of guessed that," he said. "I won't wait up. I have a feeling this is going to be a long night."

★ ★ ★

Forty minutes later Charley's seafood lasagna was out of the oven and the kitchen was clean. The house was empty, too. Richard had packed up his bags and left without another word. Which was fine with Charley. He'd said enough.

Selfish bitch. Was she really? Had it been selfish to sink her inheritance into that restaurant? She hadn't thought so at the time. Yes, she'd had to do some talking to persuade Richard they wanted to settle here. But she'd felt so sure he'd grown to love the town, the same way she had. She'd believed he was happy. Anyway, this had been all she could afford. It would've cost twice as much to start a restaurant in the city. She'd wanted to be practical. And she'd liked being a big fish in a small pond.

But somehow, she'd become a bigger fish than her husband. Looking back now, she realized that hadn't gone over well. He used to jokingly refer to himself as her kitchen slave or Mr. Charley. But he'd been the chef.

Still, she'd been the front person, the one people saw when they came in. And people had liked her. Richard not so much. She thought back to the party she'd thrown herself when she got divorced, how so many of her friends had said they'd never really liked him. Yes, Cass, was right. Love was blind. And dumb.

The doorbell rang. Richard. He was back to say he was sorry, he'd never meant those mean words. He'd stay and help her rebuild Zelda's.

You can't take him back, she told herself. *You've been a fool twice. Don't go for a third time.*

She remembered the ugly expression on his face when

she'd proved herself immune to the old Richard charm. Was she that insecure, that desperate for love? The answer was no. Hell, no.

She marched to the door and yanked it open.

And there stood the Sterling sisters, Cass and Ella, bearing gift bags, chocolates, cookies and wine. "We're here for another party," Samantha said.

Girlfriends. What would she have done without them? She could feel tears pricking her eyes. "You're just in time for seafood lasagna."

"All right," Cecily said, handing over a bottle of wine. "Let's party."

And party they did. They ate every bit of Charley's lasagna and consumed enough goodies to put themselves in a sugar coma (the gingerbread boys with their heads cut off were a huge hit). They played games—Stick the Knife in the Ex-husband (crafted by Cass), Hangman (every word was an unendearing term for Richard) and a movie trivia game Samantha had thrown together that involved bad men getting what they deserved. Then Charley opened presents—bubble bath, chocolate, more cookies and the hit of the night, Man Away Spray, which was really an old can of bug spray wrapped in a funny label Cecily had made.

"I hope you've got an extra can of that for yourself," Samantha told her sister.

Cecily stuck her tongue out at her sister, then returned her attention to Charley. "Next time Richard comes near you, aim this at him."

"I doubt he'll ever come near me again," Charley said, and felt a moment of melancholy. "Especially after I threw that bottle of wine at him." Just remembering the shock on his face was enough to make her feel better and she actually giggled.

"I'd love to have been a fly on the wall for that," Cecily said.

"Heck, I can top that," Cass told them. "I once threw a flour canister at Mason."

Samantha shook her head. "We're a violent bunch."

"Men drive us to it," Cass said.

The final present, this one from Ella, was the hit of the evening. Charley read the words engraved on the silver pendant, *True to Myself,* and teared up.

"First to thine own self be true," Samantha murmured.

"And if you find yourself having trouble doing that, call one of us. We'll get you through," said Samantha. "That's what friends are for," she said again.

"Absolutely." Cass nodded. "Men may come and go but girlfriends are forever."

"To girlfriends," Cecily said, raising her glass.

"To girlfriends," everyone chorused.

Yes, that was all she needed, Charley told herself.

But later that night when she finally went to bed, she remembered there were a few things men were still good for. Yes, she had her friends and they were fabulous, but when it came to sharing dreams and building a life (and a sex life), marriage was still the gold standard. At least it was for her. No matter how many parties she threw herself, no matter how many friends she had, in the end she still went to bed alone.

Maybe she'd always be alone. She hugged a pillow and let the tears fall.

17

Ella was closing out the till on Thursday when someone tapped at the door of Gilded Lily's. Good customers would sometimes have a wardrobe emergency and need help after hours, and she always opened up for them, but today she was in no mood. She was pooped and didn't want to open up for anyone.

It had been a long day. Dani's bridesmaids had come by to pick up their dresses, and that had been the only bright spot. Hildy Johnson had come in looking for something to wear to a Christmas party and kept insisting she was one size smaller than she really was. Of course, nothing fit and she finally left in a huff. Darla, the mayor's sister, had returned a bracelet with a faulty clasp. She didn't have a receipt—hardly surprising since Ella had sold her that bracelet two years ago. Two bargain-hunters had spent an hour wandering around, asking questions and getting free fashion advice and then left with their wallets still securely in their purses. Of course, this often happened in retail, but it was discouraging when you spent so much time and tried so hard to help people and got nothing in return. Finally, Charley had come in for some retail therapy and had spent a small fortune, then left wearing a smile that never quite reached her eyes.

That had been depressing, partly because Ella felt bad for her friend but also because watching Charley was a little like hanging out with the Ghost of Christmas Yet to Come. Was this her future, loneliness and disappointment? Retail therapy?

With a sigh she looked up from her work and saw that her visitor wasn't a woman but a man with dark hair and gorgeous dark eyes. Oh, no. What did he want? A snatch of the Christmas carol "Jingle Bells" came jingling into her mind. *Oh, what fun it is to ride in a one-horse open sleigh.* No. No more rides in the sleigh bed.

She opened the door and stood there, her brain and her mouth not quite connecting.

It turned out she didn't need to say anything. He spoke first. "I thought you might be going somewhere after work and I wanted to ask you to come back to the house. I have something waiting there."

"What?"

"Just come home and you'll see."

Home, there was an interesting choice of word, considering that house wasn't their home anymore.

"Will you do that, El?"

He looked so earnest.

So what? He always looked earnest.

Except she was tired of avoiding the house and she hardly ever got to see Tiny. "Okay."

He grinned like a little boy who'd just impressed his mom with his school art project for Mother's Day. "Good. I'll wait for you in the truck."

She shut the door after him and realized she was smiling. *What are you smiling about? Nothing's changed. No one has changed. People don't change.*

Scrooge did. Of course, Scrooge wasn't a real person.

With a sigh, Ella fetched her purse. Then she locked up the shop and got into the truck with Jake. He had the radio tuned to her favorite station, one that played solid Christmas songs this time of year, and Rascal Flatts was singing "I'll Be Home for Christmas." She wasn't going home now. She was going to a house. *I'll be at a house for Christmas.* Boy, that sure didn't have the same ring.

You'll have a home someday, she told herself, snapping off the radio. This had been a starter marriage. Someday she'd have the real thing. Or maybe she'd end up like her mother, keeping men at a distance, keeping them as friends. Being a single mom, bossing her daughter around.

Whoa, where had that come from? She immediately shied away from the disloyal thought. Her mother never bossed her around. She simply gave advice. Good advice.

She could imagine what kind of advice her mother would give her if she were here right now. *Don't go back to the house with him. What are you thinking?*

Oh, what fun it is to ride... No, no. That was a bad thought.

The truck cab was heavy with silence. Boy, had that been rare back when they were happy.

Ella sighed and looked out the window at the houses

on their street. Every one of them was all dressed up for Christmas. The Bennetts had their living room light on, and through the window she could see Cheron and Harold decorating their tree. Judging by the cars parked on the street, Sam Moyle, her former math teacher, and his wife, Selma, were hosting a party of some sort, and his brother Ben, who happened to live next door, was walking across the lawn with his wife, Marliss, who carried a huge platter of Christmas cookies. Everyone was in the holiday spirit. She wished she could join them.

Farther up the road, the houses were fewer and the trees denser. At the end of it sat their house. She wished they'd gone ahead and put up...lights! Jake had strung multicolored lights all along the roof. She turned to him, tears in her eyes, and stated the obvious. "You put up lights."

He smiled at her, his look tender. "I thought you'd like it."

She did. "Thank you," she murmured. Her gratitude felt out of place and awkward. Why was she thanking him? And why was he doing this? They weren't married. The house was sold. This was crazy.

Inside the smell of onions greeted her. She looked questioningly at him.

"I made dinner," he said.

"Meat loaf." It was the only thing he knew how to cook. That and, "Baked potatoes?"

He nodded.

She loved meat loaf. It was something Mims had considered beneath her and she'd never made it, but for Ella meat loaf spelled family.

"I thought we should have one last dinner together," Jake said, helping her out of her coat.

Their last supper.

He led her out to the kitchen, where she found the table set and decorated with a small vase of red and white roses. He'd even put on the tablecloth they'd bought at a garage sale three years ago.

"Sit down," he said.

She sat and watched, Tiny glued to her side, while Jake dished up meat loaf and baked potatoes with all the trimmings. And salad from the grocery store deli. Salads, easy as they were to prepare, were beyond him. Then he pulled a bottle of champagne from the fridge.

"Champagne?" she asked. There was nothing to celebrate.

"Why not?" He filled their glasses. Then he sat down across from her and raised his.

"What are we toasting?"

He shrugged. "To happier times, past and future."

She could do that. "To happier times," she said, and they clinked glasses.

The meat loaf was delicious, full of chopped peppers and onions and coated with barbecue sauce. She was going to miss Jake's meat loaf. She was going to miss a lot of things, but she was better off without him. Still, it was hard to remember that just now, and every bite she took came seasoned with guilt. Which was ridiculous. She had nothing to feel guilty about. She'd carried her weight in this relationship, working eight to five, five days a week. And she hadn't chased after other men.

"Why are you doing this?" she asked.

"I figured it might be our last chance to talk."

"There's nothing to talk about. It's too late."

He set down his fork and leaned back in his chair. "It's

never too late. I've always loved you and I still do. You know that."

"Do I?"

He frowned. "You believed in me once. Why did you stop?"

Now she set down her fork. "You really need to ask? You know why. You couldn't be trusted."

"I was never unfaithful to you. I tried to tell you that."

Right. She rolled her eyes.

"But you listened to your mom instead of me."

"My mother was right," she said hotly.

"Why, just because she's your mother?"

"No, because she had proof."

"Those pictures looked like proof because you wanted them to. You chose to believe her over me. How do you think that makes me feel as a man? I know you love your mama, but you promised to build a life with me. And you didn't. You always kept bringing your mother into our relationship. And maybe that would've been okay if she'd liked me, but she never did."

"I…" Ella stopped, unsure how to finish that sentence.

"Do you remember how happy we were?"

She remembered, more often than was comfortable.

"We could still build a good life."

Somewhere deep down, past the hurt and anger, something glimmered, like a small candle determined to hold back the dark.

"And I want to. I think you do, too, El, but you've got some tough choices to make."

"What kind of choices?" she asked suspiciously.

"You're gonna have to choose whose side you're on, your mom's or mine."

"I was never on anyone's side," she protested.

"Oh, yes, you were. When it came time to choose sides, you always took hers."

"That's not true!"

"It is, El, and you know it. You stood in church before God and all our friends, and you promised to stick with me no matter what—sickness, health, for richer or poorer—but in the end you listened to your mom. You chose her over me, and all because of something you imagined. A phone number and a message and some pictures that didn't tell the whole story."

Ella shoved her plate away, no longer hungry. In fact, she felt slightly ill. Tears were sneaking into her eyes now, turning Jake's face to a blur. "They told enough."

"Jen was never interested in me. Those pictures are bogus."

Ella looked at him in disgust. Was he still insisting on that same tired story?

She got up to leave but he caught her arm. "Come and hear the band play the song I wrote for you tomorrow night. Meet this other woman you were so sure I was hot for."

She chewed on her lip, torn.

"At least give me that, El. Let me prove I never cheated on you."

She frowned. "Why now?" What was the point?

"Because I want you to know the truth. Hell, I should've done this back when everything first hit the fan, but I was mad. And proud, too proud to beg. But I've come to realize that my pride isn't worth a damn. I'd rather have you. So will you come? Will you do that much for me?"

All right. She could do that much. She nodded.

He smiled. "Good." Then he nudged her plate back toward her. "Tiny will love this, but I made it for you."

They finished their dinner in silence. She half expected him to bring out the eggnog, try to kiss her, something, but instead he simply said, "Why don't you go watch some TV? I'll clean up in here."

"I think I'll take Tiny for a walk," she said. Tiny needed the exercise and she had a lot to process.

She had even more to process Friday night at the Red Barn. She felt awkward joining the other women at the band's usual table. These women had stuck with their men. She'd been the defector.

"Hi, Ella," Larry's girlfriend, Chrissie, greeted her. "Glad you're back."

She wasn't back exactly. She was just…here. Sort of. Not much had changed since the good old days when she'd come and hung out on the weekends. Pretty much the same crowd of cowboys and farmers inhabited the place. The old hardwood floor was still scuffed and scarred, the table lamps were still cheap and the bar was still hoppin'.

There was one small change at the band table, though. A new member had joined Chrissie's and Guy's wives, Taylor. This woman had to be Tim's new lady, but Ella had a hard time imagining him with this tough-looking customer. Her hair was cut short and she wore jeans and a black T-shirt and she was the only woman at the table who hadn't bothered with makeup. She wasn't fat by any means but she wasn't the petite girlie-girl type Tim normally went for.

"This is Tanya," Chrissie said. "Jen's partner."

Partner. Partner? Partner! "You mean… I mean…" Ella could feel her face flaming.

"You mean what?" Tanya asked, her eyes narrowing.

"I mean, I thought…" Ella put her hand to her mouth. She was going to cry, she was going to laugh, she was going to…remember her manners. "Oh, my gosh, it is so great to meet you."

Tanya looked at her like she was nuts.

Jake's voice drifted over to her from the bandstand. "And now I want to play a song I wrote for someone very special. It's called 'To Find Heaven.'"

Ella fell onto the chair next to Chrissie and let the song wash over her.

"'Sometimes this world is a hell of a place. And heaven feels so far away. But every time I've held you and you've made me come undone. That's the closest I have come.'" As he sang Jake looked at her with eyes so full of love she had to wonder what madness had possessed her to think they didn't belong together. And give their love—*almost* give their love—away to the green-eyed monster.

"'I'm close to heaven with you, closer than I've ever come. There's no hell I won't walk through to find heaven, girl, with you,'" Jake finished.

They had gone through hell, thanks to her. The band was just coming off break, and a moment later Jake was at her side, hugging her. "Hey, El. I see you've met Tanya."

Tanya didn't seem all that happy about it. Once more Ella's face sizzled. She managed to nod.

Now his keyboard player Jen had come up beside him. "And this is Jen."

"Hi," Jen said. She sat down, placed an arm around Tanya's

shoulders and smirked at Ella. "I'm your competition. Nice to meet you."

"Still think I was cheating on you?" Jake asked softly.

What a fool she'd been. What a stupid, insecure, untrusting fool. "Oh, Jake!" She threw her arms around him and kissed him.

"Get a room," Larry cracked.

"You are such a jerk," his girlfriend said, swatting his arm.

Not half as much a jerk as Ella had been.

"But what about those pictures the detective took?" she asked later as they drove home.

"The detective your mom hired?"

The residual bitterness in his voice made her feel bad that she'd allowed Mims to overstep her boundaries. Still, "You've got to admit it looked bad."

"To someone with a suspicious mind," Jake said, not willing to cut either her or Mims any slack. "You remember in one of those pictures I was carrying some papers. Lyric sheets."

So he'd said. *I was just dropping off some lead sheets.*

She remembered what she'd said in response. "And it takes an hour to drop off lead sheets?"

That was when Jake had blown up. That was when everything had blown up.

"Yes," she said now.

"Well, I was. Just like I told you. Jen asked me if I had a minute to go over a couple of songs, which we did. Then she started crying, told me she was having problems with Tanya. They'd had a big fight about twenty minutes before I showed up. All I did was listen and then tell her everything would be okay. When I left she hugged me and said thanks. So, like I told you, it didn't mean a thing."

The damning picture had been a thank-you hug. One picture was, indeed, worth a thousand words. And this time those words all needed to be "I'm sorry."

"I should have told you back then that Jen wasn't into guys but, like I said, I was mad. And you know what? Even if I *had* told you, you wouldn't have believed me."

Much as she hated to admit it, he was probably right. By the time the Jen incident had happened, her insecurities had hardened into a wall of mistrust.

"El, there will always be women throwing themselves at me. That goes with the territory if a guy makes it in this business. But there's only one woman I want, only one woman I'll ever want, and that's you." He reached over and took her hand and she gave his a squeeze. "Hmm," he said thoughtfully, "I wonder if there's a song in that."

Saturday morning Axel called Ella. "I thought you'd like to go to the tree-lighting ceremony tonight. I'll come by the shop and pick you up."

"Sorry, I can't," she said.

"Oh." He sounded shocked. "Why not?"

She grinned at Jake, who was standing next to her in the kitchen, flipping pancakes for their breakfast. "I'm back with Jake."

There was a moment of shocked silence on the phone. Then, "You can't be serious."

She smiled at her ex-husband, who was grinning from ear to ear. "I'm afraid I am. But thanks for the offer."

"Ella, I don't know where your head is," Axel said.

She didn't, either, actually, but she knew where her heart was.

"Sorry," she said. "It wouldn't have worked out between us." She still hated jazz.

The family had just come home from church when Cass's cell phone rang. It was her stepfather, Ralph. Probably calling from the airport. They were due to fly out today and had a layover in Detroit.

"How's it going?" she asked. Neither Ralph nor her mother was particularly fond of flying, but Mom had said nothing was going to keep her from coming up for her granddaughter's wedding.

"Not so good," Ralph said.

Cass could feel a dark cloud creeping up on her sunny Sunday. "What's wrong?" she asked, dreading the answer.

"Your mother had a fall."

The cloud shot out thunder and lightning. Cass fell onto the nearest chair. "Oh, no."

"What's wrong?" Dani asked, sitting opposite her.

"Grandma fell," Cass said, then asked Ralph, "Is she hurt?" Dumb question. Of course she was hurt or Ralph wouldn't have been calling.

"She broke her wrist. She has to have surgery on Friday."

The day before the wedding. *Poor Mom. Poor me,* Cass added as a new, more selfish thought occurred. There went her support system. She'd been counting on her mother to help her hold it together while dealing with Mason and his family. Now she was on her own.

She chided herself for being so egocentric and asked if she could speak to her mother.

"I'm afraid she's with the doctor right now," Ralph said. "We'll keep you posted, though."

"Thanks," Cass said. "Tell her I love her. We're going to miss you guys."

"Not as much as we're going to miss you," Ralph assured her.

"So what happened?" Dani asked as Cass set aside her cell.

"Grandma broke her wrist. She has to have surgery on Friday."

Dani looked horrified. "She's not coming to the wedding?"

"She can't travel the day after surgery," Cass said.

"It won't be the same without her."

Now Willie was back from the kitchen (always his first destination after church) with a bag of chips. "When are we eating?"

"It's not all about you," Dani told him. Then to her mother, she said, "Maybe Grandma will be well enough to fly by Saturday."

No, it wasn't all about Willie, but it certainly was all about the bride-to-be. Cass leveled a look at her daughter, who had the grace to blush. "Even if she was up for it, they wouldn't get here in time."

Dani fell back against the couch cushions. "This blows."

There was an understatement. Cass patted her leg. "Don't worry. We'll have plenty of family for your big day." Half of them unwanted.

"I know. I just feel bad Grandma won't be here."

Not half as bad as I feel. "I know, and I know she's disappointed. But Uncle Drew will be recording it, so at least she'll get to see you walking down the aisle later on."

Dani's scowl lessened to a frown. "Poor Grandma. Gosh, I really wanted her there."

Cass gave Dani a hug. "But the most important people will be there—you and Mike."

That coaxed a smile out of her daughter.

"Now, come on, let's make dinner," Cass suggested. "Amber, Willie, that means you, too."

"Aw, Mom," Willie protested. "I hate cooking."

"But you like eating, and if you want to eat well when you're out in the big bad world, you'd better know how to cook. Anyway, it's tacos, and that's easy."

"Tacos! All right!"

"It's your turn to grate the cheese," Amber informed him. "I had to last time."

Willie groaned. "I suck at grating cheese. I always scrape my fingers."

"Be a good sport," Cass told him, and then told herself the same thing. Having her mother missing from Dani's wedding party had hardly been part of her plan, but—as she'd told her kids—not all recipes turned out as you planned them.

She said as much when her brother called to console her.

"Wow, sis, you're sure taking this well," he said.

She was sure pretending to take it well, anyway.

By the time her friends arrived for their Sunday chick-flick night, she was tired of pretending.

"Not having your mom here for such an important event, that's awful," Ella lamented.

"Dani's really disappointed," Cass said. "And I've got to tell you, even though I put on a good face for her, I'm not doing so well, either. I was counting on Mom being here to help me get through this."

"We'll get you through," Samantha promised.

"Absolutely," Charley seconded.

"Speaking of getting through things, how are you doing?" Cecily asked her.

Charley's eyes turned steely. "I'm doing just fine. I've decided to become a man-hater. Too bad I've got to work with one rebuilding the restaurant."

"Who'd you end up hiring?" Samantha asked.

"Masters Construction."

"Ethan Masters?" Samantha cocked an eyebrow.

"He's new in town, isn't he?" Cecily asked.

Samantha nodded. "And newly single from what I hear. I met him at Bavarian Brews the other day."

"Quite a hunk of beefcake from what I hear," Cass said, looking speculatively at Charley.

"Hey, you go for him if you want," she said, holding up a hand. "Me, I'm so done with men it isn't even funny."

"Never say never," Cecily said.

"Yeah, you never know what might happen," put in Ella, who was beaming.

Cass looked at her speculatively. "Okay, you've been acting like a woman who owns a diamond mine ever since you got here. What gives?"

"Well." After a dramatic pause, she announced, "Jake and I are getting back together."

This produced squeals of delight and hugs all around.

"You two belong together," Cecily said.

"That's what we decided." Ella dropped her gaze, suddenly self-conscious. "You know, I was wrong about Jake. I mean, yes, he's a flirt, but he never cheated on me."

"I smell a story in there somewhere," Samantha said.

Ella's face turned pink. "I met the keyboard player Friday. She has someone. I guess this is where you all say I told you so."

"We wouldn't dream of it," Cass said.

"But we did tell you," Cecily added with a wicked grin.

"I'm glad Cupid is being good to you," Charley said. "Jake really is a nice guy."

Ella nodded. "Now, if we can just figure out a way for him to make a little more money."

"You've been able to live okay on what you guys earn," Cecily pointed out.

"But you're right to be thinking about how you can earn more," her sister said. "Especially if you want kids...."

"It would be hard to raise a family on what we're making," Ella admitted, and the pink in her face deepened.

"A family?" Cecily looked at her speculatively.

"I mean, we'll probably end up having kids," Ella stammered.

"You'll figure it out," Charley said. "One thing's for sure, you'll have lots of aunties to help out."

Poor Charley, Cass thought. It seemed she was auntie to half the babies in town, and the rare times she wasn't at the restaurant, she was always watching someone's kid. At the rate she was going, was she ever going to have children of her own? Cass hoped she would, hoped her friend wouldn't give up on love.

She was in no position to encourage Charley to stay hopeful. She herself had given up years ago. Love was overrated.

It did produce children, though, and she'd gotten three good ones out of the bad deal she'd made with Cupid. And now she was about to add a son-in-law and, down the road, grandchildren. Everything was coming together for the wedding and it was going to be beautiful.

But as she watched Cecily's movie pick of the week, *National Lampoon's Christmas Vacation,* she couldn't shake the feeling that she was going to wind up living the sequel.

18

Monday morning Ella met Mims at Bavarian Brews to make her big announcement. So far she was finding it difficult to work up the nerve.

"Ella, baby, what's wrong?" Mims asked.

"Wrong? Nothing."

Mims raised a perfectly sculpted eyebrow. "You could have fooled me. You're fidgeting. And you ordered decaf."

Ella took a deep breath. "I have news." And it was good news, so she shouldn't be so nervous about telling her mother.

Mims smiled encouragingly. "Well, my darling, let's hear it."

"Jake and I are back together."

A disapproving frown devoured her mother's smile. "Ella, you can't be serious."

She'd never realized before how often she saw that frown. Ella lifted her chin. "I am."

"After the way he's behaved? Have you gone insane? My God, we need to find you a shrink." She took her cell phone from her purse. "I'm calling Gregory and getting the name of his."

"I'm not seeing a shrink and I'm not leaving Jake," Ella said firmly. "You were wrong about him, Mims."

Mims gave Ella her snootiest look, the one she reserved for incompetent store clerks. "Oh?"

"He wasn't seeing that keyboard player."

Now Mims looked heavenward as if praying for strength to deal with her obstinate daughter. "Ella. Baby. I don't know what he said to you."

"Everything those pictures didn't. I was wrong not to give Jake a chance to tell the whole story."

She'd wanted to believe her mother was right. She was already jealous of the attention Jake got from other women, already prone to suspicion when she found Jen's note and phone number in his pocket. She'd had springs on her feet, ready to jump to conclusions. And once she had those incriminating pictures, she'd closed her mind and her heart to anything Jake had to say.

"Those pictures—"

Ella cut her off. "He wasn't having an affair with that keyboard player. She has someone else."

"Now, maybe," Mims conceded, "but not then."

"Not then, either. Jen's not into guys. She's got a girlfriend."

"A…girlfriend?"

"I should never have divorced him."

"Oh, yes, you should have," Mims insisted. "If not her, it would've been someone else. And he's never going to have any money. He's never going to amount to anything."

"There's more to life than money," Ella said.

There went the motherly eyebrow again. "When was the last time you tried living without it?" Before Ella could say anything, she added, "I won't always be here as a safety net for you, Ella. I want you to be secure."

"I am secure. I'm secure with Jake."

"You think you can be secure with a selfish man who always puts himself first?"

Brandon Wallace, one of Jake's softball team buddies, and Todd Black, who were sitting at a table behind them, suddenly began to laugh like some kind of all-knowing Greek chorus.

Mims shook her head. "Men like him, they use other people. They say all the right things, but their actions never line up."

"Are you talking about Jake or my father?" Ella retorted.

"Both."

Ella heard another guffaw from the table behind them. And something else, some kind of country song.

"Ella, baby—"

Ella held up her hand for silence. That voice, it sounded like Jake's. She got up and moved to stand by the table, trying to subtly peer over Brandon's shoulder. Sure enough, there on YouTube was Jake and his band. When had he done this? And what was it? Now Mims was standing next to her.

Brandon glanced over his shoulder at them and his eyes got bigger than those of any deer looking into a truck's headlights. "Ella, hi," he said, and quickly closed the page.

"Brandon, that was Jake," Ella said.

His deer-in-the-headlight eyes shot to his buddy.

Okay, what was the problem? Jake was on YouTube. That should be good news.

"Uh, no, it was some—somebody else," Brandon stuttered.

"Bring that back up," Mims commanded.

Brandon and his pal exchanged uh-oh looks as he obliged.

Sure enough, it was Jake. "Oh, my gosh, he's going to be famous," Ella cried. Another thing her mother had been wrong about.

Then she heard the lyrics. What kind of sick song was this? Next to her, Ella could feel her mother stiffening. She listened in horror as the song proceeded on its nasty route, Jake mocking her mother, offering Santa beer for life if he'd just haul Mims away. That was supposed to be funny?

Mims didn't stay to hear the second verse.

"I didn't see you guys sitting there. Sorry, Ella," Brandon said sheepishly.

He wasn't half as sorry as her husband was going to be. Make that ex-husband. Again.

When Ella didn't come home Jake figured she and her mother were shopping. But the hours dragged by and no Ella. His afternoon guitar students came and went, and still it was only him and Tiny in the house. Finally, it was almost dinnertime and he was hungry—for more than food.

He called her cell and received a very stiff hello.

What the hell was going on? "Hey, where are you?"

"I'm with Mims."

"Did you guys go to Seattle or something?"

"No. I'm at her place."

"Oh." Disappointment and confusion made it difficult for his brain to come up with any other words. Finally some surfaced. "Uh, when are you coming home?"

"Not tonight." The words came out so cold he nearly got frostbite on his ear.

"Okay, what's up?"

"What's up? You really need to ask?"

"Yeah." How else was he going to find out what could have gone wrong between last night and today?

"Well, why don't you look on YouTube? That might give you a clue," she said. Then all he heard was dial tone.

He didn't need to hear any more. Now he knew what the problem was. Somehow, someway, she'd seen him singing THE SONG. She'd been with her mother today and that meant mama-in-law had heard THE SONG, too. *Shit.*

He sat on the couch with his laptop and brought up "Merry Christmas, Mama." He almost dropped it when he saw how many views they had. That was great—in a parallel universe. Here in Jake's world it was a disaster. There he was, big, dumb, guitar-playing dope, dissing his former mother-in-law for all the world to see. He shut the laptop and fell back against the couch cushions. What was he going to do now?

The invasion had begun. Louise, Cass's former mother-in-law, and Maddy, her former sister-in-law, stopped by the bakery midmorning to announce that they had arrived. Days early. "We don't want to miss the bridal shower," Louise had said. Next thing Cass knew, they were stealing Dani away for shopping and lunch. Cass was not invited, which she told herself was fine, since someone had to wait on the customers. The snub stung, though, and she could only imagine how many more she was going to endure before their visit was over.

The next torture began when Mason showed up at the house with his trophy wife, who also wanted to attend the shower—oh, joy. He looked as fit as he was on the day they got married and had only a scant salting of gray in his brown hair. Father Time was treating him much more kindly than Cass. Men. They always stuck together.

Babette, standing next to him, was arm candy with her petite figure and her perfectly highlighted, shoulder-length hair. Looking at her, Cass felt every extra pound on her body. And here was another treat. They'd brought their dog, Cupcake.

Some dog, Cass thought. The yippy apricot Pomeranian resembled an overgrown powder puff. Cass was not a fan of little dogs. She much preferred real dogs like Ella's Saint Bernard, Tiny, dogs who had a purpose in life beyond trying a person's patience.

"Oh, you brought Cupcake," Amber said as Babette walked in holding the stupid thing like a baby. Amber reached out a hand to pet it and the dog growled and barked at her. She yanked back her hand.

"No, Cupcake, this is family. Remember?" Babette cooed to the minibeast. "She doesn't know where she is."

She's in Icicle Falls, invading my house. And for longer than she'd originally agreed to, no less. She must have been insane to go along with this.

"She just needs time to warm up. She's really very sweet," Babette explained to Cass.

Compared to what?

"Thanks for putting us up," Mason said.

He was managing to be civil. She could, too. "No problem," she lied. Dani had given up her room and was sleeping in Amber's, a sacrifice she was more than willing to make to have her father here. They were a full house, but not as full as they would've been if Mom hadn't broken her wrist. If Mom and Ralph had made it, Mason and Bimbette would probably have been on the sleeper sofa.

At least she'd been spared having to see *that* every morning when she got up. "Dani will show you to your room. Dinner's just about ready." After that, the women would be off to Dani's bridal shower, which Cass was determined to enjoy even if it killed her.

Dinner was lasagna with garlic bread and Caesar salad. Size-six Babette passed on the lasagna, had a few bites of salad and fed most of her garlic bread to the dog, who came to the table and sat in her lap.

"I take it you don't like lasagna," Cass said, trying (not very hard) not to be offended.

Babette wrinkled her pert little nose. "It's so fattening."

And that was why Babette was a size six and Cass was… not. She should have gone on a diet when she first heard this highlighted Barbie doll was coming.

Oh, what did she care? She didn't have to look good for anyone.

This last thought didn't prove comforting. She dished herself up a second helping of lasagna.

After dinner Mason and Willie got busy looking for a guy movie to watch while the women cleaned up in the kitchen. Babette cleared the table, all the while talking about the "amazing" Murano glass she'd bought when Mason took her to Italy. Cupcake helped by trying to get into the garbage. And Cass reminded herself that they were only here for a few days.

Then it was off with Dani and Amber and Ms. Size Six to pick up her ex-mother- and sister-in-law at Olivia's B and B and take them to Samantha's place for Dani's big night.

They were already standing outside the door when Cass pulled up under the port cochere. Maddy had gone lighter with her hair and it looked like she'd gained weight. She'd gotten divorced shortly before Cass and Mason. Like Cass, she'd obviously shed a husband and gained a couple of dress sizes. Louise, on the other hand, had gotten thinner. She looked like a stick with a wool coat. Even her lips were thin. That probably had something to do with the fact that they were pressed together in a semifrown.

"It's almost seven," she said as she got in the backseat. "We're going to be late."

Ah, yes, how Cass remembered that charming critical spirit. "Don't worry. Samantha lives five minutes from here. We'll be right on time," she assured Louise.

She was wasting her breath. Her former mother-in-law wasn't listening. She was already gushing a greeting to Dani. "And here's our bride. I'm looking forward to meeting all your friends, darling."

And they were looking forward to meeting her. Not.

"Thanks for picking us up," Maddy said. She checked out the interior. "Is this the same car you had way back when you were with Mason?"

Wouldn't that have been a fun bit of information to spread

when she got back home and saw her friends? "Not quite. How've you been, Maddy?"

"Wonderful. I've just gotten engaged."

"Well, congratulations," Cass said, determined to be magnanimous.

"How about you? Did you ever find anyone?"

Maddy had a way with words. "I haven't been looking. I've been too involved with my business."

"Still single, then? Well, maybe you'll catch the bouquet. Dani, you'll have to throw it in your mother's direction."

Oh, that was cute. "I think we'll save that opportunity for the younger girls," Cass said. "Speaking of bouquets, tell them about your flowers, Dani."

Her suggestion shone the spotlight where it needed to be. Talk turned to the wedding and they made it to Samantha's without Cass having to stop the car and bitch-slap her ex-sister-in-law.

"What a pretty house," Babette said as Cass pulled up to the curb.

The Prestons' house was decked out for the holidays with white lights strung along the roof and a holiday wreath on the door. Inside it was just as lovely. Samantha was an amateur photographer, and a winter shot she'd taken of Icicle Falls frozen in action hung over the fireplace. To the side of it, several candles were arranged on the mantelpiece, and the scent of bayberry filled the house. The living room was packed with women, all dressed in their holiday finery and Samantha's coffee table was piled high with beautifully wrapped presents and gift bags.

Samantha herself looked chic in black jeans, ballet slippers and a green sweater that showed off her red hair.

"Thank you so much for including us," Babette said once Cass had introduced them. "It's so exciting to see our Dani getting married."

Our Dani. Cass managed to smile and grind her teeth simultaneously.

"You're welcome." Then before Babette could get too chummy, Samantha got down to business, offering to take everyone's coats.

Dani's bridesmaids, Mikaila and Vanessa, came running up to her, all squeals and excitement and adorableness. Looking at them, Cass wondered if she'd ever been that cute. Hard to remember ancient history, but she was pretty sure she'd once been equally happy and carefree. She was still happy, she reminded herself. And seeing all her friends and neighbors here to show their love and support for her daughter had proud-mama tears welling up.

Samantha had gone all out and her dining room table practically groaned under the weight of appetizers and cookies.

"When did you have time to do all this?" Cass asked as she handed over her coat.

"Me? Are you kidding?" She nodded to where her younger sister stood, chatting with Lauren Belgado. "Bailey's back. Wait till you taste the chocolate dessert she made."

"Can't wait," said Cass. Too late to start dieting now, she reasoned.

But first she needed to make the rounds and thank everyone for coming. Oh, yeah, and introduce the in-laws.

"It's lovely to meet you," the mother of the groom said to Louise.

Yeah, well, wait until you get to know her, thought Cass.

"We're delighted to be here," Louise said.

She'd certainly been delighted to tell Samantha how lovely her house was. So much roomier than Cass's, but then those old houses weren't really designed for modern living.

Who said? It had taken all Cass's restraint not to kick the gray-haired biddy in her skinny butt.

Now Louise was busy telling Mike's mother how lucky her son was to be getting such a sweet girl.

"Oh, we know it," said Delia, giving Cass an encouraging smile—one suffering daughter-in-law to another. Delia and Cass had become good friends over the past few months and had come to agree on several important things. Yes, their children were young to be getting married, but they were both mature, well-grounded kids and they'd be fine. And they were each getting a great mother-in-law, which was more than either Cass or Delia could say. And, no matter how strongly tempted, they would neither take sides nor interfere in their children's lives.

Once all the guests had arrived, Samantha's younger sister Bailey, who'd come home early to cater the wedding, took charge, making them all play a game, some sort of word scramble involving necessities for a successful wedding. Cass couldn't help smiling at one of them—*reacter,* which, unscrambled, spelled *caterer.* Good advertising.

Then it was time to open presents. Amber was happy to be put to work making a practice bouquet using ribbons from the package and a paper plate, while Dani's friend Vanessa kept track of who gave her what. Dani was over the moon with Cass's, which was a box filled with essential baking tools. Like her mother, she loved to bake both at work and at home, and Cass knew Dani would use every item. Delia gave her a cookbook and the Sterling women gave her a gift card to Hearth and Home. Ella had made a wedding towel cake. Louise, big spender that she was, had given Dani a 9" x 12" glass pan and Maddy had gone one better by getting her a set of ramekins. Her bridesmaids got her fun gifts—personalized bride flipflops and a sexy cookbook loaded with aphrodisiac recipes. But the hit of the shower was Babette's present—a huge Victoria's Secret gift bag packed with lingerie. Even perfume.

"Oh, thank you! I love this fragrance," Dani said happily.

"I know you do," Babette told her, smiling.

It was like they were best friends. Cass popped an entire snowball cookie in her mouth.

"That's quite the gift," said Dot, who was sitting next to Cass with her foot propped on a footstool.

It was hard to swallow...the cookie. "Yes, it is," Cass agreed, and went back to the refreshment table. *This is not a competition,* she reminded herself. *Try to remember you're a grown-up and be grateful your daughter has so many people in her life who care.*

That attitude adjustment made it much easier to enjoy the shower. And it hardly fazed Cass when her former mother-in-law eyed her second plate with disgust. They were small plates.

Bailey had created a special drink for the bride that she'd dubbed Wedding Night Bliss, a frothy white concoction consisting primarily of coconut juice and white chocolate liqueur, for which she was now taking orders. "I can do alcoholic or virgin," she said.

"I'd better make mine a virgin," Babette said.

"And I know why," Maddy murmured, with a conspiratorial grin. She leaned across Dani and said to Cass in a stage whisper, "She's pregnant."

Cass lost her grip on her plate and two cookies bounced onto the floor. "P-pregnant?" she stammered.

"Wow, I didn't know that," Dani said.

"They're thrilled about it," Maddy confided.

And Maddy would know, of course, Cass thought cynically, since she specialized in minding other people's business.

The rest of the evening became mechanical. Cass smiled and said all that was right while inside she battled with her less noble half once more. This time it was a losing battle. It was hard to shake the sense of injustice she felt. After doing such a lousy job with his first set of kids, Mason the absent father was getting a second chance with his hot young wife. Everything was going great for him the second time around.

You could have remarried.

As if she'd wanted to. She liked being on her own. No one to foul up her plans, no one to disappoint her, no one… well, no one.

That wasn't altogether true. She had her family and her friends and her business. She didn't need anyone else. Heck, she didn't have time for anyone else.

But her nest was starting to empty. In another ten years she'd have time. How was she going to fill it? She'd never given that any thought. She'd been so busy, and middle age had been a lifetime away. Now here it was. She found herself feeling relieved when the party ended.

She helped carry Dani's loot out to the car and load it in the trunk, then looked on with a motherly smile while her daughter hugged Louise and Maddy goodbye at the lodge. She kept her smile as she, her daughters and Babette drove back to the house and Dani said to Babette, "I didn't know you were pregnant."

"Well, I'm only three months," Babette said, and glanced nervously in Cass's direction.

"Congratulations," Cass said, and tried to mean it. After all, there was no sense resenting Babette. She deserved a chance at happiness just like anyone else.

"Thanks," Babette said. "We're excited."

Mason had been far from excited when she got pregnant with Dani. "How did that happen?" he'd protested. As if it'd been all her fault. Of course, he'd backpedaled and said they'd make it work. And they had. They'd made it work by her doing everything. Well, maybe this time around he'd be more involved.

Mike had joined Mason and Willie, and they were on their second action flick when the women walked in the door, but they stopped it to help unload the trunk and then showed the proper interest in all of Dani's presents. Mike was especially interested in Dani's Victoria's Secret goodies.

"That's quite the haul," Mason said when she'd finished.

"We have so many great friends," Dani said happily, falling onto the couch next to Mike.

"You can say that again," he said.

"Man, you sure get a lot of stuff when you get married," Willie observed.

"You *need* a lot of stuff when you get married," Mason informed him.

"But it's all girl things," Willie said.

"Oh, not all of it," Mike said, picking up the Victoria's Secret bag.

That made Willie, big man on campus, actually blush.

He leaned over his chair, reaching down to the plate sitting on the floor, only to discover Cupcake devouring the one remaining sugar cookie on it. "Hey!" he yelled.

Cookie in mouth, Cupcake made a dash for the kitchen. "She ate my cookie!"

"Oh, Willie, I'm sorry," said Babette, who had squeezed in next to Mason on the other end of the couch.

"You know better than to leave food on the floor," Mason told him.

Cass bridled. This was her house. Willie could leave food on the floor if he wanted. "He's not used to having to worry about anything coming along and stealing his food," she said.

Mason shrugged off her comment, much as he'd shrugged off almost everything she'd had to say when they were married. She glared at him. That, too, bounced off him.

No glaring on the night of your daughter's bridal shower, she scolded herself. *And no more of these negative feelings.* At this rate she'd never get to sleep. And, unlike everyone else in the house, she had to be up before dawn.

She excused herself to go get ready for bed. Cupcake, now lurking by the stairs, yapped at her. *Good night, bitch.*

It was going to be a long week.

The next day wasn't any better for Cass. Her workday was an endless stretch of baking and waiting on customers, and the customer service turned out to be a one-woman operation once Dani disappeared to run errands in the afternoon and never returned. When Cass finally called her on her cell to find out where the heck she was, she learned Dani was out with Grandma and Aunt Maddy.

"Sorry, Mom. I've got so much to do."

"You've also got a job," Cass said. "I need help here."

"Okay, I'll get there as soon as I can," Dani promised.

Cass ended the call feeling guilty. It was unfair to expect Dani to work the week before her wedding. She'd been wrong and she'd apologize to her daughter—if she ever saw her.

In addition to realizing she was being unfair, she came to another conclusion. With her right-hand woman leaving, she was going to have to hire help.

This left her feeling a little low. Dani had been her baking sidekick, working alongside her for the past six years, first coming in after school and washing down tables and cleaning up in the kitchen, then taking on more responsibility as she got older. Cass had delighted in watching her daughter's skills develop and her creativity bloom, and she'd come to depend on her. Their shared passion for baking had kept them close. Now Dani was leaving, making plans to go back to school and get a catering degree. She'd be setting up both a business and a new life a hundred and seventy miles away.

Not the edge of the earth, Cass reminded herself. Why was it so hard to let go of that vision of Dani and her family here in Icicle Falls, of living close to her grandchildren? Family was important. Grandkids were important.

Maybe they'd been important to Louise, too.

Oh, no! Where had that come from? No place Cass wanted to visit.

She reined her thoughts away from the past and turned them toward the future. What was she going to do with Dani gone? Maybe she could teach Amber how to work the cash register and get her to come in after school on weekdays, even convince her she could sacrifice some of her social life to work on Saturday mornings. But Amber was more into clothes than cookies. Even if Cass could persuade her to put in some hours, that wasn't going to be enough, not with the way her business had been growing.

It was time to put an ad in the classifieds. Her daughter would be a tough act to follow, though. Maybe impossible.

That's life, she reminded herself. Children grow up and move on. She'd been perfectly happy with the growing-up part, and the moving on. It was just this moving *away* thing that upset her.

The future was out of her control. All she had was the present, and here in the present she had customers to wait on.

She'd just sent Darla on her way with a gingerbread house when Willie called to report that Cupcake had eaten his shorts.

"She *what?*"

"She ate my shorts!"

There was a gross visual. "How on earth did she manage that?"

"I don't know," Willie said grumpily. "I came home and found 'em all shredded. I hate that dog."

That made two of them. Still… "Did you leave your dirty clothes on the floor like I'm always asking you not to?"

"Yeah," he said grudgingly.

"And I'm guessing you didn't bother to close your bedroom door when you went to school."

"I shouldn't have to."

"No, you shouldn't. But if you don't want the dog going

after your socks next, it might be a good idea to keep the door closed."

"Gee, thanks, Mom," Willie grumbled, and hung up.

Life was tough all over. Dani never made it back to the bakery, leaving Cass to soldier on alone.

Her daughter was apologetic when they met with the ex-in-laws for dinner at Der Spaniard later. Cass apologized, too, for being such a slave driver, and even managed a friendly greeting for Louise, along with a compliment on her Christmas sweater.

Louise accepted the compliment with as much grace as the cactus on the reception desk, which was also decked out for the holidays with colored lights and looked a lot cuter.

Once everyone was seated and the orders had been placed, talk turned to the happy couple's upcoming move.

"Spokane has some great wineries," Babette said. "We'll have to come check them out. After the baby's born," she added, and put a hand on her tummy.

Cass kept smiling.

By the end of the evening, the smile was wearing thin and she was glad to leave the restaurant. Mason picked up the tab. Mr. Generous.

Let him, she decided. She was tired of competing with him, tired of keeping score.

To prove it she offered to make coffee for everyone and serve up the cream puff swans she'd brought home from the bakery. Louise declined the invitation, claiming exhaustion. Yes, shopping all day could be wearing. Maddy said she'd come, though, promising to be there as soon as she'd dropped off Louise.

Won't that be fun? More smiling all the way home. Mouth

muscles aching, Cass opened the front door and led everyone into the house.

And got an early Christmas present. Lovely. This was the icing on the cake.

19

It wasn't hard to figure out what she'd stepped in. Soft, squishy, stinky—a welcome-home present from Cupcake. With a growl, Cass lifted her foot to remove her shoe, while behind her Amber said, "Eew, gross."

"What?" asked Willie, lumbering in behind her.

"Watch where you step," Cass cautioned. "Amber, get some paper towels."

"What's wrong?" Babette asked. She halted just inside the door. "Oh."

"Yes, *oh*," Cass agreed. "That dog," she said through gritted teeth.

Now Mason was inside. "What's this?"

"If you can't guess, I'll be happy to let you take a sniff of my shoe," Cass snapped.

Her son, probably fearing that he'd get drafted to help

with cleanup, made himself scarce, leaving the three adults to deal with the smelly problem.

"I knew we should've taken her for a walk before we left," Babette lamented.

"And lost her," Cass muttered.

"Cute, Cass," Mason said in disgust.

Amber returned with the paper towels, and Mason snatched them and got to work. Amber beat a hasty retreat, but Babette bent to help, all the while saying how sorry she was.

Cass ignored her. "Cute?" she retorted. "Kind of like you bringing that animal here without even asking if it would be okay?"

"Mason said it was all right," Babette protested. "I had no idea."

Cass glared at him. "Seriously?"

"I'd forgotten how uncooperative you could be."

"Oh, that's rich coming from you of all people," Cass snarled as she wiped off the bottom of her shoe.

"I'm so sorry," Babette said again.

Now the verbal battle began in earnest. "*You* don't need to be sorry," Cass told her. "It's the inconsiderate jerk you're married to who should be sorry."

"Hey, you're the one who invited us to stay," Mason said, his voice rising.

"Because I was suffering from temporary insanity."

"Temporary?"

"Oh, that is funny."

The door opened to reveal Dani and Mike.

For a moment all was silent as Dani stood gaping at her squabbling parents. Then she burst into tears. "Why do you guys have to do this?" she wailed. "Are you going to fight on my wedding day, too?"

Without waiting for an answer, she turned and fled, Mike following her.

"Now look what you've done!" Cass snapped at Mason. *"Me?"*

Babette was crying, too. And here came Cupcake, trotting out to see what all the fuss was about. "You bad dog," Babette scolded.

Bad? How about demon-possessed? Cass tossed her smelly shoe out on the front porch and then stomped off to the kitchen.

"Don't make coffee," Mason yelled at her. "We're going out."

"Fine," she shouted. *Go out and don't come back.*

She didn't bother with the coffee but she did help herself to two cream puff swans. No sense letting them go to waste. Then she set the rest out on a plate. Willie and Amber would finish them off.

And now, after eating too much and saying too much, it was time for bed.

A knock on the front door reminded her that not everyone had gotten the message that the party was off. She opened it and there stood Maddy.

"Mason's car is gone," she told Cass.

"Sorry. I should've called you. We had a change of plans."

"A change of plans." Maddy repeated the words as if she were learning a foreign language.

"Yes, a change of plans," Cass said, trying to hold on to her patience.

Maddy pointed a finger at her. "You and Mason had a fight, didn't you?"

"Good night, Maddy," Cass said, and shut the door. Not in Maddy's face, not really. All right, she'd shut it in Maddy's face. Guilt prompted her to open the door again. Maddy was already marching down the porch steps. "We'll do it another time," Cass promised.

Maddy graciously accepted the offer with a one-fingered salute and kept walking.

Cass shut the door again and started upstairs. She met Amber coming down, holding the cause of all the commotion. Cupcake growled at Cass and let out an ear-piercing bark. *Bad Mom.*

"Are you and Daddy still fighting?" Amber asked in a small voice.

Nothing like a final dose of guilt to help a woman sleep well. Cass sighed. "We do that sometimes."

"Sometimes?"

"Okay, we do that a lot. But everything will be fine." She gave her daughter a pat on the arm. "There are cream puffs in the kitchen just dying to be eaten."

Amber nodded and continued on down to the empty living room, while Cass went upstairs and shut herself in her bedroom. What a lovely evening this had been.

And whose fault was that?

She tried to ignore the sobering thought as she got ready for bed, but it refused to be ignored. It followed her into the shower. Then it followed her to bed, where it camped on her pillow and nagged her for hours. She lay there, trying to not face it, as muted voices drifted up from downstairs. Dani was probably back, talking with Mason about her terrible mother. Eventually she heard footsteps on the stairs, and then in the hallway as, one by one, everyone made their way to bed. Had Willie done his homework? Amber had asked for help with her math earlier. Cass had completely forgotten. Great. Mother of the year.

Now the nasty thought was bouncing up and down on the bed. *Whose fault? Whose fault?*

She rolled over on her side and squeezed her eyes shut, told both the thought and herself to go to sleep.

It didn't. Neither did she.

At 1:00 a.m. she decided to see if warm milk really did help a person sleep and padded downstairs to the kitchen. To her surprise, she found Mason already there, seated at the kitchen table with a mug of cocoa and a book. He looked up at her entrance and frowned.

"I couldn't sleep," she said. "Hard to do when you've got a guilty conscience."

He grunted. Then he raised his mug. "Want some?"

"I'll have some hot milk," she said, and sat down at the table.

"That's for sissies."

"Sissies who have to be up early in the morning. The chocolate will keep me awake." Just like that nasty thought. Okay, it was now or never. She took a deep breath. "Mason, I'm sorry. I've been a rotten host."

He shrugged and put a mug of milk in the microwave.

"My attitude stinks," she admitted.

He turned and faced her. "I hate to say it, Cass, but it's stunk for a long time."

Her first instinct was to fire back an angry retort, but she didn't. Instead, she did something she hadn't done in years. She stopped and considered what he'd said.

The microwave dinged and he removed her cup and brought it to the table. Then he sat down and looked at her. "You know what I like about Babette?"

"The fact that she's young and gorgeous?"

He shook his head. "The fact that she's there for me."

Okay, now she was done holding back. "What, and I wasn't?"

"Not really." He took a sip of his cocoa and regarded her over the rim of his mug. "Come on, Cass, let's be honest."

"Okay," she agreed. "Let's. If you want honesty, try this on for size. I hate it that you've been Mr. Absent Father for years and now all of a sudden you come waltzing in like you're Super Dad. You write a few checks, throw around a few bribes and everyone loves you. It makes me feel like everything I've done for the kids all these years doesn't matter."

He set down his mug with a heavy sigh. "I'm sorry you feel threatened, Cass. You've been a great mom. Nobody would say any different, certainly not me. I'm just trying to be a better dad. I'm tired of feeling left out. And if you want to know the truth, I always felt left out."

"Left out?" What was he talking about?

"It was always you and the kids, with me on the outside looking in, trying to figure out how I fit into the family. Sometimes all I felt like was a paycheck."

"That's all you were," Cass said bluntly. "You were so busy becoming important you didn't have time for us."

"I did it all for you," he protested.

"So you always said. But what good did that do when we never saw you?"

His jaw was set, which meant he was dealing with strong emotions. "I didn't want to be a loser like my dad. I wanted to be successful. And I wanted you there for me, Cass. You never were. Everything I ever did you resented."

"That was because it took you away." How often had she told him that? Had he never listened? Well, duh. Of course he hadn't. That had been part of the problem.

"Well, you got your revenge. You moved far enough out of reach that you made it damned hard for me to be anything *but* away. If I hadn't finally gotten a job in Seattle we'd still have been squabbling about when I could see the kids."

"I didn't want revenge. I only wanted a new start."

"Are you sure that's all you wanted?" he pressed.

She sat back against her seat. That *was* all she'd wanted, wasn't it? She'd been so angry, so bitter.

So out to get him? "I don't know now," she said. "I honestly don't know."

He shrugged. "It's all water under the bridge."

Troubled water.

"We probably didn't belong together in the first place."

He was right, but the statement stung, anyway.

"Still, you were so damned hot I couldn't resist you," he added with a hint of a smile.

She took the hint and managed to give him one in return. Then sighed. "If I hadn't gotten pregnant…"

"I'd have married you, anyway. You have to know that."

She nodded, accepting the truth of his statement. They'd been hot for each other, sure that what they had would last forever.

"But the instant-family thing had me panicked. I had to do something to provide for you."

Hence rushing into the navy. And that hadn't pleased her. Neither had anything else he'd done to try and better himself. "I'm sorry I wasn't more understanding," she said, and meant it.

"Past history." He shoved away his mug. "But it feels good to hear you say it. And I'm sorry I let you down."

"Well," she said thoughtfully, "you didn't let me down completely."

"Yeah?"

"You gave me three great kids."

"We gave each other three great kids," he corrected.

"I guess they were the one thing we did right." What she and Mason once had together was definitely past history, but their children were the present and the future. And that was worth keeping in mind.

"Think we can work on being a team instead of adversaries?" he proposed. "For the kids' sake?"

She should have been the one proposing that, and she should have done it a long time ago. "I'm willing to try." After all, they'd be sharing these kids and probably grandkids for a lifetime.

"Me, too." He got up and took his mug to the sink.

"Mason?"

He turned, a questioning look on his face.

"You chose a nice wife."

He nodded. "I think so."

"I still hate her dog."

He smiled. "Me, too," he said, and left the kitchen.

Cass glanced at the kitchen clock and decided she'd better get back to bed. She didn't bother to finish the milk. She didn't need it anymore.

★ ★ ★

Jake tossed his cell phone aside and slumped against the couch cushions.

Tiny laid his head on Jake's leg and looked up at him in doggy concern.

"My life's in the toilet," he told the dog.

Ironic considering that his song was now up to 7400 views.

"You've got to take that thing down," he'd said to Larry.

"Are you nuts? Do you know how many views we're up to?"

"Yeah, and I don't care if we're up to a million."

"What the hell is the matter with you?"

"I'm trying to get back with Ella."

"So?"

"So my mother-in-law saw it."

"Ex-mother-in-law, dude," Larry had reminded him.

"She won't be an ex-mother-in-law once Ella and I are back together. And we were—until that song."

"I feel your pain," Larry had said. "Women. But, hey, what are you gonna do?"

"Take the song down, for starters."

"No can do, buddy."

"I can't get her back as long as that song is up there!" Jake had shouted.

"If her mom already saw it, it's too late, anyway. I'm not taking it down."

"You have to!"

"Hey, man, you may be our lead singer but I'm still the leader of this band. Now, I let you have your no-drinking onstage rule and your one-drink-during-practice rule, but

I'll be damned if I'll let you screw things up for all of us just 'cause you're hot to get in your ex's pants."

It was a good thing they'd only been talking over the phone. Otherwise, Jake would have punched Larry's lights out. "You need to take that song down," he shouted.

"No, you need to get your shit together," Larry had said, and hung up.

And now, after that happy conversation, here came a call from Billy Joe Brown, a Nashville talent manager who had seen him on YouTube, wanting to know if he was under management. Did he have a CD in the works? Where had his band played? What were his plans for the future?

To win back his wife—that was his plan. But Jake had been properly professional, and he and Billy Joe left it that he'd talk to his band, then call him back.

"The sooner, the better, son," Billy Joe advised. "When the snowball starts rolling you want to take advantage of it."

Well, the snowball had started rolling, and it had rolled right over Jake's love life.

Next to him, Tiny let out a groan.

"Yeah, I know. It's not all about me, is it? Tell you what, let's go for a walk and then get some firewood."

Tiny barked his approval of the plan.

Some people (Jake's ex-mother-in-law) thought that dogs couldn't understand human vocabulary, but Jake didn't agree. Tiny understood a lot. For sure he understood what *walk* meant. That translated into bounding across snow-covered lawns, sniffing and peeing on every shrub that crossed his path.

He also understood what *firewood* was. It was an exciting chore. Jake had a sled reserved for hauling in the wood that he harnessed to Tiny, so he could pull it from the shed to the house. It was more work harnessing Tiny and load-ing and unloading the wood than it was simply bringing in a couple of armloads, but Saint Bernards needed a purpose. So did humans. A man needed to do what he was put on earth to do.

He probably hadn't been put here to diss Ella's mom.

Once he'd brought in the wood it didn't take him long to get a roaring fire going. He grabbed his guitar, plunked down on the couch and stared into the flames. How many times had he sat here like this on a winter's day, dreaming of a future filled with success? His dreams were finally start-ing to come true, but they wouldn't mean anything without Ella by his side. He was living in ashes.

He strummed his guitar. "I'm living in ashes. The fire is gone."

The song began to flow, and soon he was so caught up in what he was creating that he lost all track of time. He never heard the door open, never heard Ella walk into the room. He'd just finished singing his last chorus when he opened his eyes and there she stood by the fireplace. Was he hal-lucinating?

The hallucination spoke. "That's a beautiful song," she said softly. "Why couldn't you have put that up on YouTube?"

If he had they'd be solid now. He shook his head. "I don't know." That was a lie. He knew exactly why he'd put up his snarky holiday greeting to his ex-mother-in-law. He'd been angry.

And immature.

"That was a mean thing to do."

Yes, it had been.

She opened her mouth to say something else, then seemed to think better of it and started to leave the room.

"Wait," he begged. "What were you going to say?"

"What does it matter?"

"It matters a lot."

She pursed her lips and studied him. At last she spoke. "I know I married you, Jake, and I owed you my loyalty. I did a lot of stupid things. I was jealous for no reason, and toward the end I know I wasn't very supportive."

You could say that again. Jake wisely kept his mouth shut.

"But maybe if the shoe had been on the other foot, *you'd* have gotten jealous. And maybe you'd have jumped to the same conclusions."

She had a point there. "Maybe," he conceded.

"And you can't blame Mims, either. She was only trying to help."

Was that what you called it?

Ella bit her lip. Sure enough. "You always want to make me choose—you or Mims. Do you know how impossible that is? What would you have done if I'd asked you to choose between your mother and me?"

Jake gave a snort. "That would never have happened because my mom likes you." *And my mom's cool and yours is a bitch.* "Anyway, your mom never wanted to share. She's hated me ever since I asked you to the senior prom."

"No, only since you picked me up for prom in that beat-up old truck," Ella corrected him. The memory brought a reluctant smile to her lips.

He grinned. "We took some rides I'll never forget in that old truck."

Ella sobered. "Oh, Jake."

Just then the doorbell rang. Jake swore. "Don't answer."

"I have to. It's Mims."

"Don't tell me, let me guess—you two are going out to dinner." The wicked witch of the Pacific Northwest, sweeping in again, just when she was most not wanted.

"We're going to dinner at—"

Jake cut her off. "Schwangau."

Ella nodded.

Big surprise there. Mims didn't like Mexican, and a pizza joint was beneath her. She sure as heck wouldn't be interested in Big Brats or Herman's Hamburgers. Now that Zelda's was closed for repairs, the hoity-toity Schwangau was the only place this side of Seattle where Lily Swan would deign to eat. Why the hell couldn't she find someone her own age to go to dinner with?

Ella hurried down the hall. Jake could hear her opening the door, could hear Lily saying, "You ready, baby? I don't want to keep Axel waiting."

Axel! Who'd painted him back in the picture?

"Let me get my coat," said Ella.

There it sat on a nearby chair, along with her purse. For a moment Jake considered hiding them.

Now she was back, her expression unhappy, and he wasn't sure if she was unhappy about the conversation they'd been having or about the fact that her mother was taking her away. "I have to go," she said, not looking him in the eye.

"El," he pleaded. They could work this out if they could just have some uninterrupted time to talk.

She shook her head and rushed off, putting on her coat as she went.

In less than a minute he heard the door shut.

"*Now* what am I supposed to do?" he asked Tiny.

Tiny whimpered in sympathy.

Jake fell back against the couch cushions. "They're a matched set, aren't they?" he mused. "Hard to find a woman who doesn't come attached to her mama."

What was that about, anyway? Men left home and their moms accepted it. Why was it so hard for them to let go of their daughters? Or their daughters to let go of them? Was it some kind of female thing?

"You take one, you get the other," he informed Tiny. "No extra charge." He thought he'd been marrying one woman, but he'd gotten a twofer. Well, sort of. He would have if Lily Swan had ever approved of him.

She sure didn't approve of him now, thanks to that song. Who'd think one song could do so much damage?

"You should have known," he told himself. "Songs are powerful."

Hmm. Yes, they were. A song had gotten him into this latest mess. Could a song get him out?

20

"Axel, I'm glad you could join us on the spur of the moment like this," Mims said after the waiter had taken their orders.

"My pleasure." He looked inquiringly at Ella. "I thought you'd have plans with Jake."

Lily spoke for her. "She doesn't. She and Jake are through for good."

"Really?" Axel sounded dubious.

"I don't want to talk about it," Ella said.

He nodded. "Well, this is some snowfall we're getting, isn't it?"

Ella gazed out the window at the scene of snowcapped shops lit by old-fashioned streetlights. When it snowed like this, she and Jake liked to be tucked in their house in front of a roaring fire.

He'd built a fire for her.

Who cared? What he'd done to her mother was unfor-
givable.

But was it understandable? She could still remember his
angry words when they had their final fight, right before he
accused her of not trusting him, and told her to go ahead and
get that divorce. "I blame this on your mom. She's wanted
me gone from the minute we got together."

"That's not true!" Ella had protested, but of course it was
true. Weren't mothers supposed to be happy when their
daughters found someone to love?

"Ella?"

Her mother's voice brought her back to the present.

"I'm sorry. What?"

Mims shook her head. "Where were you just now?"

With Jake. "It doesn't matter." Except it did. "You know,
sometimes I don't understand why you never gave Jake a
chance."

Both her mother's eyebrows shot up. "You must be joking."

"No, I'm not."

"Maybe I should go," Axel said.

"No, stay. We're not going to talk about this anymore,"
Mims said firmly.

Ella fell silent. Fine. She wouldn't talk at all. The waiter
arrived with their salads, and she concentrated on the baby
greens on her plate.

Axel tried to step into the breach with talk of plans to
tour the California wine country.

Who cared? Ella broke her vow of silence. "I made a
mistake."

"It's a little late to change your order now, baby," Mims said.

"No, I mean about Jake."

Axel stood. "You know, I'm going to leave you ladies to sort this out."

"Oh, Axel," Mims began.

"Good idea," Ella agreed. "Don't worry about dinner. My mother will pick up the check."

Axel nodded and left, and Mims let out an offended huff. "Really, Ella. That was high-handed."

"No more high-handed than you inviting him in the first place," Ella said in a tone of voice she rarely used with her mother.

"Well, you weren't seeing that—"

"Jake. His name is Jake. And what's Axel got that he hasn't?"

"Money, for one thing. Sophistication."

"Oh, Mims, he's a fathead. And he's controlling. Every time he asked me out it was to something he'd already de-cided on. I don't want to be controlled." Heaven knew she'd been controlled enough growing up. "By anyone," she added.

"Are you implying that I control you?"

She was on a roll now. *May as well keep rolling.* "You do. Actually, you always have. When I was growing up I never got to pick out my own school clothes."

"Of course you did, once you developed some fashion sense."

"Any friends you didn't like you weeded out of my life."

"For your own good," Mims insisted.

"There was nothing wrong with any of my friends, ex-cept that their moms worked at the Sweet Dreams factory

or as cashiers in the grocery store." Mims had nothing to say
to that and Ella moved on. "You're the one who decided I
should work for you at the shop."

"And why shouldn't you? You have a flair for clothes."

"I have a flair for decorating, too. That's what I wanted
to do." So she should have spoken up and said so instead of
just going along. Well, she was done going along now. It
was time to be her own woman.

"That was ridiculous," Mims said. "Go work for someone else when we had a family business? Ella, I don't know
what's gotten into you."

"I want to be me. I don't want to be an imitation you. I
want to be happy."

"You are happy," Mims said. "We're happy. We've always
been happy, just the two of us."

Your mom never wanted to share.

Jake's words washed over Ella, a shower of icy reality.
He was right. Surely, on some level, she must have known
this. Maybe she'd never wanted to see it. Her eyesight was
twenty-twenty now. The big question was, what was she
going to do with her new, improved vision? Something every
grown woman had to do at some point—claim her own life,
for better or for worse.

She took a deep breath. "Mims, you know I love you."

"And I love you. There's nothing I wouldn't do for you.
I gave up a modeling career for you."

Okay, that didn't ring true. "You once told me that mod-
els burn out early. That you'd already peaked."

This made her mother frown. "Well, I hadn't. I could
have done any number of things if we hadn't moved here."

"Then why didn't you do those things?"

Mims sat there staring at her. "I...I just didn't."

Ella fell against the seat and stared back at her mother. "You ran away. You ran away from your life."

"I did not!" Mims said hotly.

"You got pregnant and you up and ran away. Why didn't I ever meet my father?"

Mims stiffened. "We've had this discussion before."

"*It didn't work out and I have no idea where he is.* That's a discussion?"

Mims set her fork down with enough force to break the table. "Really, Ella. What do you want from me?"

Ella slammed down her fork, too. "My life! And I don't want it to turn out like yours. I don't want to end up alone." Had that just come out of her mouth?

For a moment, she and her mother sat looking at each other in shocked silence. Finally Mims said, "There's nothing wrong with my life, and I'm not alone. I have you. We have each other. That man you were with, he was only going to bring you heartache."

"Like yours did?" Ella asked softly.

Mims squirmed in her seat. "I didn't need him, anyway. You don't need a man to be happy, baby, believe me."

"Are you all that happy, Mims?"

Her mother looked at her like she'd uttered some sort of blasphemy. "Of course I am!"

They fell into another strained silence as the waiter arrived to carry off their salad plates. As soon as he'd left, Ella asked, "Who *was* he?"

Mims rolled her eyes. "Oh, not this again. How many times have you asked me that question?"

About a million.

"What does it matter? The man's never been a part of your life."

"And why was that?"

"I've told you, we went our separate ways long before he even knew about you."

"Maybe he'd like to know about me."

Mims shook her head in disgust. "I doubt it."

"All you ever told me was that he was a model. Do you have any idea how many magazines I looked through growing up, studying each man, wondering if he could've been my father?" And wondering why, with two beautiful people as parents, she hadn't turned out more beautiful herself. Not that it had mattered after she met Jake.

"Ella, I'm not having this conversation."

Ella sighed. "I'm sorry he hurt you. Did he leave you for someone else?"

The expression on her mother's face said it all. "I told you, I'm done talking about this."

Some women told the whole world when a man left them, scattered their bitterness like so many seeds. Mims had put up a fence around her past and sown her bitterness inside, where it grew into mistrust. So was it really surprising that she'd been more than ready to believe Jake was cheating on her daughter? Her mother's mistrust, Ella's insecurity—what a deadly combination that had been!

It wasn't too late for Ella to recover from the ripple effect of her mother's long-ago liaison but maybe Mims never would. "Oh, Mims. I'm sorry. I'm sorry you were so badly hurt."

Now Mims looked like she was going to cry. She reached across the table and laid a hand over her daughter's. "I got the best part of him when I got you. And everything I've done has been for you, so you'd have a stable life."

"I did have a stable life," Ella assured her.

"And it hasn't been so bad, has it?"

"Of course not. But, Mims, I have to live my *own* life. You know yourself that eventually little girls grow up and leave home. You left home to be a model."

"And my mother never spoke to me again."

This was one story Ella had heard in plenty of detail. Sadly, her grandparents had died when she was young. Maybe that was why Mims had clung to her so tightly. She was all her mother had. "I never left you, though," she said.

"He'd have been happy if you did," Mims said, and it didn't take a genius to figure out she was referring to Jake. "And he showed his true colors with that awful song."

The sounds of a guitar strumming intruded on their conversation. Ella looked up to see Jake approaching, his guitar strung over his shoulders.

"What's he doing here?" Mims said sourly.

Singing, obviously. "'This is just a thank-you to the women in my life,'" he crooned. "'To the mama who shared with me the beauty who's my wife.'"

A new song. He'd written a new song to make up for what he'd done! As Jake sang on, Ella stole a look across the table to see how Mims was receiving his peace offering. She was studying her salad plate, and wiping at a corner of her eye.

"'So here's a simple thank-you from a humble man, to the women in my life who make me who I am,'" Jake concluded.

The other diners applauded but he ignored them, keeping his gaze focused on Mims. "Lily, I know we haven't always gotten along, but I'd like to find a way to change that," he said. "I hope this song will be a beginning. I'm gonna sing it with my band and put it up on YouTube."

"Thank you," Mims said stiffly.

To Ella he said. "I have one more song. This one's for you." He began to strum and silence descended on the restaurant. Not a single fork clinked, not a glass was raised. Everyone, including the waitstaff, listened as Jake sang about the rough ride they'd had over the past year.

It had been, but maybe the ride had taken them to a new place, someplace more solid.

Now he was into the chorus, and every word held the promise of a better future.

By the time he'd finished, most of the women were blowing their noses or dabbing at their eyes, and that included Ella.

"I didn't get a chance to tell you, a talent manager from Nashville called me."

"A talent manager?" Ella smiled across the table. "He's going to make it, Mims."

Her mother grimaced, then—reluctantly—nodded.

"When you finish your dinner, how about you both come back to the house for dessert."

"We don't have any dessert," Ella said.

"Oh, yeah, we do. I called Cass and told her I had an emergency. She sold me a red velvet cake."

Ella's favorite, and the only dessert for which Mims had a weakness. Ella turned to her mother.

She was trying hard to look put upon. "I don't know. I have plans…"

"Well, if you do…" Jake began.

"I can change them."

Jake grinned. "Great. I'll see you girls back at the house."

He left and Ella turned to her mother. "I still love him, Mims. I tried not to but I can't seem to stop."

Her mother sighed. "Well, you could've done better. But I suppose you could've done worse. Time will tell."

Not exactly a movie ending, Ella thought, but a not a bad new beginning, maybe for all of them. And the best Christmas present she could ask for.

It was Friday and the sign on the door of Gingerbread Haus read Closed for My Daughter's Wedding. Cass had taken the wedding cake home to decorate.

Late-afternoon shadows were stealing the light as she stepped away from the kitchen table to admire her magnum opus. It was a work of art, worthy of a baked-goods museum—a three-tiered pile of cake presents wrapped in fondant of white and red with silver frosting ribbon and dusted with delicate white snowflakes.

"Mom, it's beautiful," said Dani, who had joined her to admire the finished product.

The awe in her daughter's voice made the stiffness in Cass's back disappear. "I'm glad you like it."

"Like it? I love it!" Dani hugged her. "Now I'm glad you talked me out of cupcakes."

That was saying a lot.

Dani had just taken a picture with her cell phone when Mason entered the kitchen. "We're all ready to go to— Whoa, that is something else."

Cass smiled as she watched him approach the cake as though he was Indiana Jones moving toward lost Incan treasure. She'd come a long way from doll cakes and butterflies, and she couldn't help feeling gratified by his admiration of her art.

"And to think I used to make fun of your doll cakes," he said.

Now Babette joined them, with Cupcake trotting along behind. "Oh, that is gorgeous!"

Babette went up another notch in Cass's estimation.

A moment later Louise and Maddy were in the kitchen. "We've been standing by the door forever," Maddy complained. "Are we leaving for the holiday lights parade or aren't we?"

"We were just looking at the cake," Dani said. "Isn't it beautiful?"

Louise studied it. "Hmm. Very nice."

Nice. Damning with faint praise. Cass felt a sudden desire to shove a pie in her former mother-in-law's face, but since there was no pie handy (probably just as well), she forced a smile and said, "We should get going."

"I didn't think you'd be able to come with us," Louise said.

Just one more day of her, Cass told herself. "I didn't, either," she said, pretending her unexpected presence was a pleasant surprise to Louise. "I thought this would take me longer." She'd figured she'd be decorating right up until the rehearsal, so the original plan had been to skip the parade and appetizers at Olivia's, finish the cake, then take it to the inn and set up before the rehearsal. Now she liked the idea of being able to join her family for all the festivities. Well, most of them.

"I don't understand why it took you so long to decorate," Louise said. "There isn't much to it."

Where was a good cream pie when you needed one?

"Fondant's very hard to work with," Dani said, springing to her mother's defense.

"Really?" Louise sounded like she didn't believe it.

"Let's go," Mason said. "We're all going to roast standing around here with our coats on."

Everyone trooped out of the kitchen, Cupcake dancing along with them and yapping. Willie and Amber had been waiting patiently on the couch—easy to do when you had a phone to play with—but now they both stood and the party was complete. Quite an impressive group.

We look like one, big, happy family, Cass thought. Boy, were looks deceiving.

At the door, Babette knelt and gave the furry little monster she called a dog a kiss on the head. "No, baby, you have to stay here and guard the house."

Mess up the house, more likely. Cass hoped Willie had shut his bedroom door. Otherwise, he'd be missing more shorts.

"The cake really is gorgeous," Maddy said to her as they paraded down the front walk.

"Thanks," Cass said. Maybe Maddy wasn't so bad, after all. Maybe this whole weekend wouldn't be so bad, after all. Life is good, she concluded with a smile.

Life is really good when you're a dog and you've discovered the world's biggest doggie treat sitting on the kitchen table.

The visiting exes had all been charmed by the parade, which consisted mostly of cars and horse-drawn sleighs decked out in lights and bearing various festival princesses and dignitaries and, of course, Santa. Now they all walked back to the house to get their cars for the drive to the lodge.

"The town looks like a giant snow globe," Babette said, taking in the twinkle lights everywhere. "I can see why you like living here," she said to Cass. Then to Mason, "I wouldn't mind having a condo up here."

Please God, no, Cass thought. She'd made her peace with Mason, but that didn't mean she wanted him and Babette living right around the corner.

Before she could speak, Mason said, "Cheaper to rent a condo once in a while."

Thank you, Mason.

"Anyway, I'm not sure Cass would want us here all the time."

Cass decided to change the subject.

A few minutes later they were back at the house. Louise said she needed to use the bathroom, Babette wanted to freshen her makeup and Mason offered to help Cass load the cake. It was too cold to wait outside, so everyone trooped into the house. Surprisingly, Cupcake wasn't at the door to greet them with her high-pitched bark. Or anything else, thank God.

"Where's Cupcake?" Babette wondered.

"Did you shut your bedroom doors?" Cass asked the kids.

"Uh, yeah," Willie said in a tone of voice that plainly stated he'd learned his lesson.

"Cupcake," Babette called, and walked through the dining room. "Cupcake." Now she headed for the kitchen. "Cup— Aaah!"

Cupcake…kitchen. Cass connected the dots and her heart

dived to her feet. She rushed in past a stunned Babette and found Cupcake, destroyer of all, on the table and up to her furry face in frosting. She'd obviously used one of the kitchen chairs as a doggie stepstool to get to it. And get to it she had. There wasn't a layer of cake the little beast hadn't sampled.

With a shriek, Cass shooed the dog off the table. Cupcake yelped and scrammed, trailing cake and icing behind her, and the rest of the family entered the kitchen to see what was going on.

"Oh, Cupcake," Babette moaned. "Oh, Cass." That was as far as she got before bursting into tears.

Mason hesitated, torn between helping his distraught new wife and calming his former one.

There was no calming Cass. "That dog, that damned dog! Look what she's done. I'm going to kill her!"

"My cake," Dani wailed. Now she was crying, too.

"You shouldn't have left it on the table," Louise said. "You should've known that stupid dog would get it. In fact, I don't know why you brought it home."

Because, between waiting on customers and dealing with some family member calling her at the bakery every other minute with questions and needs, she'd thought it would be easier. Because she'd wanted to be where the family was. She'd wanted Dani to see her creation taking shape. She'd... Oh, she'd been stupid, that was all there was to it. She shoved her fist into a ruined layer and squeezed, pretending it was Cupcake's neck.

"Cass, I'm so sorry," Babette said in between sobs. "Your poor cake." Her eyes got big and she gasped. "Oh, no, and poor Cupcake. This is going to make her sick. Mason, we've got to find a vet." She whipped out her cell phone and strode from the kitchen past Willie and Amber.

"That cake is shit city," Willie observed.

"Shut up," Amber snapped at him. "It's okay, Mom," she said, hurrying over to Cass. "Maybe you can fix it."

"You'll never be able to fix that," Louise predicted. "The stupid animal has had its mouth all over the thing."

"Uh, let me know if you need me to do something," Mason said, and beat a hasty retreat.

Cass didn't blame him. She wished she could run away, too.

Accidents happened all the time, and she had mended many a gingerbread house over the years and many a cake, too. But never one that had been practically bulldozed. She stood staring at her ruined work of art, her brain frozen.

"Do you have anything in stock at the bakery?" Maddy asked.

Two cakes that would feed twelve, six gingerbread houses and two dozen gingerbread boys, a dozen cream puff swans a-swimming… And a partridge in a pear tree. Cass began to laugh hysterically. She caught her former mother- and sister-in-law exchanging concerned glances. *The person responsible for the wedding cake has gone around the bend.* She fell onto a kitchen chair, willing her brain to cook up something.

Sheet cakes. She'd have to throw together some sheet cakes. Now, there was a memorable wedding present for her daughter.

Babette was back in the kitchen now. "Mason's taking Cupcake to the vet," she announced.

"Good for Cupcake," Cass muttered.

"Oh, my gosh, that's it!" Babette cried.

"What's it?" Louise demanded.

"Cupcakes. We could make cupcakes," Babette said glee-fully.

"Oh, yes," Dani exclaimed.

Just what her daughter had wanted all along.

And Babette had been the one to suggest it—a bitter icing to top off this disaster. What made it even worse was that Cass didn't see how she could pull it off.

Dani was looking at her hopefully. Heck, everyone was looking at her.

"All right, cupcakes it is." They wouldn't be fancy and she'd have to bake all through the night, but she'd get them done. Sleep was overrated, anyway.

Her daughter rushed to hug her. "Thank you, Mama. You're the best!"

Not the best at sharing, though. She still hated that it was Babette who'd promised to deliver Dani her heart's desire. But Babette was in her daughter's life to stay and *someone* needed to learn to share. There was no time like the present.

"We can all help," Babette said eagerly.

"I could use it," Cass admitted.

"Then let's get cracking." Louise rolled up her sleeves. "Tell us what to do, Cass."

"Okay," Cass said. "Dani, you take Amber and Willie and go on over to the lodge. Your father can join you there once he's dropped the dog off at the vet's."

"But the rehearsal dinner," Dani fretted.

"Will still happen," Cass assured her.

"Without you?"

"Never mind me," Cass said. "You've got your whole bridal party and Mike's family. You go and have fun."

"I can't leave you to bake all by yourself," Dani protested.

"You won't," Babette told her. "Remember, she'll have us."

"Absolutely," Maddy agreed.

"Family pulls together," Louise added, making Cass wonder if the woman's body had been taken over by aliens.

"I'm going to the bakery," Cass said. "I can bake more cupcakes more quickly over there. You all go to work here."

"I'll run to the store and get cake mixes." Babette started out of the kitchen.

"Don't forget butter and powdered sugar," Louise called after her, searching the cupboards.

"I've got plenty of both at the bakery," said Cass. "Stop by there on your way back."

"What should we do with this?" Maddy asked, pointing to the cake.

"Let's eat it," Willie said, and stuck a finger in the frosting.

"It's got dog drool all over it," Amber said in disgust.

Willie made a face, then said, "I'll eat around the drool."

"You don't have time," Amber told him. "We have to get to the rehearsal."

"I'll take a piece with me."

Cass didn't stick around to hear any more of the conversation. She had things to do.

She'd just put her first batch of cupcakes in the oven when she heard pounding on the bakery door. Thinking it was Babette coming by for frosting supplies, she hurried to answer.

It was, but she also had Samantha and Bailey with her.

"Sam, what are you doing here?" Cass asked.

"Kidnapping you," Samantha said.

"What?"

"I'm here to make sure you get to the rehearsal and the dinner."

Cass shook her head. "Maybe Babette didn't tell you, but we've got an emergency."

"She did and that's why we're here," Bailey said. "I'm taking over for you until after the dinner."

"Mom and Cecily are baking," said Samantha. "So are Ella and Charley. And Blake will be taking my cupcakes out of the oven in…" She checked the time on her cell phone. "Five minutes. Then I have to get a new batch in." She grinned. "Our secret chocolate cupcake recipe."

"How did you— I don't understand."

"Babette found me and I spread the word," Samantha said. "Half the women in town are busy baking even as we speak. So, come on. You have some mother-of-the-bride duties to perform."

Cass blinked back tears. "Thank you."

"Don't thank me, thank Babette," Samantha said. "She's the one who sounded the alarm."

Her beautiful cake was ruined and that made Cass sad. But her daughter's day *wasn't* ruined, thanks to friends and former in-laws pulling together. And that was amazing.

Even more amazing, she was becoming downright fond of Babette.

21

Dani's wedding was one to remember and, happily, not because of any more wedding disasters but because everything was perfect. Sitting with Babette in the transformed big meeting room at Icicle Creek Lodge, Cass watched teary-eyed as Amber came down the aisle to Pachelbel's *Canon,* looking much older than the fifteen years she now was in a sophisticated red satin dress. Dani's friends Vanessa and Mikaila, both in gray satin, were next, two girls barely into their twenties and just beginning their lives.

Now, here came Dani, walking an indoor garden path lined with white roses, silver netting froth and greenery, carrying a bouquet of red and white tea roses. Her baby, all grown up, a snow princess, escorted by her beaming father. Cass was so glad her brother, Drew, was here, recording the whole thing.

"Who gives this woman to be wedded to this man?" asked Pastor Jim once they'd reached the front of the room.

"Her mother and I, with all our love," Mason said. His part in the ceremony over, he sat down between Cass and Babette and, much to Cass's surprise, took her hand and gave it a squeeze. She smiled and squeezed back. It was so much better to be allies than enemies.

Pastor Jim made sure his talk was short and sweet. "I wish I could promise you that your life together will always be just like this day—perfect. But it won't, and I think you already know that. There are going to be times when you'll look at each other and ask, 'Why did I pick you?' So I want you to file away in your minds what you're thinking, what you're feeling, right now. Remember the good you see in each other right now. If you do that, you'll be fine."

Cass swallowed a lump. Maybe she and Mason would have been fine if she'd had a Pastor Jim to advise them when they first got together. Too late for those regrets now. She'd chosen the life she had and it wasn't so bad. In fact, it was pretty darned wonderful.

One of Dani's musical girlfriends played her guitar and sang the wedding song Jake had written for Ella as Dani and Mike poured colored sand—his silver, hers gold—into the tall crystal vase that had been Cass's mother's. Cass watched as the colors mingled and swirled. Two becoming one. Not just two people, she thought, looking to where Mike's mother, Delia, sat alongside her husband and mother, dabbing at her eyes with a tissue. Two families. No, make that three, she amended as Babette linked her arm through Mason's.

The couple exchanged vows and then Pastor Jim grinned. "And now, the moment we've all been waiting for. By the powers vested in me, I now proclaim you husband and wife. Mike, you may kiss your bride."

And kiss her he did, while his buddies hooted and everyone broke into applause. Then, to the surprise of everyone, including the mother of the bride, the bridal party danced their way down the aisle to a pumping rock song.

So, of course, as the ushers (including Willie, who'd decided he wasn't so averse to wearing a tux, after all) sent them on their way row by row, the guests did, too. It was a short walk to the huge dining room where the reception would be held. The room was lovely to begin with, but Heinrich and Kevin had turned it into something magical with white and silver floral arrangements and silver mercury-glass votive candles. Looking at all the flowers, greenery and netting, Cass knew they'd gone *way* beyond her budget. What a wedding gift!

With the help of Charley's waitstaff from Zelda's, Bailey had the food well in hand. And the cupcakes—every imaginable flavor—were to die for. Cass vowed to get the recipe for Janice Lind's banana cupcakes if it was the last thing she did.

"You'll never get it out of her," Dot predicted when Cass stopped by her table to visit with her and Tilda and some of her Chamber of Commerce pals.

"I'll just have to get my hands on some truth serum," Cass joked.

"Well," Louise said later as they all stood watching Dani and Mike feed each other cupcakes, "you did it."

"No," Cass corrected. "*We* did it. Thanks, Louise."

Her mother-in-law shrugged. "Anything for my granddaughter."

Cass couldn't help smiling.

Now Babette and Mason joined them. "What a lovely wedding," she told Cass. "Thanks for letting us stay with you. It was great to be a part of everything."

"I'm happy it worked out," Cass said, and realized she meant it.

"It's so lovely up here. I really have fallen in love with this place," Babette continued.

"I think we should all stay for Christmas," Louise said. "That'll give us a little more time with Dani and Mike before they leave for Spokane."

"Good idea," Maddy chimed in.

"Christmas?" Cass repeated weakly.

"But all our presents are back at the house," Babette protested.

"You don't want to miss out on those," Cass added, grabbing at straws.

"We can do presents anytime," Louise said. "Let's make a party out of this. Anyway, with all these cute shops, I'm sure we can find some small gifts to open."

"And that's why all my exes are still here," Cass told her friends at their chick-flick party the next evening.

They'd moved the festivities to Ella's house, figuring Cass would be beat. And she was. But she was also happy. Probably a sloppy sentiment hangover. Now she lounged on Ella's couch, Tiny keeping her company. She had no illusions about being his favorite, though. He was only there because she'd been slipping him bits of her cookie.

"Sounds like you're going to have some Christmas," Cecily said. "I don't envy you."

"Me, neither," Charley agreed.

"Speaking of Christmas, are you going to be okay?" Cecily asked her.

Charley nodded. "Absolutely. I'm off tomorrow to stay with my sister in Portland. I need a break anyway, otherwise I'm going to kill that Ethan Masters."

Cass had heard from Cecily about the angry sparks that flew every time Charley had to deal with the tough-as-nails owner of Masters Construction who was going to be restoring Zelda's. Maybe those sparks were fueled by more than their disagreements. Cass hoped so. Charley was too young to spend the rest of her life without someone.

She's not that much younger than you, whispered a little voice. *Yeah,* Cass told it, *but I'm too set in my ways.* She didn't need a man. She had her business and her kids. *Who are growing up and leaving you,* the voice reminded her. Well, they wouldn't *all* leave. She hoped some of them would stay in town.

"I have some news," Ella said. The way she was beaming, it came as no surprise when she announced, "I just took an early pregnancy test. And I passed!"

"Oh, my gosh! Congratulations," Cecily cried, and jumped from her chair to hug her friend.

"Good," Charley said. "Another baby to play with."

"Not unless you want to come to Nashville." Ella smiled as she spoke. "That's the rest of my news. We're moving."

"Wow, that's fast," Cass said in astonishment.

"The house was already sold. Plus Jake's got a talent manager interested in him."

"Thanks to the YouTube song?" Cecily asked.

Ella nodded.

"How many views is that up to now?" Samantha asked,

then let out a low whistle after Ella told her. "Looks like he's really got a hit on his hands."

"That *has* to have made your mom happy," Cecily said.

"She's okay with it. Sort of," Ella added with a grin. "Mainly because he wrote a nice one and put that up, too."

"So, what's your mom going to do?" Samantha asked.

"She says she'll come visit, but she's not moving down there. Too many rednecks."

"I kind of like rednecks," Charley said.

"Me, too," Ella said, making her friends smile. Then she turned serious. "We have one problem though. Tiny. We can't take him with us. We'll be living in an apartment. Plus he's a mountain dog. He needs cold, mountain air. It wouldn't be fair to make him swelter in the South."

"What are you going to do with him?" Cass asked, rubbing the dog's head.

"We need to find a good home, preferably here."

Cass remembered how Amber had fawned over Cupcake. The kids had been bugging her to get a dog for years. She'd always resisted, though, claiming that between them and the bakery she had enough to take care of.

Dani was moving. Cass needed to fill the hole in her home and her life.

She hadn't had a dog since she and Mason were first married. It would be nice to have one to come home to.

But did she have to start out with one the size of a horse?

Better that than a yippy, spoiled Pomeranian.

As if sensing a need to prove how lovable he was, he laid his head on Cass's lap and looked up at her with big, brown eyes. And drooled on her. Well, every male had his faults.

"He likes you," Samantha said.

"You want to come live with us?" Cass asked, and Tiny barked.

"Let me run it by the kids," she said to Ella.

"As if they're going to object," Samantha scoffed. "Just say yes. You know you want to."

"Okay, yes. But when Jake makes it big and comes to Seattle, you owe me concert tickets. Front row," Cass added with a smile.

"Front row," Ella agreed, beaming. "So, are you guys ready for my movie pick?"

"Let's have it," Charley said. "What are we watching?"

Ella's smile grew bigger as she pulled a DVD out of her purse. "The perfect movie. *It's a Wonderful Life.*"

"You know," Cass said with a smile. "You're right. It is."

She had to remind herself of that on Christmas Day when she tripped over Cupcake, lost her balance and dropped the red velvet cake she was bringing out to the dining room table for her open house.

"Oh, no," Babette wailed as she hurried to help clean up the mess. "Oh, Cass, I'm so—"

"Sorry," Cass finished with her. "Oh, well, we've still got cookies. And appetizers. And if you eat them you're dead," she informed the dog, who was now in the living room, seeking protection in Amber's lap.

"You hear that?" Babette said to Cupcake. "Bad dog!"

Of course, everyone who showed up for the party thought the little beast was adorable.

"Maybe you should bring Tiny over so they can get acquainted," Cass whispered to Ella.

Ella smiled. "You're evil."

"Thanks. I try."

"It's a great party," Ella said, looking around.

Indeed, it was. And it was made even better when her mother called from Florida. "Get the guest room ready. We'll be flying up in time for New Year's and I'll be setting off airport security all the way. So tell Dani not to leave before I get there."

"Don't worry. She'll still be here."

"Hopefully your other guests will be gone."

"They will," Cass said.

"I'm so proud of you," said her mother. "Not everyone could have pulled off hosting her exes the way you have."

She *had* pulled it off. Somehow, they'd all gotten through. Nearby Charley was laughing at something Cecily had said, and Jake and Ella had settled in on the couch and were acting as much like newlyweds as Dani and Mike. Louise had cornered poor Delia, and Maddy was showing off her engagement ring to Drew, who was looking for a way to escape.

As Cass surveyed the room she caught sight of Mason standing by the Christmas tree with Willie and Amber. He smiled at her and saluted her with his glass of eggnog.

She raised hers back. *Merry Ex-mas.*

Actually, it was.

★ ★ ★ ★ ★

RECIPES & BAKING HINTS FROM CASS WILKES

We thought you might enjoy the recipes for some of our wedding cupcakes. These are so good you won't be able to eat just one. But before we get to the recipes, let me give you a few tips on baking cupcakes.

1. Use cupcake liners. They're not only pretty, but your cupcakes will rise higher and be easier to take from the pan.
2. When pouring your cupcakes, fill the liners two-thirds to three-quarters full. If you fill to the brim your cupcakes will overflow and you'll have a mess.
3. Most standard 2½ inch cupcakes are baked from 15 to 22 minutes. Don't overbake your cupcakes or they'll be dry.
4. When making a cake or cupcakes, add a package of plain gelatin to the mix. This will keep your cake from cracking.

Okay, now, you're ready to go.

SAMANTHA STERLING'S CHOCOLATE GANACHE MARSCARPONE CUPCAKES

(courtesy of *New York Times* bestselling author Jill Barnett)

MAKES I DOZEN

What you'll need in addition to the ingredients

Paper baking cups
1 cupcake holer or grapefruit spoon
muffin tin

Ingredients

For cake:

¼ lb. (1 stick) butter
1 cup sugar
1 cup all-purpose flour
4 extra-large eggs, room
   temperature
1 Tbsp. vanilla
16 oz. chocolate syrup such
   as Hershey's

For cream filling:

½ pint heavy whipping cream
1 small container mascarpone
   cheese or 4 oz. whipped
   cream cheese
1 tsp. vanilla
1-2 heaping Tbsp. sugar

For ganache:

⅓ cup heavy whipping cream
6 oz. high quality chocolate
   chips such as Ghirardelli
   (semisweet or milk
   chocolate)
½ tsp. instant espresso

Directions

For your cake, cream the butter, sugar and eggs and beat
until fluffy. Add the chocolate syrup and vanilla and mix,

then sift in flour and mix. Line muffin tin and pour the mix into each cupcake liner until ¼ inch away from the top of the liner. Bake at 350° for 13 to 18 minutes, until the tops of the cupcakes spring back. Cool.

For your ganache, heat chocolate chips and ⅓ cup heavy cream and espresso powder over boiling water, stirring constantly, until completely melted and glossy. Dip the top of your cooled cupcakes in the chocolate (twice if you want a thicker ganache layer). Let cool. Samantha (and Jill) usually make them the evening before a party and let them set overnight so the ganache is firm.

The next morning you can use your cupcake holer to take out a small part of the center of your cupcake, or you can simply use a melon baller or small grapefruit spoon.

For your mascarpone cream filling, mix in a bowl with a hand mixer, ½ pint whipping cream, 4 oz. mascarpone or whipped cream cheese, sugar and vanilla. Mix until very stiff. Then spoon into a quart-size plastic storage bag, cut off the tip and pipe into the center of the cupcakes, piping it up about an inch above the ganache.

Cupcakes don't have to be refrigerated unless it's hot out. (In fact, worrying about storing them is never a problem. These babies go in a hurry!)

CASS'S RED VELVET CUPCAKES

Yes, they're everywhere now, but this particular recipe comes with Cass's top-secret frosting recipe. (She got it from Sheila Roberts, who kept both the frosting and the cake recipe a secret since she first got it from a Southern belle at the age of sixteen. We don't really know how many years ago that was, since Sheila has been lying about her age since she turned thirty, but we do know it's quite a long time.)

Ingredients

2 oz. red food coloring

3 Tbsp. powdered chocolate milk mix (such as Nestle's Quik)

½ cup shortening

2¼ cup cake flour

1 tsp. soda

1 Tbsp. vinegar

1 tsp. vanilla

2 eggs, beaten

1 cup buttermilk
(Note: if you forgot to buy buttermilk, you can substitute milk with a small amount of vinegar added to it.)

1 tsp. (scant) salt

Directions

Mix food coloring and chocolate powder in a small bowl. Cream the shortening and sugar. Combine beaten eggs and food coloring mixture, then add it to the shortening mixture. Sift flour and salt together and add alternately with buttermilk. Add vanilla. Remove from mixer and add one at a time by hand, first the soda, then the vinegar. Pour into muffin tins lined with paper baking cups and bake at 350° for

15 to 20 minutes, until the cake springs back when touched. As with the chocolate cupcakes (or any cake), don't over-bake. Cool and then frost with Red Velvet Cake Frosting.

FROSTING FOR RED VELVET CAKE

Ingredients
¼ lb. (1 stick) butter
8 Tbsp. shortening
3 Tbsp. flour
1 cup sugar (*Make sure you use pure cane sugar.*)

⅔ cup milk, room temperature
1 tsp. vanilla

Directions
Combine, one at a time, the butter, shortening, sugar and flour, beating well after each addition. Add milk and vanilla and beat well. Will keep in refrigerator.

Note: Use pure cane sugar for this frosting. The cheaper beet sugar is coarser and will leave your frosting tasting grainy.

CASS'S WEDDING CUPCAKES

MAKES 2 DOZEN

Ingredients

2¼ cup sifted flour

2½ tsp. baking powder

1 tsp. salt

1½ cup sugar

½ cup butter, room
temperature

1 Tbsp. oil (for added
moistness)

1 cup milk

2 eggs

1 tsp. vanilla

Directions

Sift flour, salt and baking powder into a bowl. Then add
sugar, butter, vanilla and two-thirds of the milk. Beat with
mixer at medium speed for two minutes. Add remaining
milk and unbeaten eggs and beat 2 minutes longer. Pour
into muffin tins lined with paper cupcake liners and bake at
350° for 18 to 20 minutes. Cool. Frost with Rose Frosting.

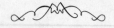

ROSE FROSTING

Ingredients

2½ cups powdered sugar
3 Tbsp. butter, room
  temperature

3 Tbsp. milk, room
  temperature
⅛ tsp. rose water ★

★ *Note: You can find rose water in the specialty section of a high quality grocery store. This is a powerful flavor so use sparingly. Remember, you can always add more, but if you add too much your guests will think they're eating soap.*

Directions

Sift your powdered sugar, then mix in all your other ingredients. Sifting the powdered sugar and using room temperature butter and milk will help prevent lumps in your frosting. Add your favorite pastel food coloring.

JANICE LIND'S BANANA CUPCAKES

Ingredients

2½ cups cake flour
2 cups sugar
2½ tsp. baking powder
1 tsp. salt
1 tsp. soda
1 Tbsp. oil (for added
  moistness)

1 tsp. banana extract
⅔ cup butter
2 eggs
1¼ cup mashed ripe bananas
1¼ cup coconut milk

Directions

Sift flour, soda, baking powder and salt into a mixing bowl.
Add sugar, butter, bananas and half the coconut milk. Beat
with mixer at medium speed for two minutes. Add eggs, banana extract and remaining coconut milk and beat for two
more minutes. Pour batter into your cupcake liners and bake
at 350° for 15 to 20 minutes, until cake springs back when
you touch it. Cool. Frost with Red Velvet Cake Frosting.
(Cream cheese frosting also works well with this recipe.)

Merry Christmas and happy baking!
—Cass

Come back to Icicle Falls for another visit this spring! Can't wait? Turn the page for an excerpt from What She Wants *by Sheila Roberts, available in April 2013, everywhere books are sold.*

What *do* women want?

Jonathan Templar and his poker buddies can't figure it out. Take Jonathan, for instance. He's been in love with Lissa Castle since they were kids, but, geek that he is, she's never seen him as her Mr. Perfect. He's got one last shot: their high school reunion. Kyle Long is equally discouraged. The pretty receptionist at his office keeps passing him over for other guys who may be taller but are definitely *not* superior. And Adam Edwards might be the most successful of Jonathan's friends, but he isn't having any success on the home front. His wife's kicked him out.

When Jonathan stumbles on a romance novel at the Icicle Falls library sale, he knows he's found the love expert he's been seeking—Vanessa Valentine, top-selling romance author. At first his buddies laugh at him for reading romance novels, but soon they, too, realize that these stories are the world's best textbooks on love. Poker night becomes book club night…and when all is *read* and done, they're going to be the kind of men that women want!

1

Working in such close quarters with a woman that you could bump knees (thighs, and maybe even other body parts) with was probably every man's dream job, except Dot Morrison's knees were knobby and she was old enough to be Jonathan Templar's grandmother. And she looked like Maxine of greeting card fame. So there was no knee (or anything else) bumping going on today.

"Okay, you're good to go," he said, pushing back from the computer in the office at Breakfast Haus, Dot's restaurant. "But remember what I told you. If you want your computer to run more efficiently, you've got to zap your PRAM once in a while."

"There you go, talking dirty to me again," Dot cracked.

A sizzle sneaked onto Jonathan's cheeks, partly because old ladies didn't say things like that (Jonathan's grandma sure didn't), and partly because he'd never talked dirty to a woman in his life. Well, not unless you counted a *Playboy* centerfold. When talking with most real-life women, his tongue had a tendency to tie itself into more knots than a bag of pretzels, especially when the woman was good-looking. This, he told himself, was one reason he was still single at the ripe old age of thirty-three. That and the fact that he wasn't exactly the stuff a woman's dreams were made of. It was a rare woman who dreamed of a skinny, bespectacled guy in a button-down shirt.

Those weren't the *only* reasons, though.

Never sure how to respond to Dot's wacky sense of humor, he merely smiled, shook his head and packed up his briefcase.

"Seriously," she said, "I'm glad this didn't turn out to be anything really bad. But if it had I know I could count on you. You can't ever leave Icicle Falls. What would us old bats do?"

"You'd manage," Jonathan assured her.

"I doubt it. Computers are instruments of torture to anyone over the age of sixty."

"No worries," he said. "I'm not planning on going anywhere."

"Until you meet Miss Right. Then you'll be gone like a shot." The look she gave him was a clear sign that something was about to come out of her mouth that would make him squirm. Sure enough. "We'll have to find you a local girl."

That was all he needed—Dot Morrison putting out the word that Jonathan Templar, computer nerd, was in the market for a local girl. He didn't want a local girl. He wanted…

"Tilda's still available."

Tilda Morrison, supercop? She could easily bench-press Jonathan. "Uh, thanks for the offer, but I think she needs someone tougher."

"There's a problem. Nobody's as tough as Tilda. Damn, I raised that girl wrong. At this rate I'm never going to get grandchildren." Dot shrugged and reached for a cigarette. "Just as well, I suppose. I'd have to spend all my free time baking cookies for the little rodents."

Sometimes it was hard to know whether or not Dot was serious, but this time Jonathan was sure she didn't mean what she said. She was just trying to make the best of motherly frustration. Dot wanted grandkids. Anyone who'd seen her interacting with the families who came into the restaurant could tell that. It was a wonder she made any money with all the free hot chocolates she slipped her younger patrons.

She lit up and took a deep drag on her cigarette. It was about to get downright smoggy in her little office at the back of the restaurant kitchen.

"I'd better get going," Jonathan said, gathering his things and trying not to inhale the secondhand smoke pluming in his direction.

"You gonna bill me as usual?"

"Yep."

"Don't gouge me," she teased.

"Wouldn't dream of it. And put your glasses on to read your bill this time," he teased back as he made for the door. Dot had a habit of overpaying him, always claiming she'd misread the bill. Yep, Dot was a great customer.

Heck, all his customers were great, he thought as he

walked over to Sweet Dreams Chocolate Company, where
Elena, the secretary, was having a nervous breakdown thanks
to a new computer that she swore was demon-possessed.

"Thank God you're here," she greeted him as he stepped
into the office.

People were always happy to see the owner and sole
employee of Geek Gods Mobile Computer Service. Once
Jonathan arrived on the scene, they knew their troubles
would be fixed.

He liked that, liked feeling useful. So he wasn't a mountain
of muscle like Luke Goodman, the production manager at
Sweet Dreams, or a mover and shaker like Blake Preston,
manager of Cascade Mutual. Some men were born to have
starring roles and big, juicy parts on the stage of life. Others
were meant to build scenery, pull the curtains, work in
the background to make sure everything on stage ran well.
Jonathan was a scenery kind of guy. Nothing wrong with
that, he told himself. Background workers made it possible
for the show to go on.

But leading ladies never noticed the guy in the background.
Jonathan heaved a sigh. Sometimes he felt like Cyrano de
Bergerac. Without the nose.

"This thing is making me loco," Elena said, glaring at the
offending piece of technology on her desk.

Samantha had just emerged from her office. "More loco
than we make you?"

"More loco than even my mother makes me," Elena
replied.

Samantha gave her shoulder a pat. "Jonathan will fix it."

Elena grunted. *"Equipo desde el infierno."*

"Computer from hell?" Jonathan guessed, remembering some of his high school Spanish.

Elena's frustrated scowl was all the answer he needed.

"While you're battling the forces of evil technology, I'll be meeting with Ed about his surprise birthday party for Pat," Samantha told Elena. "When Cecily comes in, tell her I'll be back in a couple of hours. Try to keep my favorite secretary from turning the air blue," she said to Jonathan.

"No worries," he said. Then he turned to Elena. "I'll have this up and running for you in no time."

No time turned out to be about an hour, but since Elena had expected to lose the entire day she was delighted. "You are amazing," she told him just as Samantha's sister, Cecily, arrived on the scene.

"Has he saved us again?" she asked Elena, smiling at Jonathan.

"Yes, as always."

Jonathan pushed his glasses back up his nose and tried to look modest. It was hard when people praised him like this.

But then, as he started to pack up his tools, Cecily said something that left him flat as a stingray. "I heard from Chantelle Bates that you guys have your fifteen-year reunion coming up."

"Uh, yeah."

"Those are always fun, seeing old friends, people you used to date," she continued.

This was worse than Dot's cigarette smoke. Chatting with Cecily always made him self-conscious; chatting with Cecily about his high school reunion would make him a nervous wreck—especially if she started asking about women he used to date. Jonathan hit high speed gathering up his tools and his various disks.

"Are you going?" she asked him.

"Maybe," he lied, and hoped she'd leave it at that.

She didn't. "I moved back just in time for my ten-year and I'm glad I did. There were some people I wouldn't have had a chance to see otherwise."

There were some people Jonathan wanted to do more than see. Some people with long, blond hair and... He snapped his briefcase shut and bolted for the door. "So, Elena, I'll bill you."

"Okay," she called.

The door hadn't quite shut behind him when he heard Elena say to Cecily, "He needs confidence, that one."

He needed a lot more than confidence.

He grabbed some bratwurst and sauerkraut for lunch at Big Brats, then fit in two more clients before going home.

May's late-afternoon sun beamed its blessing on his three-bedroom log house at the end of Mountain View Road. (He'd originally planned for two bedrooms but his folks had talked him into the extra one. "You have to have room for a wife and children," his mother had said. Good old Mom, always hopeful.) Fir and pine trees gave the house its rustic setting. The pansies and begonias his mother and grandmother had put in the window boxes, as well as the patch of lawn edged with more flowers, added a homey touch. Someone pulling up might even think a woman lived there. They'd be wrong. The only female in this house had four legs.

But Jonathan often pictured the house with a wife and kids

in it—the wife (a pretty blonde, naturally) cooking dinner while he and the kids played video games. He could even see himself as an old man, sitting on the porch, playing chess with a grandson. Naturally, he would've passed the house on to his own son, keeping the property in the family.

His grandpa had purchased the land as an investment when it was nothing more than a mountain meadow. Gramps could have made a tidy profit selling it but instead he'd let Jonathan have it for a song when Jonathan turned twenty-five.

He'd started construction when he was twenty-seven. A cousin who worked in construction in nearby Yakima had come over and helped him and Dad build the house. Dad hadn't lived to see it finished. He'd had a heart attack just before the roof went on, leaving Jonathan on his own to complete both his house and his life.

Jonathan had become the man of the family, in charge of helping his mom, his grandmother and his sister cope. He'd been no help to his grandmother, who had tried to outrun her loss by moving to Arizona. He hadn't been much help to his mother, either, beyond setting her up with a computer program so she could manage her finances. He'd tried to help Julia but he'd barely been able to cope himself. He should never have let Dad do all that hard physical work.

"Don't be silly," his mother always said. "Your father could just as easily have died on the golf course. He was doing what he wanted to do, helping you."

Helping his son be manly. The house was probably the one endeavor of Jonathan's that his father really took pride in. It wasn't hard to figure out what kind of son Dad had really longed for. He'd never missed an Icicle Falls High football game, whether at home or away. How many times had he sat in the stands and wished his scrawny son was out there on the field or at least on the bench instead of playing in the band? Jonathan was glad he had no idea.

"I love you, son," Dad had said when they were loading him into the ambulance. Those were the last words Jonathan heard and he was thankful for them. But he often found himself wishing his dad had said he was proud of him.

As he pulled up in his yellow Volkswagen with *Geek Gods Mobile Computer Service* printed on the side, his dog, Chica, abandoned her spot on the front porch and raced down the stairs to greet him, barking a welcome. Chica was an animal shelter find, part shepherd, part Lab and part…whatever kind of dog had a curly tail. She'd been with Jonathan for five years and she thought he was a god.

He got out of the car and the dog started jumping like she had springs on her paws. It was nice to have a female go crazy over him. "Hey, girl," he greeted her. "We'll get some dinner and then play fetch."

He exchanged his slacks for jeans and his business shirt for a T-shirt that cautioned Don't drink and derive. Then, after a feast of canned spaghetti for Jonathan and some Doggy's Delight for Chica, it was time for a quick game of fetch. It had to be quick because tonight was Friday, poker night, and the guys would be coming over at seven. Poker, another manly pursuit. Dad would have been proud.

The first man to arrive was Kyle Long, Jonathan's old high school chess club buddy. Kyle didn't exactly fit his name. He was short. His hair was a lighter shade than Jonathan's dark brown—nothing spectacular, rather like his face.

But his ordinary face didn't bug him nearly as much as his lack of stature. "Women don't look at short guys," he often grumbled. And short guys who, like Jonathan, weren't always so confident and quick with the flattery, well, they really didn't get noticed.

The grumpy expression on Kyle's face tonight said it all before he'd even opened his mouth. "What's with chicks, anyway?" he demanded as he set a six-pack of Hale's Ale on Jonathan's counter.

If Jonathan knew that, he'd be married to the woman of his dreams. He shrugged.

"Okay, so Darrow looks like friggin' Ryan Reynolds."

Ted Darrow, Jonathan's nemesis. "And drives a Jag," Jonathan supplied.

"But he's the world's biggest ass-wipe," Kyle said with a scowl. "I don't know what Jillian sees in him."

Jonathan knew. Like called to like. Beautiful people gravitated to each other. Jonathan had seen Jillian when he'd gone to Kyle's company, Safe Hands Insurance, to install their new computer system. She was hot, with blue eyes, blond hair and supermodel long legs. Women like that went for the Ted Darrows of the world.

Or the Rand Burbanks.

Jonathan shoved that last thought out of his mind. "Look, you may as well give up. You're not gonna get her." It was hard to say that to his best friend, but friends didn't let friends drive themselves crazy over women who were out of their league. Kyle would do the same for him...if he knew

Jonathan had suffered a relapse last Christmas and had once again picked up the torch for his own perfect blonde. The road to crazy was a clogged thoroughfare these days.

Kyle heaved a discouraged sigh. "I know." He pulled a bottle opener out of a kitchen drawer and popped the top off one of the bottles. "It's just that, well, damn. If she opened those baby blues and looked my way for longer than two seconds, she'd see I'm twice the man Darrow is."

"I hear you," Jonathan said, and opened a bag of corn chips, setting them alongside the beer.

Next in the door was Bernardo Ruiz, who came bearing some of his wife's homemade salsa. Bernardo wasn't much taller than Kyle, but he swaggered like he was six feet.

"Who died?" he asked, glancing from one friend to the other.

"Nobody," Kyle said grumpily.

Bernardo looked at him suspiciously. "You mooning around over that bimbo at work again?"

"She's not a bimbo," Kyle said hotly.

Bernardo shook his head in disgust. "Little man, you are a fool to chase after a woman who doesn't want you. That kind of woman, she'll only make you feel small on the inside."

Any reference to being small, either on the inside or the outside, never went over well with Kyle, so it was probably a good thing that Adam Edwards arrived with more beer and chips. A sales rep for a pharmaceutical company, he made more than Jonathan and Kyle put together and had the toys to prove it—a big house on the river, a classic Corvette, a snowmobile and a beach house on the Washington coast. He also had a pretty little wife, which proved Jonathan's theory of like calling to like since Adam was tall and broad-shouldered and looked as though he belonged in Hollywood instead of Icicle Falls. Some guys had all the luck.

"Vance'll be late," Adam informed them. "He has to finish up something and says to go ahead and start without him."

Vance Fish was the newest member of their group, a confirmed bachelor somewhere in his fifties, which made him the senior member. He'd built a big house on River Road about a mile down from Adam's place. The two men had bonded over fishing lures, and Adam had invited him to join their poker group.

Vance claimed to be semiretired. He owned a bookstore somewhere in Seattle called Pleasures and Treasures, which sold books and antiques. He'd recently added Sweet Dreams Chocolates to his inventory, making himself popular with the Sterling family, who owned the company. He dressed as if he was on his last dime, usually in sweats or jeans and an oversize black T-shirt that hung clumsily over his double XL belly, but his fancy house was proof that Vance was doing okay.

"That means we won't see him for at least an hour," Kyle predicted.

"What kind of project?" Bernardo asked. "Is he building something over there in that fine house of his? I never seen no tools or workbench in his garage."

"Something to do with the bookstore," Adam said. "I don't know what."

"Well, all the better for me," Kyle said gleefully. "I'll have you guys fleeced by the time he gets here." He clapped his hands together. "I'm feeling lucky tonight."

He proved it by raking in their money.

"Bernardo, you should just come empty your pockets on the table right from the start," Adam joked. "I've never seen anybody so unlucky at cards."

"That's because I'm lucky at love," Bernardo insisted.

His remark wiped the victory smirk right off Kyle's face. "Chicks," he said in disgust.

"If you're going where I think you're going, don't," Adam said, frowning at him.

"What?" Kyle protested.

Adam pointed his beer bottle at Kyle. "If I hear one more word about Jillian I'm gonna club you with this."

"Oh, no," said a deep voice, "I thought you clowns would be done talking about women by now."

Jonathan turned to see Vance strolling into the room, looking stylish as ever in his favorite black T-shirt, baggy jeans and sandals. In honor of the occasion he hadn't shaved. Aside from the extra pounds (well, and that bald spot on top of his head), the guy wasn't too bad-looking. His sandy hair was shot with gray but he had the kind of craggy brow and strong jaw women seemed to like even in a big man. All that big-man sexy stuff was wasted on Vance, though. He wasn't interested. According to Vance, women were a mistake men made under the influence of testosterone.

"We're done talking about women," Adam assured him.

Vance clapped him on the back. "Glad to hear it, 'cause the last thing I want after a hard day's work is to listen to you losers crab about them."

"I wasn't crabbing," Kyle said sullenly.

Vance sat down at the table and eyed him. "It's that bimbo

where you work, isn't it? She got your jockeys tight again?" Kyle glared at him but Vance waved his anger away with a pudgy paw. "You know, women can sense desperation a mile away. It's a turnoff."

"And I guess you'd be an expert on what turns women off," Adam teased.

"There isn't a man on this planet who's an expert on anything about women. And if you meet one who says he is, he's lying. Now, let's play poker." Vance eyed the pile of chips in front of Kyle. "I think you need to be relieved of some of those, my friend."

"I think not," Kyle said, and the game began in earnest.

After an hour and a half Vance announced that he had to tap a kidney.

"I need some chips and salsa," Adam decided, and everyone took a break.

"Did you get the announcement in the mail?" Kyle asked Jonathan.

No, not this again.

"What announcement?" Adam asked.

"High school reunion," Kyle said. "Fifteen years."

Jonathan had gotten the cutesy little postcard with the picture of a grizzly bear, the Icicle Falls High mascot, lumbering across the corner. And of course, the first thing he'd thought was, *Maybe Lissa will come.* That had taken his spirits on a hot-air balloon ride. Until he'd had another thought. *You'll still be the invisible man.* That had brought the balloon back down.

"Yeah, I got it," he said. "I'm not going."

But Rand probably would be. Rand and Lissa, together again.

With *that* thought, his balloon ride was not only over, the balloon was in a swamp infested with alligators. And poker night was a bust.

Just like his love life.

★ ★ ★ ★ ★